Murder in Death's Waiting Room

Janis Patterson

S~AB
SEFKHAT-AWBI BOOKS

Murder in Death's Waiting Room

Cover Art from BookGraphics.net

Formatting by Rik – Wild Seas Formatting (http://WildSeasFormatting.com)

ISBN - 978-1-941520-16-1

Published by Sefkhat-Awbi Books
www.JanisPattersonMysteries.com.

This Book is Dedicated to

my wonderful in-laws

Wendy Knight

and

Larry Stubblefield

and to

CAPT Hiram M. Patterson, USN(Ret)

the most wonderful man in the world

and

and a great big Thank You

to

Dr. Thomas Risser

for being my guide to getting the prescription medicines correct

Books by Janis Susan May

The Avenging Maid
Family of Strangers
The Devil of Dragon House
Shadowed Legacy
Passion's Choice
The Jerusalem Connection
The Egyptian File
Inheritance of Shadows
Lure of the Mummy
Timeless Innocents
Welcome Home
Miss Morrison's Second Chance
Curse of the Exile
Echoes in the Dark
Dark Music
Quartet: Four Slightly Twisted Tales
Lacey
The Fair Amazon
The Other Half of Your Heart
The Fortunes of Love
The House in the Pines

Books by Janis Patterson

A Killing at El Kab
Murder and Miss Wright
The Hollow House
Beaded to Death
Exercise is Murder
Murder to Mil-Spec (anthology)

Books by Janis Susan Patterson

Danny and the Dust Bunnies (childrens)

Written with Aletha Barrett May

The Land of Heart's Delight (memoir

Chapter One

***R**ehabilitation center indeed!* Flora Melkiot thought with a mental sniff. She had decided upon arrival that physical sniffs were likely to overwhelm one with unpleasant odors. *More like a dumping ground for everything that limps, cries, drools or wears diapers.*

The fact that she was a patient too didn't temper her opinion. Her being here was solely the fault of her idiot daughter Clarissa. It had only been a little traffic accident; Flora could have managed quite well on her own with a broken wrist.

At least she cherished the dream that she could have; her eldest child – a soft spoken, decorous and painfully conventional daughter who had been a trial to Flora since she was in diapers – refused to countenance the possibility. Probably regarding the accident as a heaven-sent opportunity to enforce her own will, Clarissa had swooped up from San Antonio, bamboozled the doctors and spirited Flora away from her home at the Olympus House in Dallas and the few of her friends who were still living to the Cold Creek Health Care Facility, a rehabilitation/nursing home whose primary attraction seemed to be its proximity to Clarissa.

The only ones here who looked the least bit healthy were the nurses and attendants. Everyone else…

Nothing but a waiting room for the Grim Reaper, Flora had thought mournfully when she had finally wakened to Clarissa's saccharine mewlings about 'poor Mama' and the labored breathing of her roommate.

"You couldn't get me a private room?" had been Flora's first coherent words.

"Now, Mama, they don't have private rooms here… part of the rehabilitation is interaction with your peers…" Clarissa had temporized, not thinking that her mother would object to being regarded as equal with those who limped, cried, drooled or wore diapers. The resulting disagreement brought attendants flying in from three separate departments.

That had been over a week ago and, outwardly at least, Flora had become resigned to her fate. After due reflection, she had decided it was better not to make a public spectacle of herself with a cast on her right wrist (of course she had to have injured her writing hand), an assortment of bruises and her hair whacked off short. Flora had worn her hair black, long and bound into a sophisticated chignon for most of her adult life; changing your style, she declared, was a sign of insecurity about your Self.

Flora was never insecure about anything.

Still, until her hair grew out a little, at least enough to cover the stitches in her scalp, she was just as happy to be away from Dallas and all its gossips. Especially since the tell-tale grey (which in actuality was now pure white) that Ramon had hidden so successfully for years was beginning to blaze from her roots.

"Good morning, Mrs. Melkiot," chirruped this morning's day nurse. She was blonde, brainless and relentlessly cheerful. "How are we feeling today?"

Flora scowled. This irritating angel of mercy reminded her of the equally brainless and equally irritating blonde who worked in the office at the Olympus House, though she was not as expensively dressed or well put together. Flora disliked them both intensely.

"As you have just now entered the room I have no idea at all how you are doing. My wrist itches. My head itches. And I am bored. It is not as if this place is overloaded with scintillating conversation!" Flora cast a deadly glance at the snoring lump that was her roommate.

The nurse, whose name Flora was sure was Candy or Cookie or something equally gooey, continued smiling. The daughter had been insistent that her mother not know a stroke victim who slept a great deal and could not speak had been specifically chosen for her roommate. Clarissa was not only conventional, she was extremely smart and had no illusions about her mother's temperament.

"You're not here to converse, you're here to get better. Now we need to get you up and dressed."

"Why? There's nothing to do here."

"You need to get to therapy."

"Bah. I don't need therapy. I just need to get home."

The nurse smiled even more sweetly. "Then I guess I'll just have to get Al in here to bathe you."

Flora glared. The nurse continued to smile, though by now it was beginning to look a little worn.

On her first day here the humiliation of being completely, intimately, thoroughly bathed by a handsome boy barely older than her college student grandson had sent Flora into a temper tantrum that had been heard all over the facility. Repeating the experience was a threat the nurses trotted out any time they wanted Flora to do something she did not want to do. Flora was well aware they used it as a tool to control her. She also knew that they'd do it without a qualm.

Accustomed to running her own life and a number of other peoples' whenever she could manage it, Flora Melkiot found that lack of autonomy, even in something so little as bathing, was anathema.

"I can bathe myself," she growled.

"Then you'd better get about it," the nurse said, her smile broadening. "It's almost time for breakfast and therapy starts at ten o'clock."

* * * * *

From the first Flora had thought therapy was a joke and, when she saw her partner for today's session, it was a bad one.

The therapy room was a large, determinedly cheery room full of, in Flora's opinion, absolutely idiotic things. There was a walking ramp perhaps ten feet long with sturdy handrails, several bicycle pedal things, a couple of raised platforms covered with mats and several large tables holding all kinds of stuff. There was a large fabric container filled with balls of various sizes and several chairs were dotted around the room. A variety of walkers and canes were parked by the door, as neatly as cars in a lot. They, and the elderly occupants, were the only things that kept the room from looking like a day care facility for super-sized toddlers.

"They took another shot at me in the hallway last night," Flora's partner confided in a soft voice.

"Really."

Mrs. Badham was a sprightly little gnome of a woman with sparkling eyes and a ready laugh, both of which were in direct contrast to the silent shufflers who mostly populated Cold Creek Health Care Facility. She was also mad as a hatter, making up stories about anyone and everyone and believing them utterly. In spite of herself Flora almost admired the old woman's riotous imagination.

"Let me get your security belt on, Mrs. Melkiot..." Terry Williams, a pretty woman of middle years who was head physical therapist and therefore had to work with Flora when everyone else flatly refused, tightened a length of webbing around Flora's waist. It was thick and sturdy and looked as if it would be more at home hoisting crates. "Don't want you to fall, do we?"

Flora smiled tightly. She truly believed she could stand everything else about this place if the staff weren't so relentlessly cheerful! It was like continually chewing on a saccharine tablet.

"All right now, let's toss the ball and work on your coordination." Terry handed an almost weightless beach ball to Flora and hauled Mrs. Badham to her feet, using her security belt as a handle. "Let's try this standing up, shall we? You need to work on your lower body strength."

Flora lifted the ball effortlessly toward Mrs. Badham. It was the same way she had played ball with her children and grandchildren before they could walk.

The ball bounced off the old woman's veined and flailing hands and skittered across the room.

"Good try!" chortled Terry. She trotted after the ball. "I'll get it!"

"They know I know," Mrs. Badham whispered. "They'll do anything to get rid of me."

"I doubt that," Flora said astringently. *At least,* she added, *not as long as the ridiculously high daily charge was being paid.*

"But I know…"

"Let's try again!" This time Terry gave the ball to Mrs. Badham, who sent it to Flora with about the same energy and accuracy as her infant children and grandchildren had.

Flora returned the ball. This time Mrs. Badham knocked it to the other side of the room. Repeating her mantra of "Good try!" Terry went after it.

"I know too much!"

Flora really did not want to be caught in this woman's world of imaginary plots and conspiracies, but there seemed no other way to communicate with her. She sighed.

"Killing you would cause more problems than it would solve. Their best bet is to make you look crazy so no one will listen to you."

Listen to me! Flora thought with a mixture of anger and dismay. *I sound as crazy as she does!*

"You're right…" Mrs. Badham cocked her head as she thought, her white-candy-floss hair wobbling. "I'll just keep taking notes. Somebody will know what to do… I don't want to put myself in more danger."

"Very wise."

They threw the ball back and forth, on one or two occasions actually completing a toss and catch. Terry was getting the major benefit of the workout, running back and forth to catch the ball. If she worked like this all day Flora could not understand why the therapist was still so chunky.

Only once or twice did Terry look as if she might think Flora was missing the throws and tosses on purpose. Serenely Flora ignored her quizzical glances.

"All right," Terry puffed, tossing the ball into the large canvas container. "Mrs. Badham, why don't you just sit here and rest a minute? Helen will set you up on the pedal machine when she's through with Mrs. Kirkland. Now why don't you come over to the table, Mrs. Melkiot?" She turned her attention to Flora, who had been edging toward the doorway hoping to escape, and was almost able to hide her expression of unholy glee. "Let's try something different for you today."

Flora sat gingerly at the large round table. Like the rest of the furniture at the center it was drab, serviceable and rubber-edged. The top was cluttered with what looked like children's toys – puzzles, building blocks, yarn loops.

Terry took the top off a plastic tub and dumped out a large glob of neon-bright yellow clay. As Flora watched it oozed from an exact replica of the container to a shapeless blob on the table. A bumpy blob. There were a couple of brilliantly colored plastic pegs sticking out of it.

"So this is where old movie monsters come to retire," Flora muttered.

Terry didn't crack a smile.

"Now take this and knead it like this…" In demonstration she squooshed it through her fingers. It returned to a shapeless blob almost immediately. The effect was slightly repellent. "And when you find one of these little plastic pegs, take it out, clean it by rubbing against the clay and drop the peg in this box."

Flora regarded the thing with distaste. "Why?"

"This will help build strength in your hands and arms and help your small motor skills. Now let me see you do it." She plopped the whole thing into Flora's hands. "Both hands now."

The play dough and modeling clay Flora had bought for her children and grandchildren hadn't felt like this. It was slick and resistant and almost slimy, if something dry could be considered slimy. A peg jabbed her palm.

"Don't push!" An authoritative voice boomed through the room.

The woman coming through the door was smartly dressed in a pantsuit and silk blouse in glaring contrast to everyone else. The staff wore scrubs and most of the patients wore either pajamas and robes or summer-weight sweat suits.

Flora frowned. This was all it took to make the morning just perfect. The night before she had been introduced to Mrs. Cattermole, Mrs. General Brian Cattermole as the woman was prone to say at any and all times, and one meeting had been enough. Just because her late husband had held an exalted rank in the Air Force Penelope Cattermole thought she had the right to order everyone else around. Flora never ceased to be amazed at the little arrogances people took upon themselves.

"Yes, Mrs. Cattermole," said the nurse's assistant. Small and shy, she invariably had the bad jobs pushed off onto her by her more determined coworkers. Escorting Mrs. Cattermole was definitely one of the least desirable chores. It was obvious to everyone – except Mrs. Cattermole herself – that she needed help; her walk was lurching and the cane she held was at the moment vacillating more between hindrance and offensive weapon than balancing aid.

Charlie, one of the few male therapists, came forward and took Mrs. Cattermole's arm. "I've got her, Nora. You can go."

The little aide frankly ran.

"Welcome to the therapy room, Mrs. Cattermole," Charlie said in his smooth way. A dangerously handsome man, he was too smooth and determinedly pleasant almost to the point of unctuousness; Flora would not have bought a used car from him, but most of the old ladies here doted on him and all but fought over his attentions. "I thought this morning we'd do some basic testing to see what your abilities are... that is, if you approve of the idea."

Flora thought she might just gag.

Penelope Cattermole gave him a straight look. "Don't patronize me, young man. I'm not one of these silly old women to be gotten around with smiles and soft words. My husband was General Brian Cattermole of the United States Air Force and I don't like being condescended to by the hired help!" Her voice was thickened and slurred as a result of her stroke, but still she managed to form understandable if somewhat mangled words and spit them out, as pointed and deadly as darts.

Charlie blinked. For one instant there was silence in the usually noisy therapy room as all the oldsters held their breath either from fear or outrage. He swallowed, then went on without dimming his toothpaste-commercial smile one bit.

"I wouldn't dream of it, Mrs. Cattermole. Will you sit here?" With the grace of a practiced courtier he held out a chair at the table next to Flora's.

At one time Penelope Cattermole had been an extraordinarily handsome woman; not beautiful, which implies a pleasing prettiness, but handsome, which goes beyond the mere arrangement of facial features. Even now, with the left side of her face showing the ravages of a recent stroke, she was impressive. Coupled with a strong personality, she would have been a worthy match for any number of generals on either side.

Slowly, clumsily, Mrs. Cattermole sat down, uttering

a little sigh when she was done. His smile still firmly pasted in place even though she was looking at him with a suspicion most people reserved for unrecognizable things found too late in the back of the refrigerator, Charlie pulled out an array of what looked like toys and puzzles and began his tests.

Flora looked over at Terry. "Perhaps you should be glad you got me instead."

Terry smiled, the gesture as plastic as the yellow goop Flora was manhandling. "We like to work with all our patients."

Flora pulled a plastic peg from the mess and flipped it at her.

"I think I'll get us some coffee." Terry plucked the sticky peg from the front of her scrubs with dignity and strode over to the miniscule counter that held a Mr. Coffee, a microwave and, underneath, a tiny refrigerator.

Assailed by unfamiliar feelings that in someone else might be considered shame, Flora tore at the sticky clay and removed every peg in it. One of the troubles of being treated like a child was that one started acting like a child. Single and married and widowed, Flora Bernice Donahgey Melkiot had been a strong-minded, independent (bone-stubborn, according to her late husband Morris) woman. The coddling and loss of freedom at this place had seriously eroded her sense of autonomy.

Well, that was going to stop! She was stuck here until she got well – Clarissa had seen to that! – so the best thing for Flora to do was get well quickly.

Convinced that if she had just put her mind to it she could have become a great artist, Flora began to sculpt the therapy clay, pulling it and tweaking it and silently swearing at it.

Terry set a pink plastic mug in front of Flora, then sat down, still holding her own. "What a lovely flower," she said in honeyed tones.

Flora had been creating a rather unconventional and

hopefully contentious Madonna and Child. She squished the hopeful image back into a finger-marked blob. "Nothing," she muttered. "This clay's the wrong texture."

"It wouldn't have held anyway. It's made not to keep a shape. Make anything you like out of it and in no time at all it will be back to a puddle."

Flora eyed the yellow lump as if it were possessed of some alien intelligence. "Nasty stuff."

"But very helpful. I see you got all the pegs out." Terry sounded indulgent.

"It was a hard fight, but I won."

"Okay, let's do five minutes on the pedal machine and that'll be all for today."

Flora took a sip of her coffee. It was just grocery-store stuff, pallid and bitter, but it was the first real coffee Flora had had since coming to Cold Creek. What they served in the dining room did not even deserve the name of coffee, or much of anything else that could be mentioned in polite society. *One had to adjust*, she thought philosophically and tried not to remember the new shipment of Gevalia French Roast that had arrived just before the accident. It would be waiting for her when she got home. And in spite of what Clarissa might think, she was going home again, and soon.

Terry set the small frame with undersized bicycle pedals on the table in front of her. Flora had a vague memory of these things being marketed once as weight-reduction devices – pedal away the pounds while you sat and watched TV, or some such nonsense. Not that she ever had to worry about losing weight; she was still the same weight she had been when she married. Its distribution, though, seemed to have shifted somewhat.

"Now you just grab the pedals and turn them. This will develop your upper body strength – "

There was a crash from the other table. All activity in the room stopped as everyone turned to look.

"And I tell you I cannot! I am a better judge of what I

can do than you are!" With her good arm Penelope Cattermole sent another box of plastic things flying.

"Now, Mrs. Cattermole…"

She eyed him poisonously. "I know your type, young man. My late husband General Cattermole would not have had anyone like you in his unit."

There was a visible struggle behind his eyes, but Charlie kept a bland expression on his face. "Your doctor wanted us to ascertain a baseline level of ability so we can help you get well as quickly as possible…"

"I will be well as soon as I can get some rest without officious little people bothering me all the time. I am going back to my room!"

It was painful to watch her struggle to her feet and stagger towards the door. Charlie ran to help her, only to receive a solid thunk from her cane across his shins. Mrs. General Cattermole's progress was unsteady and pathetic, but also somehow magnificent, a triumph of will over failing flesh and bone.

"Bitch!" Charlie muttered, unaware that in the dead silence of Mrs. Cattermole's exit everyone could hear.

Chapter Two

Naomi Case rubbed the back of her neck. Lord, how she hated new patients! Especially the ones who were here involuntarily. Yes, they were old and sick, but they hadn't admitted it yet; they still thought they could do everything the way they always had. Once the patients realized they were little more than children again and obeyed their orders like they should, they could be darlings, but while they fought her they were tiresome.

Like Mrs. Cattermole. Mrs. General Brian Cattermole. Lord, that woman could give Jesus Christ Himself a temper! She wanted a private room. She wanted her own furniture. She wanted her personal maid to look after her. She wanted special meals. She wanted things that Naomi hadn't even known existed.

Until now Naomi thought Flora Melkiot had been her most tiresome patient who wasn't positively mental, even more so than old Mr. Moretti who tried to put his hands everywhere, but even Mrs. Melkiot appeared almost normal compared to Mrs. Cattermole. Oh well, this might not be the best job in the world, but it was keeping her family fed and housed and there was enough left over for her accounting classes. Once she graduated and got a job as an accountant she'd go into an office and never have to deal with crazy old people or their dirt again!

The idea was as seductive as a drug. No one in her family had ever worked in an office before. Naomi could picture herself in a pretty suit, sitting in an office, working on a spreadsheet or analyzing a profit/loss statement.

She'd have a big desk and a bookcase and a leather chair and a window…

"You feeling okay?" Melanie Jenks' voice had a definite Texas twang that somehow seemed to fit perfectly with her long and bony face. She dumped a stack of dietary reports on the nurses' station counter. "Anything wrong?"

"Cattermole." Naomi told about Mrs. Cattermole storming out of therapy and how she had helped the general's widow back to her room.

"Gawd, what a bitch!" Wearily Melanie pushed a handful of her abundant dirty-blonde hair back behind her ear. "Why does she think she's so important?"

"I guess she used to be and can't get used to the idea she isn't anymore." Naomi shrugged and her full lips twisted into a wry smile. "Anyway, she's not all bad… she gave me a compliment."

Melanie snorted. "Mrs. General Brian Cattermole gave you a compliment? Go on…"

"She did. She said I was a good little nigger gal."

"I hope you decked her one."

"Why?" Naomi shrugged a second time, her mind burying the fact she had indeed felt like doing just that. "She's old. People talked like that when she was young."

"People will always talk like that unless someone tells them different!"

"Isn't going to make any difference what I say. She's too set in her ways… It'd just make my life more unpleasant. Words don't hurt me none. Leastaways, not words like that from people like her." Besides, Naomi knew reacting could cost her this job, and then how would she feed her kids or finish school?

"You're a true Christian saint," Melanie said and grabbed the morning dietary report forms. "I'd have decked her."

Naomi watched the tall, thin nurse stride off down the hallway. Melanie always looked as if she'd be more comfortable loping across pastures or fields instead of being indoors. If there were a visual definition of a country gal, Melanie Jenks was it. Lanky and horse-faced, she was still pretty in a corn-fed kind of way. As she was just going through her third divorce it was obvious the menfolk liked her, though apparently not for too long a time.

And, Naomi thought ruefully, *she probably would have decked Mrs. Cattermole if the old lady had said something about her being po'white trailer trash or some such nonsense.*

Melanie had some anger management problems which were not been helped by the newest and still ongoing divorce and what was building up to be a fairly nasty custody battle. Naomi knew a little bit about was going on, about her husband's new girlfriend, about how the two of them wanted to adopt Davy, Melanie's six-year old son. Just to add to the mix, only a few weeks before Melanie's oldest daughter, a product of her first marriage, had given birth to a badly retarded little girl.

Quickly Naomi said a prayer of thanks for her own three healthy children. Pity their dad couldn't have lived to see them turn out so well, but men would go a-soldiering and some of them did get killed. It was the way of the world, but it didn't stop Naomi's automatic spurt of anger at senseless wars.

At least he died decent, Naomi thought, *and the kids can be proud of him. And he didn't go off a-whoring like Melanie's husband.*

No, Melanie might have some anger management problems, but she sure had a bunch of reasons to be angry.

Not the least of which was walking towards Naomi at the moment.

"Good morning, Miss Enero," Naomi said politely. She kind of liked Stacey Enero, administrator of Cold Creek. A Junoesque and impeccably dressed woman in her late thirties, she was a perfectionist and an acknowledged disciplinarian whom no one wished to cross. On the other hand, everyone said that Miss Enero was fair and really seemed to care about the residents, as long as she didn't have to do anything personally to them. Some of Naomi's daydreams of the future had been influenced by Stacey Enero.

"Good morning, Naomi. Was that Melanie?"

"Yes, ma'am. She's taking the breakfast reports down to the dietician."

A tiny frown teased at Stacey's perfectly shaped eyebrows. "That should have been done right after breakfast. It's almost time for lunch."

"I'm sure Melanie knows that. She must have been with a patient."

"Yes, Melanie is one of the best nurses on staff," Stacey admitted with only a little reluctance. "I just wish she were as attentive to protocols."

"Yes, ma'am."

A quick grin tugged at the corners of Stacey's lips. "Might as well wish for snow in July, huh?"

"You got that right."

"I heard how you helped Mrs. Cattermole and what she called you. I'm sorry you had to hear it, but I'm proud of the way you handled it. Good job."

"I'm here to help."

Naomi had long since ceased to wonder at how Stacey Enero knew everything that happened. Some of the employees said she had the whole place wired for sound. A nurse who had left during the winter had said Miss Enero was either a witch or a psychic. Two of the therapists swore she had paid spies. Almost everyone agreed that she snooped. Old Mrs. Hammond, the previous administrator, had seldom left her office except when she went home in the evening. Miss Enero was seldom in it, always being out somewhere in the halls. Whatever her sources were, her almost instant knowledge of anything and everything that went on was quickly becoming legendary.

"She's going to be difficult. I'm afraid she might not settle down."

"She's a lady used to having her own way, all right."

Stacey sighed. The word 'lady' was not one she would have applied to Mrs. General Brian Cattermole other than an appellation of gender. "Well, our job is to get her back to where she can function on her own, not to change her or to like her. All we can do is do our best to see it happens quickly."

Naomi giggled as Stacey Enero hurried towards the kitchen.

* * * * *

Flora had decided on her first day that any meal in the communal dining room was almost as lethal as the cuisine and enough to kill anyone's appetite. The décor of cheerful sayings and posters and a gross over-utilization of violently colored crepe paper was enough to turn the stomach of anyone with finer sensibilities, but the food – so bland and soft and boring that it simply had to be violently nutritious – was an insult to anyone with a palate. The contrast, both visual and culinary, with the elegant gourmet restaurant restricted to Olympus House residents was as great as if they had been on different planets.

Flora had spent several days saying that to anyone who would listen, and protested loudly when informed that she could not order in from her favorite Mexican restaurant on the River Walk. It had done no good save to bring Clarissa running every meal time, finally deteriorating even her determinedly placid demeanor.

It did no good to Flora's, either, especially since she was trapped in this place.

To Flora's distress, Clarissa had somehow conned old Judge Rubio into giving her a temporary guardianship over her mother's health care until she was released from the doctor's care. That meant, Clarissa said with a loving smile, that Flora would stay at Cold Creek Health Care Facility, abide by Cold Creek Health Care Facility rules and eat Cold Creek Health Care Facility food until she was well and her doctor released her.

It was all for her own good, didn't she see that?

Flora's appeal to Dr. Jensen, the house doctor in charge of her case, including various veiled threats, produced nothing except his habitual bland smile and an assurance that everything was being done for her own good. If Flora had not been certain she had given birth to only one boy, her Jonathan, now a New York stockbroker with no inclination at all to meddle in his mother's business, she would have sworn that the doctor was Clarissa's twin brother.

She plotted fates for both of them that were almost as dire as the revenge she had planned for that treacherous old fool Enrique Rubio. He had been a friend of hers and Morris's for over forty years… how *dare* he turn on her and condemn her into a place like this? Her face twisted as she contemplated such treachery.

"I think the veal is rather good today, don't you?" asked Mrs. Rogers. Widow of a retired Army Master Sergeant, Honoria Rogers was recuperating from a bad reaction to hip surgery. She, at least, was sane, but so given to mindless, sugary platitudes and endless pictures of her grandchildren that Flora tried to avoid her. Unfortunately, the strict seating order – *It increases socialization, Mama*, Clarissa had replied to Flora's inevitable protest – made sure that she was going to be inflicted on Flora at least twice a week. Every resident had a stridently colored placard with their name on it, and the staff placed them around the tables in strict rotation.

Flora regarded the pale, flabby slab on her plate. If it was truly veal she would be surprised, but at least it was in one piece, not liquefied as it had to be for some. "As compared to what? Tofu?"

"I've heard that tofu is quite good for you," Mrs.

Rogers said. "The Orientals…"

"Crap!" snapped Mrs. General Brian Cattermole and threw her spoon across the table. It was, uncharacteristically, the first word she had said since sitting down. "Stuff tastes like sh…"

Flora raised her eyebrows. She had thought a general's wife would be above such vulgarity, but apparently not. Unfortunately the lady also had difficulty with her 'fs' and 'esses', which not only made her hard to understand, but also insured that whatever pureed veal remained in her mouth was sprayed over much of the table.

"If you please!" Flora said in a voice that made every headwaiter in Dallas quake.

Whatever her failings, Penelope Cattermole was made of stern stuff. She merely gave Flora a hard look that doubtless had annihilated many a junior officer and, turning her attention back to her plate, poked the offending pile. "Crap," she said again. "It tastes like sh…"

"Now, Mrs. Cattermole," said Melanie, pausing by the table with her own dinner tray which, Flora noted enviously, contained a gloriously juicy hamburger and no trace of veal in any form, pureed or otherwise. "That's not nice."

Penelope Cattermole looked up at her and her eyes narrowed. Her head cocked sideways and Flora was reminded of nothing so much as someone studying a new variety of bug.

"I know you," she said slowly and her eyes narrowed as if seeking focus.

"Yes, Mrs. Cattermole. I'm Melanie, one of the day nurses on your wing."

"No…" The older lady's permed curls bounced as she shook her head. One could almost see her damaged brain struggling to work. "You look so familiar…"

Melanie gave a little laugh. "I guess I just have one of those kind of faces, Mrs. Cattermole."

"No… I'll remember. I do know you…"

Melanie's smile became fixed. "Well, when you do be sure to remember to tell me. See you later, ladies."

After wiping the last Cattermole effusion off her arm and scooting her plate as far as she could away from the offender, which put her almost in Mrs. Williams' lap, Flora poked again at her veal cutlet. Flabby it might look, but it was so rubbery she could barely make a dent in it with either knife or fork.

If she dropped it, would it bounce away across the room?

They would probably just bring her another one. Perhaps even pureed.

Sighing, Flora pushed her plate away. Thank goodness her friend Rebecca had sent her the largest box of chocolates Russell Stover made. Flora truly preferred Godiva, but beggars couldn't be choosers. At least she wouldn't starve.

"Stupid girl," Mrs. Cattermole spluttered. "I never forget a face. I know her."

"Do any of you ladies need any help?" asked one of the aides. Her Mexican heritage was evident in her dark eyes and smooth, caramel-colored skin.

"I'm finished, Adelita," Flora said, struggling just a little to read her nametag, which, like all of them, was printed much too small. Her mother had impressed on her the importance of using a servant's first name as a reinforcement of their relative positions.

"You didn't eat much, Mrs. Melkiot."

"There wasn't much worth eating."

Adelita laughed obediently as she marked the slip of paper that accompanied every meal detailing how much the patient had eaten.

"I thought it was quite good," Mrs. Rogers said, scooping up the last of the gelatinous rice pudding. "After all, hunger is the best appetizer…"

"I'll tell the cook," Adelita said, then marked Mrs.

Rogers' and Mrs. Williams' meal slips. She didn't even make an attempt to talk with Mrs. Williams. The tiny, wizened little woman never spoke. "What about you, Mrs. Cattermole?"

"Crap, and you can tell that to the cook." Penelope pushed the plate away violently and sank back in her chair, muttering half to herself, "Bad enough they have to serve, but I don't like the damned greasers cooking my food…"

Flora, who was none too fond of minorities herself, was moved to say, "Really, Mrs. Cattermole…"

"The damned Mexicans and niggers are taking over this country and it won't be long before they start to kill us off, just you watch." She had shouted, her face red with anger, and her voice carried. The entire dining hall went silent as every eye swept to her.

Even though she was not at all involved Flora felt a rush of embarrassment, as if just by sitting at the same table she was somehow contaminated. Mrs. Rogers looked appalled, as if she might dive under the table at any moment. Mrs. Williams hadn't moved other than to scoop up the last bite of Flora's rice pudding.

Penelope Cattermole struggled to her feet and glared at her audience. "I'm right and you all know it, but you just aren't honest enough to admit it. They're going to take over and kill us all…"

Her face set in a determinedly sweet smile, Naomi swept across the room, her arms extended. "Why don't you let me help you back to your room, Mrs. Cattermole?"

The general's widow was not to be appeased. She swung her cane wildly, barely missing Naomi's outstretched arms, Mrs. Williams' head and a rolling cart of dirty crockery. "You'll be in with them," she snarled. "The niggers and the greasers won't be happy until they kill all us Americans."

She kept ranting until she stomped out the swinging doors. Her departure left a vacuum which ended with a rush of high-pitched chatter that sounded like a disturbed aviary.

Stacey Enero went to Naomi's side with a determined step. "Are you all right, Naomi?"

Naomi nodded. Her smile had faded to a ghastly rictus and her hands trembled. "Yes, ma'am. Miss Enero, she really tried to hit me. She could have broken my arm or really hurt Mrs. Williams! She's deadly with that thing!"

"Don't worry… we're not going to allow it to continue," Stacey said, a fire kindling in her normally cool brown eyes. "None of it!"

* * * * *

"And she really used her cane?" asked Dr. Bobby Jensen.

"Like a club."

"Hmmm. That means she has much more motor skill and manual control than I would have thought. To aim a cane…"

"It means that she's dangerous." Stacey Enero looked at her co-worker with open loathing. "She can't stay here."

"What would you like to do with her?"

"Don't ask me. I just know she can't stay here. It was bad enough that everyone had to listen to her insults and name-calling. Now that she's putting people in danger…"

"She missed them, didn't she?"

"Only by accident. I could see she was disappointed. She also put a great big bruise on Charlie's shin this morning."

The doctor laughed. The sound filled the tiny, glass-walled cubby that was the administrator's office. "Spreading things around, isn't she? General contempt for everyone."

"It's not funny, Dr. Jensen. It's bad enough that Charlie has a bruise, but if it had been Juanita or Terry or Patricia, she could have broken a bone! To say nothing of her attack on Naomi at lunch. And Mrs. Williams! That swing could have cracked her skull! You know how fragile she is."

"What had Mrs. Williams done to arouse the lady's ire?"

Stacy ground her teeth. "Nothing, and Penelope Cattermole is no lady!"

"Don't let her hear you say that, or she'll come after you with that stick of hers."

"She's not going to have the chance. I took it away along with her walker and until she leaves she's restricted to supervised wheelchair mobility."

Bobby Jensen sat forward, his attention for once fully engaged. He didn't like it when things didn't flow along as smoothly as a sonata.

Convinced he was born to be a composer, Bobby had become a doctor because his father and grandfather had been doctors and it had been the course of least resistance. He had taken the position of medical supervisor at Cold Creek simply because it was the only place he could find where his patients could be expected to die. A little dope to kill their pain, a little charm to ease their anxiety… the position was a piece of cake which he would happily give up when his music began to be appreciated.

His latest project was a symphony on which he had been working the last three years. The four years before that had been spent on the first three acts of a five act opera based on the life of Disraeli. Before that lay the half-complete carcasses of half a dozen magnum opuses – or was the correct plural opii? Somehow the realization that to gain fame and fortune as composer one had to actually finish and sell something had not yet impressed itself on Dr. Jensen and, as he had just passed his forty-fifth birthday, probably never would.

"That's not going to do her rehabilitation any good."

"She's not going to be here long enough for it to affect her rehabilitation."

"Have you called the family?"

Stacey riffled the pages of the thick file on her desk. "Doesn't appear to be any. Her husband's dead and there aren't any other relatives listed."

"How did she get here, then?"

"She's one of our contract patients from the military hospital. I'm going to send her back."

Bobby scowled, his face suddenly somber. A long, balding oval, it was not a face made for serious expressions. "That's an experimental contract. It could queer the whole deal if you send her back." As well, he realized all too much, as making him look bad; his father, long unimpressed by his son's lackluster career, had at least approved of his potential military influence.

"I'm not going to have the staff and patients here put at risk from one crazy old woman," Stacey snapped. "I've already started the paperwork."

The truth was, he was right. She had agonized over the decision. As operational administrator of Cold Creek Health Care Facility, it was her duty to make sure the books balanced, the laundry was done and the patients were taken care of. The medical administrator's job was all facets of health care and rehabilitation. Decisions as potentially far-reaching as this should be agreed upon by both, but Stacey knew that easy-going, non-controversial Bobby Jensen would never ally his name with such a move. Between him and the incompetent Mrs. Hammond Stacey had been amazed that the patients were as well taken care of as they had been.

"Stacey…"

"Mrs. General Brian Cattermole is leaving, Dr. Jensen," Stacey said in her most authoritative voice, "and that is that."

Not even to herself would Stacey admit just how big of a relief it would be to see the back of the old bitch. She hadn't drawn an easy breath since seeing the woman's name on the entrance form. But now it was over, the decision made. Mrs. General Brian Cattermole was leaving Cold Creek and that meant Stacey was safe.

Chapter Three

Flora Melkiot didn't like television. Of course, she had several sets back in her condo at the Olympus House – Morris had insisted on them and they had entertained him a little during those last horrid, house-bound months of his life. There was a large screen model in the living room, a smaller portable in the bedroom and a miniscule machine that combined television, radio and CD player on the kitchen counter, but other than the nightly news or one of Flora's favorite crime shows they were seldom on.

At Cold Creek, every room had a television, each of which seemed to be continually turned on to full volume, but always to a different station. Soap operas were popular, both in English and in Spanish, as were screaming game shows in both languages. Flora couldn't stand any of them.

That was one advantage of her semi-comatose roommate; Mrs. Gutierriez awoke barely enough to slurp down most of her meals, which were delivered on a tray, and be wheeled to the rehab room twice a day for some gentle usually passive exercise. The rest of the time she slept; that meant Flora was in complete control of the remote, which remained safely hidden in her nightstand drawer ever since an unwise and suitably chastised nurse had turned on the set to wake Flora up the first morning.

Secure in her small TV-free zone, Flora could handle the various snores and snorts of the lump that was Mrs. Gutierriez. She turned on the small CD player she had insisted Clarissa bring her and selected some Mozart. She didn't really understand Mozart, or any classical composer for that matter, but some of the tunes were pretty and it was her duty as one of the social arbiters of the Olympus House, if not of Dallas itself, to at least appear classically literate. Besides, if she kept the volume low enough not only did she not have to listen, it acted almost as white noise to negate the hall full of blaring TVs.

Clarissa had also brought her a bag full of paperback books, an eclectic selection of the mysteries and thrillers Flora loved. Flora didn't care so much for paperbacks – hardbacks looked so much better on the shelves – but she did have to admit that they were easier to handle with one basically immobile arm. Some of them she had read before, but that didn't matter. At least Clarissa had pretty much stuck to the authors Flora had specified, even as she remonstrated with her mother for such bloodthirsty tastes. If Clarissa had had her way, Flora would be stuck reading the emotional effusions of Danielle Steel and Nora Roberts, if not Barbara Cartland.

"And I tell you, old woman, you better watch your step!"

The voice was low and harsh, but quite audible.

The next one wasn't; it too was low, but so unintelligible that it was impossible to hear the words or even swear that there were words.

"I don't want to hear it. Just keep your mouth shut if you know what's good for you," said the first voice.

More gurgling.

There was the blare of a commercial touting something that was new, better and completely different. Or maybe it was a game show. They often sounded alike.

Flora found herself straining to listen.

"I don't care," the voice said, even lower and harder to hear than before. "I'll kill you if I have to."

The words were as overwrought as on any soap opera, but not for a moment did Flora think she was listening to a television. The sound was different; the voice sounded like a real person, not a trained actor trying to sound like a character, though it was impossible to tell if the speaker were male or female. She couldn't hear well enough to know what the person actually sounded like, merely that the voice never came from the highly polished dream-world of soaps.

Her curiosity had been forced almost to dormancy by the staleness of life at Cold Creek, but Flora could feel it reviving. She struggled out of bed – not an easy task when one arm was weighted heavily with plaster and the much-too-high bed was covered with books that made an awful crash on the industrial linoleum floor.

By the time Flora had wiggled into the horrible flat terry house shoes Clarissa had bought her and struggled to the door, the hall was empty save for a small cluster of people at the nurses' station in the center of the hallway.

No wonder, Flora thought with a rush of disgust and glared at the bland terry scuffs. *Those books made enough noise for a herd of elephants and these dratted shoes made me so slow anyone could have gotten away. Drat Clarissa for not bringing my mules down!*

Flora glanced out the window at the uninspired so-called garden, then peered down the hallway. Two of the aides, pretty Mexican girls who played at teaching Flora Spanish, were going into a room about halfway down, but otherwise the hall was still deserted. Most of the doors were at least partway open and from them poured a cacophony of TV babble.

Sniffing, Flora realized there was something else in the air… a faint, ammoniac scent of urine. She wrinkled her nose fastidiously. They did work at keeping the facility clean, but some things were just beyond the realm of possibility. At least it wasn't a common or overwhelming problem.

For a moment Flora listened, trying to sort out the noise in her head. No, there was nothing going on that could possibly be what she had heard. First of all, there had been no syrupy, overwrought music. Secondly, she doubted if any of the actors, even the ones playing the grubby parts, could sound as real as the voice she had heard.

Where could that voice have come from?

Cold Creek Health Care Facility was a single story building built sort of along the lines of a spider, if one could imagine a six-legged spider. In the center was the nurses' station, a great round area chopped into a number of smaller ones, including two locked metal drug cabinets. One leg was devoted to the rehabilitation exercise room, laundry facilities, kitchen and dining room; another to a reception area where patients could relax with their families (a blaring TV was in there, too, so Flora could never figure out how anyone could talk to someone else, let alone relax), administrative offices, beauty parlor, a chapel so determinedly interfaith it became just another room but with colored windows and pews, and a small clinic.

The other four legs were patient rooms, two people to a room, twenty rooms to a hallway, arranged ten to each side. One of those four legs housed the permanent rehab residents, physically impaired but mentally normal-enough people who were to live out their lives in this place. Another leg housed those bedridden ones who were almost or totally absent mentally; it was closed off by a door from the rest of the building, a fact for which Flora was very thankful. The brochure called it perpetual care; Flora thought that sounded like a cemetery plot, which wasn't really too far off. In her opinion to be condemned to this place forever was like being buried alive. At least she could look forward to going home sometime, hopefully soon.

After exploring her hallway and the common areas, Flora didn't care to see any more. Her room was the last one on Corridor D. To the left of her door was the outside wall and a window overlooking the bleak expanse of rock and cacti that the brochure called 'designer landscaping.' No one ever used the garden in spite of the bench set in the middle of it; probably they wouldn't even if they could get out there. To the right was the hallway, a vast expanse of doors leading to the nurses' station.

After reassuring herself of the non-interfering nature of her roommate, Flora had had no interest in her neighbors. To one accustomed to the rarified sphere of the Olympus House and Dallas society, the residents of Cold Creek Health Care Facility held very little interest.

At least until now.

Finding who lived in what room was easy; on the wall outside each door someone had put gaudy, hand-lettered signs, almost childish in their naiveté, announcing the inhabitants. Flora had noticed her own – in shades of pink and green, decorated with impossibly yellow sunflowers – checked that the spelling was correct, then promptly forgotten about all of them.

The forever silent Mrs. Williams (first name Marie) and that dratted Penelope Cattermole were across the hall. Mrs. Cattermole didn't have sunflowers, Flora noticed; her name was red on a gray ground, and Flora was not amused to see that it was written Penelope Cattermole (Mrs. General Brian). The Cold Creek staff was split on the usage of names; some thought the use of an honorific gave dignity, while others thought the use of first names promoted intimacy. The signs reflected this dichotomy, reading Marie Williams (Mrs.), Flora Melkiot (Mrs.), and so forth. All but Penelope (Mrs. General Brian) Cattermole's.

Wonder how big of a tantrum she had to throw to get that? Flora thought.

Although she had loved her late husband Morris dearly, even when he was alive Flora had preferred to be known as herself instead of an appendage to him. But then, she thought, she was an individual in her own right – patroness of the arts, mover and shaker in Dallas society, friend of the powerful; she had even helped solve a baffling murder in the Olympus House itself not too long ago. [*Exercise is Murder, 2013*] Flora Melkiot didn't have to derive her persona from her late husband's existence or job.

She could have, though, Flora reflected; there were over thirty Melkiot's Gems and Jewels stores in Texas alone. Whatever else Clarissa was, she was a good judge of character; her husband Bill Fullerton now ran the jewelry chain and was almost as good at it as Morris had been.

Next to Williams and Cattermole were Eula Badham and Hortensia Bernal. Next to Flora and her roommate Adela Gutierriez were Leonora O'Brien and Judy Lloyd. All three doors were partially open; all three rooms had their TVs on, and all to different stations.

Flora shrugged. Maybe the quality of acting on the soaps was improving.

Still…

Shrugging, Flora turned back to her room. There was a new Robert W. Walker thriller in her stack and, Heaven knew, nothing really exciting would ever happen at a boring little nursing home in San Antonio. She couldn't be that lucky.

* * * * *

The TV was on, but Penelope Cattermole didn't see it. She sat and stared at the wall. Anyone looking at her might think she was afraid from the way that she trembled, but anyone who knew her could tell she was angry. Furious, raging, seething, and her emotions were made the more intense because she was imprisoned in a crippled shell of flesh that would not obey her commands.

How dare anyone talk to her like that? The General would have had their head! They thought they could push her around just because she was old and sick.

They had another think coming. She might be slower, and she might be older, and her body might not respond as it should, but she was still Penelope Cattermole – Mrs. General Brian Cattermole! – and she did not take that kind of shit from anyone!

Anyone.

Slowly, crookedly, her withered lips turned up in a smile. The effect was chilling.

* * * * *

Languidly Flora stretched loops of cotton knit around the pegged board. Terry had been called away just as Flora had arrived at therapy and no one had told her in what order to put the loops, so Flora was creating a work of art. Wooden pegs and colored cotton loops commonly used to create thin potholders were a strange medium for artistic creation, but Flora believed a true artist such as she could work with anything to hand.

What was growing under her fingers was a glorious abstract, all reds and yellows and oranges, obviously representing the creative temperament. Flora could see it hanging in one of those little galleries down in the Dallas design district, or maybe some trendy shop Uptown or on Oak Lawn.

On the other hand, she wasn't so sure she wanted her name linked with the Oak Lawn crowd.

"They're going to kill me, you know."

Flora sighed as Eula Badham slipped into the chair beside her. Two times in one day!

"No one kills little old ladies in nursing homes," she said, trying to decide between a burgundy loop and a crimson one. Burgundy spoke of the despair of the artist, but there weren't really enough burgundy colored loops to do anything with.

"Yes, they do. They shot Mrs. Rausch night before last and killed her dead." Eula's cloud of white hair bobbed as she shook her head emphatically.

"Then they're terrible shots," Flora said, regretfully putting the burgundy aside. "I spoke to Mrs. Rausch at breakfast this morning."

And a boring experience it had been, too; the woman had never been anything but a hausfrau and now wanted nothing more than to return to her kitchen. Almost her entire conversation was a request for someone to take her home. Flora would never choose to have a conversation with a person who had such obvious mental disabilities, but good manners dictated that she at least speak to everyone seated at her table. Flora would never be faulted on her manners.

Eula looked around carefully in case spies were lurking behind the exercise bikes, then leaned forward to whisper, "That's a double. The gang put her in here so they could learn what we know."

"What gang?"

"The gang that's laundering gambling money through this place, of course. It comes up from Mexico, you know."

Flora sighed. On the news last night there had been stories about gambling money being laundered in Vegas and illegal aliens coming up from Mexico in record numbers. Somehow those two legitimate stories had gotten scrambled in Eula Badham's short-circuiting brain and compressed into the confines of this nursing home. Flora didn't know whether to laugh, cry or scream.

"And you know the man in D-12? The man in the wheelchair?"

Flora nodded. Vaguely she remembered seeing a balding older man in that area who seemed both younger and in better health than most of the inmates.

"Well, he runs the gang. He owns this place and lots of other things, but he lives here to make sure everything goes all right."

Giving a skeptical sniff, Flora picked up a loop of

violent yellow-green and held it against her creation. "I can't believe anyone with any brains or money would choose to live here voluntarily."

"He's also having an affair with the woman in C-8. She's his wife's roommate," Mrs. Badham added in a confidential whisper.

Flora's mind boggled. "You don't say," was all she could say.

Where were Terry or Charlie or someone and why didn't they come rescue her?

"They have to kill me," the little woman said mournfully. "I know too much."

"Well, then, why don't you go tell everyone? If everyone knows, there's no reason to kill you."

Listen to me! Flora's mind screamed. *Another two weeks here and I'll be as nutty as she is!*

"They won't listen to me. No one believes me." The soft little chin quivered. "They think I'm crazy, but I know what I see. When they killed my nephew they dragged him down the hall and through the door at the end of the corridor and then buried him in the garden."

Enough, decided Flora, was enough. "Your nephew was here yesterday and he looked very alive to me."

"That's because the CIA dug him up in time. They got him good doctors and hid him and his new wife down in the A hall."

Having met Eula Badham's nephew Flora would have wagered the precious young man would never have any kind of wife, new or otherwise.

"There isn't a door at the end of the hall. There's just a window."

"No, it's really a door. We're just supposed to think it's a window. There's a secret catch that opens it. I've seen them use it at night. I've hunted and hunted for it, but I can't find it."

All the pretty colors were just about used up. If Terry or Charlie didn't show up in a minute, Flora was going to go back to her room and just say piffle on doing rehabilitation today. Actually, that sounded like a pretty good idea.

"Well, if you ever find it, tell me and I'll help you break out. They keep us locked down like maximum security."

Flora had found that out the night she decided to leave, not too long after her admittance; everyone had been so kind and so helpful and so damned obstructive! They would not let her call a cab. They told her all the doors were locked after six pm, with admittance and exit only on visual recognition. Worst of all, they had called Clarissa, who had swooped down immediately full of tears and recriminations.

"They'll never let me go," Eula Badham said mournfully. "I know too much. I know they're going to kill me."

Just as Flora had begun to contemplate doing this herself with a garrote of brightly colored cotton loops Terry appeared, her bright smile only a little forced.

"Now, you know we all love you, Mrs. Badham. We're here to take care of you."

The old lady stared incredulously at her with tragic eyes. "Yes, of course you are," she said quickly and shuffled away.

"Poor dear," Terry said brightly.

"Why does she think everyone's out to kill her?" Flora knew Terry was studying psychology at one of the local community colleges. If she could get her talking, she might get out of therapy.

Terry shrugged and sat down. "Pretty standard self-aggrandizement syndrome. She's a widow and was a nice, middle-class housewife all her life. Both her children are dead and her in-law children don't give a damn about her. None of her grandchildren have ever come to visit her in the two years she's been here. Only one who seems to care at all is her nephew, and he lives so far away he can't come often."

"So she creates this melodramatic scenario with herself as the persecuted heroine so she'll feel important."

The therapist gave a sad little smile. "Pretty much. It's not all that uncommon, though most people's aren't as violent or involved as hers."

"Which we can probably blame on television." Flora made herself two silent vows. She was going to be nicer to people, most notably Eula Badham and Clarissa, and she was going to get out of here and back to her real life in Dallas as soon as humanly possible, even if she had to get a lawyer to overturn that stupid temporary guardianship.

She also vowed never to start watching TV, her favorite crime shows excepted, of course.

"Probably." The professionally perky smile popped back into place. "Now let's see what you've done here… Most people don't use the loops to make a picture... My goodness, Flora, that's a beautiful sunset. I don't think I've ever seen anyone do anything like this!"

A sunset! How bourgeois could one get? Biting back a snarl in deference to her new vow, Flora began snapping off the loops and arranging them by color.

"Holler when you get through with that and we'll play some ball," Terry said, heading off to help Charlie get Mr. Nelson out of his wheelchair and into the walking ramp.

The prospect was almost as delightful as having her beautiful abstract called a sunset. Flora grabbed at the loops and began slamming them down. She had to get out of here before she became as crazy as everyone else, some members of the staff included!

Chapter Four

Melanie Jenks could feel Mrs. General Brian Cattermole's gaze on her like hard, cold fingers. The old witch never changed. Melanie wanted to work faster, but didn't want to make the old woman think she had rattled her. Keeping a plastic smile on her face, Melanie pulled underwear and diapers from the two drawers beneath Mrs. Williams' miniscule closet.

Piling them on the steel-trayed rolling cart used for moving everything but patients, she wondered if the relatives only sent old, crappy clothes, or if the aides and housekeeping staff only stole the best. More than once she had run into an employee wearing a garment bearing the name of a patient.

Gentle Mrs. Williams drowsed in the easy chair by the window. She was a dear, as much of a dear as a vacant lump of flesh could be. She and her personal objects – a photo of her late husband, a collection of gaudy pictures and collages made by her many and untalented grandchildren, a singularly bland crucifix – still hung on the walls; they and she would be moved last, so her new room would be instantly the same as the old one.

Melanie doubted if she would notice.

Mrs. General Brian Cattermole noticed everything. She might be impaired in speech and movement, but her brain, the thinking, observing, conniving part of her brain was as crafty as ever.

Melanie glanced over her shoulder. The old woman sat bolt upright in her wheelchair, her face full of repressed fury, her gaze fixed firmly on Melanie. It was a look to chill the blood.

"Make sure you don't take anything of mine..." Her words might have been mangled, but their intent was coldly clear.

Mrs. General Brian Cattermole was a right royal bitch!

I've got to quit thinking of her like that, Melanie thought. *She's not Mrs. General anymore. The old man is dead, and she's just a sick old woman. She can't hurt anyone.*

"I wouldn't dream of it, Penelope. Your things belong here, with you."

The aged eyes flashed with anger, which gave Melanie a small glow of satisfaction. It was a small advantage, and one Melanie would use to her heart's content.

"I am Mrs. General Brian Cattermole!"

"The general's been dead for years, Penelope, and probably grateful for it. Not even you can order him to come back," Melanie said in a mockingly gentle voice. "You're just you."

Penelope Cattermole spluttered incoherently as Melanie, smiling sweetly, finished loading the cart.

"Mrs. Williams, sweetie, I'm just going to take this stuff to your nice new room and then I'll be back for you and your treasures." Melanie patted the old woman's veined and almost transparent hand; this time there was no mockery in her voice, only a genuine softness.

Mrs. Williams didn't respond, but just sat there, vague smile in place and rheumy blue eyes firmly unfocused on ... what? Melanie could never help wondering just what images that stuttering brain saw.

"Get out," said Penelope Cattermole.

Melanie only smiled.

*****

Dinner at Cold Creek was a lighter repetition of lunch, though this time without the questionable blessing of Mrs. General Brian Cattermole's presence. The meat loaf was as insubstantial and crumbly as lunch's veal cutlet had been rubbery. Flora almost envied those with so little control – or pride – that they ate it with a spoon.

Flora's dinner companions were more congenial than at lunch; she hadn't really talked to any of them before, but at least none of them seemed obviously mental and that was refreshing. Mr. Granowski was confined to a wheelchair, but his mind was a great deal more agile than his admitted ninety-odd years would suggest. Flora decided that he had been a rip and a rake in his younger years; probably still would be, if he were physically able.

Sophia O'Connor was a woman to whom Flora felt an instant kinship despite the generation or more that separated them. Bright, articulate, cultured, she was almost like an oasis of sanity in this bleak landscape of madmen and derelicts. Unfortunately she suffered from some obscure wasting disease that was never named but all too obvious to see. Already her weakened, nearly transparent body had to be secured to keep it upright in her wheelchair and her hands shook, but her voice was still steady – if frail – and her wit sharper than the blunted table knives with which they were trusted. She laughed and talked of many things beyond the narrow confines of Cold Creek Health Care Facility and never let a note of pity for herself or anyone creep into her voice.

The most memorable person at their table was one whom Flora had seen in the hallways and hated to look at.

At one time Dewayne Harbaugh must have been a fine looking man. Ghosts of physical attractiveness still lingered in the undamaged side of his face, if one looked beyond the lines left by pain and helplessness. The other side of his face hardly looked like a face at all. Twisted scar tissue, missing features, great patches of white and red and bluish glassily-healed skin that still looked like fresh wounds… the contrast to the soft chocolate of his other cheek was startling.

What was left of his body – two short stumps of legs, a misshapen trunk, one complete arm, part of another and that nightmare horror of a head – hunkered in a motorized scooter that was incongruously decorated with a red bicycle safety flag mounted on a flexible pole. He too was anchored in place by soft webbing, but instead of wearing pajamas and robes or lounging suits as most everyone else did, he was attired in a cut-off pair of blue jeans and a flashy Hawaiian shirt.

His mouth, half with large, full lips and half nothing more than a razor-thin cut in shiny mottled skin, was never still. Either he was eating or talking, or sometimes both at once. At first Flora had wondered if she would be able to eat at all with him there; then she found herself laughing with his non-stop stream of bad jokes. He allowed no pity for anyone, especially not himself, and scant charity for anyone else, including Flora.

It had been a long time since anyone had teased Flora or even dared to criticize her (Clarissa excepted, of course) but after one bad moment Flora tartly replied in kind and the table roared with laughter.

Probably none of the three would ever have entered the rarified confines of the Olympus House or Flora's carefully cultivated social circle, but in a way Flora felt as if she were back in the real world again, with people who were able to think and speak with some knowledge of intellectual subjects. Flora had never questioned that she was an intellectual. She knew if she had wanted to she could have contributed a great deal to the world's knowledge.

"I see the wicked witch isn't here," Dewayne said, ostentatiously looking around the dining room. "Anyone hear any houses falling today?"

"Surely you're giving that tiresome woman more importance than she's due," said Sophia O'Connor. She took a dainty sip from her plastic water glass.

"I assume you mean Mrs. Cattermole?" Flora asked.

"Don't you mean Mrs. General Brian Cattermole?" Dwayne grinned. "Who else?"

"Admittedly she is a most unpleasant and probably most unhappy woman," Flora said in what her friends back at the Olympus would have called her 'lady of the manor' voice. What her enemies would have called it was better left to silent speculation. "But the Wicked Witch of the West? A bit of overkill, don't you think?"

"Obviously you don't know her very well."

"I don't know her at all, other than to share a luncheon table with her today."

Dewayne's black eyes twinkled like polished obsidian. "Ah, yes, just before her demonstration of cross and jostle work. And you don't think that was enough time to know her?"

"It was certainly enough for me to know I don't wish to know her any better," Sophia said genteelly. "It makes no difference who or what her husband was, there is no excuse for the display she put on."

"I agree," Flora said, a note of surprise in her voice. The sweet potatoes – she thought they were sweet potatoes – might look like something unmentionable at a polite table, but they were delicious. "Doesn't she realize that such blatant outbreaks only emphasize her obviously low origins?"

Flora had long cherished the notion that in spite of anyone's current dress or status she could discern a person's class of origin. She also cherished the notion that other people besides she cared about such things.

"They're sending her back, you know." Dewayne said casually.

Sophia O'Connor dropped her fork. "You are kidding!"

"Good riddance to bad rubbish," said Mr. Granowski succinctly. "Woman's bad news. Nothing but trouble since she came."

"How do you know?" Flora asked quickly. Whatever his physical handicaps it was obvious that Dewayne Harbaugh had a superior intelligence system about this place, perhaps equal to her own at the Olympus House. She was always ready to learn a new technique. "Or," she added in sudden mistrust, "are you just guessing?"

Their two dining companions laughed.

"Dewayne never guesses," Sophia said.

"CIA should recruit him," Mr. Granowski said. "He could probably teach them a thing or two."

Dewayne merely tried to look modest and failed miserably.

"I just happen to find out a thing or two," he said, his eye twinkling.

"Spies or mechanical surveillance?" Flora asked sweetly, half to needle him, half out of pure curiosity.

Dewayne roared with laughter. "I like you, lady, but I ain't gonna share my secrets!"

Not yet, Flora thought, but merely smiled.

"So is it true? Where are they sending her?" Sophia asked.

"Back to wherever she came from, I suppose. I know it's a military hospital… probably either over at Randolph or Brook Army Medical. From what I can find out," Dewayne said with a fine counterfeit of modesty, "she was taken to the hospital after she was found with her stroke. She was sent here for rehab. They're sending her back. Miss Enero was adamant."

"That pretty little tamale never opens her mouth," Mr. Granowski said, an appreciative gleam in his rheumy eyes. "Never says anything about business. You must have her office bugged."

Dewayne smiled wickedly. "I'll never tell."

"Well, it's no loss," Sophia said without heat. "That Cattermole woman has been nothing but trouble since she's been here. I don't know of anyone who will miss her."

* * * * *

Stacey Enero might have her faults, but lack of courage wasn't one of them. She had been taught to face trouble head on, and just because trouble was in the guise of a feeble old woman was no need to relax her standards or her guard.

"Good evening, Mrs. Cattermole," she said pleasantly, laying a laden dinner tray on the adjustable table.

"'Bout time," was the old woman's garbled response. "Why here? Want to go to dining room."

Stacey listened politely as Mrs. Cattermole struggled with the words, waiting until she was through to speak. "No, Mrs. Cattermole. You have caused enough uproar among our guests. I am making arrangements to have you sent back to the military hospital. Until you leave you will be having your meals in here."

The faded eyes blazed. "Sent back?"

"Yes, Mrs. Cattermole. You have repeatedly upset our guests with your behavior and on more than one occasion have been violent enough to risk causing physical harm. We cannot have anyone here – guest or employee – put in danger."

Penelope Cattermole spat out a string of syllables that Stacey was glad she could not understand. The look on the woman's face was almost enough to kill at ten paces.

"I will stay here," she was finally able to articulate intelligently.

"No, Mrs. Cattermole, you are leaving. It shouldn't be more than a day or two until you go and until then you are to stay in this room. We will do everything to make you comfortable, but I can't let you go back into the community. You have caused too much trouble."

More nonsense syllables, accompanied by a great deal

of flying saliva, then the old eyes narrowed with intense thought.

"Never forget a face," she said thickly. "You look familiar…"

There was venom in that look. Even though she shook internally Stacey returned the stare steadily. "We are not acquainted, Mrs. Cattermole. Everyone looks like someone. Now, do you need me to send an aide to help you with your dinner?"

Dinner was obviously the furthest thing from the old woman's mind. She stared at the director's face as if mentally comparing it feature by feature to a mental card file. Neither the process nor her expression were particularly pleasant.

"I'll remember," Penelope Cattermole said with a startling clarity. "I'll remember."

"I'll send someone to see if you need help with your meal," Stacey said imperturbably as she turned to exit the room. Then, at the door, she stopped and turned, looking back with a serene smile on her face. "I'm sorry you felt it necessary to behave so badly, but remember whatever happens you brought it on yourself."

Without waiting for a reply Stacey stepped out and closed the door firmly behind her. Only then did she lean against the wall and draw several deep breaths, willing her heart to quit racing.

Why here, where no one knew her? Why now, after she had built herself a new life? Why now, when there was so much else needing her attention? Why?

* * * * *

Flora Melkiot always slept well. She regarded giving in to sleeplessness almost as an admission of weakness, an acknowledgement that one could not control one's own body.

At least, she had, before coming to Cold Creek Health

Care Facility. For a place theoretically devoted to rest and health, the place was infernally noisy. Flora's bedroom back in the Olympus House was silent; the windows overlooked a lovely vista many floors above the street. Even the décor was subdued, mainly in tones of grey and gold and a rich green. There Flora slept like a baby.

The uncarpeted floors of Cold Creek magnified every noise. There were cries and snuffles and the ringing of assistance bells from lights out to their good morning wake up call, but even though she was waked several times a night, Flora didn't complain. She was saving every ounce of anger and indignation to use against Clarissa and that damn fool judge for when she was ready to go home. She was going home soon, no matter what anyone said!

That day was very close.

The soft snick of a door closing created just enough sound to shatter Flora's shallow doze. It was a rule doors were never to be shut at night, simply left ajar enough to block the worst of the light from the hallway.

Then there was a strange soft slithery kind of noise, a sound so soft Flora wasn't sure she had heard it at all. There was a time that Flora Melkiot would have been out of bed and looking – purely in the interest of security, one had to understand – in a heartbeat. Now she was sleepy and more inclined to yell a complaint than investigate. She had been waked several times already and interrupted sleep made her cranky.

Grumbling, Flora turned over in bed and pulled the blanket over her head. She had to get out of here or she'd never get better!

* * * * *

Princey Doolittle's mother had always told him he was a no-account who'd never amount to much. Princey had taken great delight in proving her right. Drifting from town to town, menial job to menial job, he lived for the moment, drinking whiskey when he could afford it, beer or cheap wine when he couldn't, smoking weed at every possibility.

Not that he could drink much of anything at this place. Damned nurses always looking and prying and snooping… he hadn't found a place yet to stash a bottle that one of those bitches hadn't found it and thrown it away. In a refinement of cruelty they usually made him watch while they poured it down the drain and lectured him about the evils of drinking. Then they'd say that he could lose his job for this, but because he was such a hard worker they'd forgive him this time.

Yeah. This time. Half a dozen times was more like it. First time it had happened he'd been scared shitless, as he happened to owe some money to some very ugly people, but the second time he had realized they were just playing with his head. People were hardly lining up to be an orderly here in Death's waiting room, dealing with puke and shit and the stink of old people and their dirty laundry.

He still couldn't find a place to hide his hooch, though. Weed would have been easier, but there was no smoking of any kind on the facility grounds.

There wasn't supposed to be any drinking, either, but he'd found evidence otherwise. One night that stuck up director Enero had left her desk unlocked. Princey hadn't been going to steal anything, just make sure everything was as it was supposed to be; that was the only reason he looked in the drawers. There were a lot of dishonest people about.

Like that snooty greaser Enero. She made all the noises about how clean and liquor-free the facility was, then he goes and finds she keeps a big bottle of hooch in her bottom desk drawer. Wild Turkey, no less.

Only bad thing was, it was sealed, and he was sure she'd notice if some of it was missing. Regretfully he had put it back in the drawer, but he checked on it every night he could. Once he knew what drawer it was in he didn't have any trouble picking the lock. That was one of the useful skills he had learned during his first time in juvvie.

Princey was almost mad with frustration. It had been a long time since he had tasted any of the really good stuff and that whole full bottle just lay there, its untouched seal mocking him. Someday she had to take a drink of it, and then he would too. She had to drink it sometime, didn't she? Why else did she keep it handy in her desk?

Princey used his master key to open the director's small office and slipped inside silently. He had learned to be soundless a long time ago, but this time he wasn't for long.

He started screaming as soon as he saw the woman slumped in the high-backed executive chair, one hand in the file drawer, one half of her head missing.

Chapter Five

"Crime of passion, that's for sure." Detective Armando Camacho folded his notebook away and nodded to the crime scene techs waiting patiently with their gigantic cases of forensic magic. He didn't understand what they did or how they did it, but every day it seemed they solved cases more than he did. "Up close and personal. Lots of anger in those blows."

One blow could never have removed so much of a human face or skull. It had taken several.

Bad enough to batter anyone to death like that, Camacho thought gloomily. *But to do it to a crippled old woman...*

A police tape had been set up outside the glass-walled office, but owing to the spider-like design of the building he couldn't block off the entire hallway. That bothered him, almost as much as the crowd of residents clustered around the tape.

They flat creeped him out. They were like ghosts, half-alive people clad in robes and pajamas and muttering in vague distress. Nurses and orderlies moved ineffectually among them, trying to get them back to their rooms, but it was like herding worms.

Probably the most exciting thing that's ever happened to any of them, Camacho realized.

Not all of them, he quickly amended at the sight of the black man in a wheelchair at the front. What was left of him almost looked worse than the corpse, but this man was still alive.

Behind him stood a tall, almost painfully thin woman with a cast on her wrist and a startling halo of white roots against roughly cropped jet black hair. She looked out of place in that crowd of fading half-people, like a crow in a flock of starlings.

"Excuse me," she said, as if she had heard his thoughts. Her voice was low and strong, the voice of a much younger woman.

"Yes, ma'am?"

"It was murder, then?"

"We haven't made a determination yet."

"Hard to be anything else with half her face bashed in," said the horribly mutilated man in the wheelchair. There was cold intelligence in his remaining eye and what was left of his grin was infectious. "Except in my case, of course."

In spite of himself Camacho grinned back; briefly, before he stopped himself, a slight nausea tickling his stomach. "How did you learn that?"

The man's grin widened. "I have my ways."

"Do you have any suspects?" the woman asked.

"We're looking into all aspects of the crime," Camacho said vaguely.

"Which means you don't know anything."

"Hey, lady, give us a break. We just got here."

The man in the wheelchair snorted. "I'll bet you don't even know the victim's name."

Camacho glared at him. "And you're going to tell me, right?"

"Her name," the crow-like woman said crisply, "was Penelope Cattermole. Mrs. General Brian Cattermole, as she rather pretentiously styled herself. And she…"

The man in the wheelchair patted the woman's cast rather abruptly, cutting her off in mid-word. "Hold it. We don't want to tell him everything. Let the man work for his money." His single eye held a wicked gleam. "Come on, Flora. There's nothing more to see here."

"Was the deceased a friend of yours?"

Both of them reacted as if stung.

"Most certainly not!" said the woman, obviously offended.

"Mrs. General didn't have any friends," the man said.

"And why was that?"

"She was a most disagreeable woman," the woman named Flora said with a sniff.

"People don't kill people for being disagreeable," Camacho said reasonably.

"People will kill each other for almost any idiotic reason. I helped solve a murder in Dallas not long ago and…"

Camacho snorted. "You helped solve a murder," he said with palpable disbelief and was almost annihilated by her ferocious glare.

"Indeed I did, and if you insist on calling me a liar I suggest you call Detective John Ashdown of the Dallas Police Department!"

"I didn't…" Camacho began but the odd pair had already left, the milling group parting for her almost military bearing and his motorized wheelchair as the Red Sea had parted for Moses.

The detective gave a sigh. This was going to be one hell of a case.

* * * * *

"The nerve of that man!" Flora was all but sputtering.

Dewayne chuckled. "So you really did help solve a murder."

"Of course. I said I did, and I never lie," Flora said with a certitude of righteousness, and she really believed it, though even her friends would have had to admit that she did have a gift for remolding the truth.

"I can believe it. Let's solve this one. I've always wanted to solve a murder."

Flora stopped so suddenly Dewayne had to turn his wheelchair back to face her. She looked down at her cast, deplorably suburban duster and terry slides, then at the pathetic husk, this partial man strapped in his wheelchair, and had to stop herself from laughing. “Us? Solve this murder?”

“Us. Solve this murder.”

“Why? Neither of us even liked the creature.”

Dewayne shrugged and Flora tried not to register how grotesque a gesture it was.

“Why not? What else have we got to do? Besides, I’m bored, and I’ll bet you are too.”

That made sense. Cold Creek Health Care Facility was not overly endowed with intellectual stimulation.

Dewayne’s eye twinkled as she weakened. “And I’ll bet you that Latino version of Kojak is more interested in clearing the case than finding the killer.”

“All right,” Flora said with much more reticence than she actually felt. The same thought had danced through her mind. She did not have much respect for police officers, thinking that they were more involved in following the letter of the law than in solving a crime. Detective Ashdown’s cavalier treatment of her assistance – and his refusal to acknowledge that he probably wouldn’t have solved the Olympus House murder without her – still rankled. “How do we go about it?”

By now she and Dewayne were moving again and she fell in beside his chair as if it were the most natural thing in the world.

“Hey, you’re the one with the experience.”

“But that happened in my own building. I knew all the people involved… except the victim.”

“Laura Fenn Tyler.”

Flora stared in real astonishment. Had he dared investigate her? How? And when? “How did you know that?”

Dewayne grinned. “I have my ways.”

"Now just one minute…"

"Come on, Miss Fly…" Dewayne pushed open the door to his room. "Let me lure you into my web…"

They had lied to her. There were private rooms available at Cold Creek Health Care Facility, or at least there was one. Dewayne lived by himself in a room that was identical in layout to every other patient room – two miniscule closets, each with two drawers beneath, a single window over a boxed in heating/cooling unit, an uninspired ceiling fan with a single bulb globe.

There the resemblance ended. Instead of being the pale institutional greeny-gray that prevailed in the rest of the building, his walls were painted vibrant yellow and green and orange and red – one shade to each wall. The upholstery and bedspread were in some enormous, wildly colored jungle print. The curtains were shades of yellow, striped with a mutant green. The furniture was gleaming stainless steel and seemed somehow distorted until Flora realized that it had been adapted for Dewayne's special needs.

What was, to Flora's eyes, the most outlandish thing was the electronics. Almost one entire wall was covered with electronic equipment. There were two computer screens, great flat things that Flora would have thought were TVs except an even bigger screen hung on another wall, the table beneath it covered by piles of tapes and DVDs. The place looked like an electronics store.

"Impressive, huh?" Dewayne asked.

"Most. Is this your profession?"

He shook his head. "Not really… more like just a hobby. Sit down."

"Are you sure it's safe?" Flora eyed the big wing chair he indicated.

"Safe?"

"I've never seen a chair upholstered with flowers like this. They look carnivorous."

Dewayne laughed. "Makes me feel safe at night.

They're tame, though."

As gracefully as she could, Flora sank down into the low-slung chair. It was a comfortable piece of furniture, and quite as nice a quality as anything she had in her home at the Olympus House, though this was obviously new and her furniture genuine antiques. She had paid a great deal for what she had in her home and knew something good when she saw it, even if it was of a completely different style. In spite of the vulgar fabric, this was a very expensive chair. Flora regarded him with curious eyes.

"Now, Miss Detective, what do we do next?"

He was playing with her, Flora knew. "I thought I was Miss Fly, Mr. Spider."

"But you're in here now, and I'll bet you can't resist this mystery any more than I can."

He was right, of course. Flora was itching to get her fingers into the puzzle and straighten it out, just as she had for Detective Ashdown and that nice crippled Rebecca Cloudwebb who owned the antique shop. Solving this case would show those small minded snobs at the Olympus House and the club who had called her a meddling busybody!

"Maybe."

Dewayne laughed.

"Are you sure the victim was Mrs. General? I barely got a glance at the body when the police were going in and out." Flora was proud that however small that glimpse was, the condition of the remains hadn't overset her at all.

Dewayne nodded. "I got there when Princey was still screaming, before Melanie chased everybody out and closed the door."

"What time was that?" Flora glanced out the window at the still-dark night sky. "For that matter, what time is it now?"

"It was about three-thirty. Now it's about four-fifteen, four-twenty."

Four-fifteen? When had she last been up at four-fifteen in the morning, Flora wondered. And it didn't feel early. Or late. One of the worst things about this place was the loss of time. Meals were fixed, as were bedtimes, but the long stretches of hours in between were great slabs of grey limbo, only partially enlivened by the determinedly cheerful activities arranged by the staff. Small wonder so many people watched television all the time; it gave them a structure, a way of breaking time into manageable chunks instead of letting it wash them away in a flood of forever 'now'.

"What were you doing out and about at such an hour?"

"I'm often up all night," Dewayne replied neutrally. "I don't need much sleep."

"That's why you have a room to yourself, no doubt."

His grin was ugly. "That… and a lot of money."

"Independently wealthy?"

"No." The shutters went down in his face and his eye turned cold. Even Flora, a seasoned snoop who was not the most sensitive person in the world, dared push no further.

"Who," she asked, adroitly turning the subject, "did you see?"

"No one… the halls were empty when the screaming started." Dewayne rubbed his forehead with the effort of remembering. "At least I think so. I don't recall seeing anyone. Of course, the lights were on night-dim, so there were a lot of shadows…" He shrugged. It was indeed a grotesque action to watch. "I don't remember."

Flora nodded. At one time she would have scoffed at the notion of someone not remembering exactly what happened at so momentous a moment, but after witnessing Laura Tyler's horrible death and not being able to remember one single thing of importance about something that happened literally right in front of her she could sympathize.

"Tell me what happened."

"All right. I was sitting here working on the

computer. I heard Princey screaming…"

"Did you know it was Princey then?"

Dewayne's face solidified with concentrated thought. "I don't know. I don't think so… It all happened so fast."

That made Flora feel vaguely better. "When did you know it was Princey?"

"I dashed out into the hall, saw that the office door was open and headed that way. By the time I got there Princey was backing out the door, looking like he'd seen a ghost."

Flora waited for Dewayne to make some self-deprecating remark about his own appearance as he usually did, but his entire attention was focused on his memories.

"I'd barely reached him when Melanie got there. We both saw what was inside… then she slammed the door shut and we took Princey down to the nurses' station. Melanie got him to shut up while one of the aides called the police."

"What did you do?"

"Sat there. Not much else I could do." For the first time in Flora's hearing there was a shadow of self-pity in his voice. "I made sure I kept my eye on the office door… I can swear no one or nothing went in or out through that door until the police got here."

Which meant that the crime scene was undisturbed after its discovery, Flora thought. *Hope those thick-skulled cops take full advantage of that.* She wished she had waked and dressed – if slipping into a snap-front duster could be called dressing – more quickly. There was much she could have learned being at the scene earlier.

"Could Princey have been faking?"

Dewayne thought for a moment. "It's a possibility, of course, but I don't think so. He's not smart enough to be that good an actor. I'd swear it was real panic. I think Melanie had to give him some tranqs to get him to quit screaming."

"Tranquilizers?" Flora was startled. "I thought they had to be prescribed by a physician."

"They do. I guess she didn't want to listen to Princey's screaming until dear old Dr. Jensen could get here."

"He doesn't live here?"

"Hardly." What was left of Dewayne's mouth twisted into a knot. "Not even close. He does make it in once a day most days, but it's a good day if he stays more than an hour or two. He's got a really nice house in Alamo Heights. Two floors, five bedrooms, three fireplaces…"

"On what he earns at this place?" Flora decided she really would have to look into what Clarissa was paying for her incarceration here. "Have you been there?"

"There's no way the good doctor would invite any patient to his home. First of all, his lady wife wouldn't stand for it."

"Then how did you find out?"

"Tax appraisal site on the net. It's public information."

"Oh," Flora said thoughtfully. The internet was a vague something outside her sphere, but if there was such private public information out there perhaps she should have someone look into it to find out if any of it was about her. "How can he afford it?"

Dewayne snorted. "He probably makes less than any doctor in Bexar County, but he's the son and the grandson of very gifted surgeons and he married an oilman's daughter. He's not going to have to worry about money anytime soon."

Flora stared. She had been unimpressed with Dr. Jensen the one time he had condescended to see her, but she had had no idea of nor any interest in his personal life. She must indeed be slipping!

"If he's that wealthy, what's he doing here?"

Dewayne smiled nastily. "Waiting for his daddy to die. According to my sources he's locked out of his family's money if he doesn't practice medicine. He wants to be a composer if you please."

"A composer!" Flora was startled. "But his wife…"

"His wife controls her side of the money. She's more than willing to spend it on all kinds of nice stuff, but she likes the prestige of being married to a doctor. Being an artiste's wife doesn't appeal to her at all. So – he's here."

"Good heavens." Flora was both intrigued and revolted. It was such a tawdry little story, hardly the kind of thing to interest one of her enlightened sensibilities. She clung to that thought as the ends of her mouth twitched. "Sounds like one of those trashy soap operas."

Dewayne laughed, the good side of his mouth curling up merrily. Disconcertingly, the injured side didn't move. "Haven't you learned yet that life here is a soap opera? About the only thing we haven't had here is the evil twin thing, and I'm waiting for it."

"Maybe Mrs. General Brian Cattermole was the evil twin," Flora said and then, unable to restrain herself any longer, allowed herself a small laugh. "Or maybe it's one of those revenant-from-the-past storylines."

"You're good, lady," Dewayne said. "Who knows what's going on. Maybe some good-hearted citizen couldn't stand the old biddy anymore and just took pity on us."

All mirth gone, Flora shook her head. "No, there was anger in that death. As the detective said, it was personal. She was a weak old woman. She had a tongue like a viper, but she could barely move on her own. A quick blow or even a throttling could have removed her easily. Those hits… Either he had something against Mrs. General herself or he just didn't like weak old ladies."

Dewayne's dark eye shuttered. "And," he said almost solemnly, "this place is just full of weak old ladies.

Chapter Six

When Flora Melkiot decided to pursue something, she did it wholeheartedly. Going back to bed after such a hubbub was ridiculous, especially when she'd be waked up in just an hour or two anyway. She left Dewayne and went back to her room where, ignoring the snoring lump of Mrs. Gutierrez, she dressed as quickly as she could (this a zip-front housedress, hardly more stylish than her duster but at least definitely a day costume) and headed back toward the central nurses' station. Dressing without assistance was more difficult than she had anticipated, but Flora persevered, as she always did and accomplished her task, as she always did. Shift change had not yet happened, so she had hopes of talking to Melanie or perhaps finding the aide who had called the police. To her disappointment neither was there.

"They're being interviewed by the cops," said another one of the little nurse's aides. These young women were so alike as to be interchangeable and Flora had never bothered to learn their names, not that it would matter. She had never been awake at this hour and therefore knew none of the graveyard shift. Of course, they never called it that here at Cold Creek. Not even Flora in one of her wilder moods would indulge in such mordant humor vocally.

"Still?"

"It hasn't been that long. It's just that time is messed up."

"I guess not. Are you on duty alone?"

The girl nodded, setting her tight black curls jiggling. "There's only five of us on duty at night – two nurses and three aides – and usually it's as quiet as the – " She stopped abruptly. "Real quiet."

Flora revised her opinion and leaned forward to read the girl's nametag. Loshonda. Or perhaps Lorlanda. Either way it was not a name Flora had seen before. Whatever. Perhaps among the staff a mordant sense of humor was a survival tool.

"And since Melanie and Ladasha are in with the police, and breakfast time is coming up, Tanisha went to start calling the day shift and ask if they could come in early. I know she called Miss Enero first."

"She seems to be quite efficient," Flora said in a neutral voice. Even while admiring the woman's work she had formed a dislike of the manager, finding her unacceptably rigid for failing to agree with Flora's reasoned argument about why she should not remain confined at Cold Creek Health Care Facility.

"Oh, she's wonderful! We can talk to her and things actually get done... not like when old Mrs. Hammond was here. That was a nightmare."

Miss Enero might get some things done, Flora thought somewhat bitterly, but the woman was singularly lacking when it came to logic. Surely a blind man could see that Flora would be better off in her own home. Of course, then Cold Creek Health Care Facility wouldn't be getting a hefty sum per day for keeping her.

However, she had come to gather information, not ruminate about the injustice of her incarceration here, and she had better get about it.

"What about breakfast?" Flora asked, hoping that the girl would simply believe her to be a greedy old woman instead of a semi-professional investigator. "Does the breakfast crew come in this early?"

The girl snapped the file closed and then opened another without raising her head. "Not often. Usually they get everything ready the night before, so it only takes a little while to get things heated up."

Perhaps, Flora though, that explained why the food tasted as bad as it did. It did not, however, explain lunch and dinner!

"They only come in real early when there's a patrons' breakfast or something special," the girl said, closing that file and opening still another one.

Flora bristled at that, since in her opinion the patients should be the special ones, but she had set herself a task and she would do it, no matter how rude it was that she be forced to talk to a bouncing mass of tight black curls. Young people of her generation had been taught to stop what they were doing and face the person speaking to them. Really, young people these days had no manners at all.

"Did you know Mrs. Cattermole?"

The girl stopped writing and raised her head. Her eyes were scornful. "Believe me, everybody here knew Mrs. Cattermole. Here less than a week and two people threatening to quit because of her. She be a real danger with that cane of hers too. I be sorry the woman's dead, but ain't nobody sorry she's outta here."

Flora made the appropriate noises of agreement even as she mentally patted herself on the back. She had been right – as usual. The obnoxious Penelope Cattermole had been universally disliked.

The little aide ostentatiously went back to writing in the file, but Flora didn't care; she had gotten all she needed to know from this child. She didn't move, however; talking to the aide had been an extra. The real reason she had come to the nurses' station was that from this particular spot she had a near perfect view of the door to Miss Enero's office. It was sad that she couldn't see inside, but even if she walked to the corner the view wouldn't have been any better. Not only was there a ribbon of yellow crime scene tape across the now closed door, but a uniformed officer stood guard.

There was activity there. Not only was Camacho going in and out and telling people what to do like an overweight gadfly, but Flora could see uniformed people coming and going, most carrying suitcase-like satchels. If only she could have gotten closer she might have heard what they were saying, but she knew even if she went up right to the hallway corner she couldn't hear anything. If the guarding officer allowed her to stay that close, which he probably wouldn't. Unless they were yelling at you, she remembered, the police were very careful to speak in low tones.

Besides, if she stood any closer she ran the risk of being noticed. She knew instinctively that she could get more done if she didn't stand out. It frustrated her terribly. When she and Rebecca had worked on Laura Tyler's murder and had needed information, Rebecca had been able to pressure what information she wanted from that uncooperative detective just because her brother was a deputy chief. That was a luxury Flora would not have here, and that fool Detective Camacho had made it very clear he didn't want any help.

No one, Flora though wrathfully, *had any respect for the ability of people of a certain age.*

Well, she would certainly show them, just like she had those thick-skulled cops in Dallas!

"Godalmighty, that man wanted to know everything but my bra size," muttered Melanie, stalking into the hollow center of the circular nurses' station and grabbing at a stack of files. "How far did you get?"

"Not as far as I could," the aide said with a surreptitious glance toward Flora. "I did get about a third finished."

"Do you do all these files every night?" Flora asked, sweetly ignoring the aide's dark look.

"Yes, ma'am. Every shift change. Gotta keep everyone's records up to date." Melanie didn't raise her head. She was going at least twice as fast as the aide.

"Seems like it would be more efficient to do it on a computer."

"Yeah, doesn't it? But there's only so much money around and computers cost money, so I'd rather have that cash on my salary."

"I thought you worked the day shift, Melanie."

"I do. Girl who was supposed to work tonight has a sick kid. Asked me to sub for her."

"The detective must have found that suspicious."

Melanie's head snapped up and she fixed Flora with a cold eye. "What do you mean by that?"

"Just what I said. In all the mystery novels I've ever read if the crime occurs when someone who is not normally there is present, they are automatically the main suspect."

"If wanting to pick up some extra dough so I can fight to keep my kid away from his rotten father and that whore he lives with is suspicious, that damned policeman can kiss my ass," Melanie said with a remarkable lack of heat but a surfeit of hatred.

Instinctively Flora stiffened, although she had the feeling the viciousness in the woman's tone was not completely directed at her. As befitted a well-rounded woman she was aware of curse words and crudities, but it still offended her to hear them used, especially in conversation with her.

Melanie took a deep breath, then another and pasted a ghastly smile on her face. "Mrs. Melkiot, you aren't going to do yourself any good by being up this early," she said in a voice that sounded like sugar-coated steel. "Why don't you let me find someone to help you back to your room until it's time for breakfast? Al," she called, seeing the handsome young man.

"Because I don't want to," Flora replied, a touch of her natural asperity seeping into her carefully controlled voice.

"Yes, Melanie?" He walked over to the nurses station with the grace of an alpha lion.

"Will you please help Mrs. Melkiot back to her room?"

"They're always the innocent ones, though." Flora kept her voice level, though she most certainly did not intend to move until she was good and ready.

"They? Who?"

"The people who are there when they normally aren't."

"You shouldn't be out walking around without your security belt, Mrs. Melkiot. It isn't safe," Melanie said with emphasis. "Al will get one and take you back to your room."

"That will not be necessary," Flora returned in the soft and aristocratic voice that made those who knew her start looking for cover.

"Sure you don't want me to take you back to your bed?" Al asked in a tone that bordered on the salacious. Most of the old ladies simply loved it. Flora found it repugnant.

Her glance fell on his arm. "That is a lovely watch," she murmured. She had noticed it before, thinking it was unusual for so young a man in such a menial job to have such an expensive watch. At the time, however, she had had other things to occupy her mind.

He looked startled. "Thank you. My grandfather left it to me. It's been in our family for years."

Flora smiled. Not only was the hunk a bad liar, he was stupid. Flora was a jeweler's widow with an encyclopedic knowledge of jewelry, and not one to believe that a watch which had hit the market only three years before had been in anyone's family for years.

"How nice," she said smoothly.

Frowning, Melanie opened her mouth, but the creak of a gurney coming out of Miss Enero's office silenced her. They all turned to watch as the paramedics rolled the cart and its grisly cargo down the hallway and out of the building. The gurney had a wonky wheel which made it wobble; the body bag shuddered slightly as if something inside it was moving.

The aide crossed herself and muttered a whispered prayer. Melanie and Flora simply stared. Al moved to help a rotund old woman who was waving madly at him.

"What's going on here? Catch me up," ordered Stacey Enero, stalking in from the kitchen area. Obviously she had dressed in a hurry; she wore what looked to be the same clothes she had worn yesterday. Her worried expression darkened when she saw Flora.

"Good morning, Miss Enero," Flora said politely. "Though I'm not sure 'good' is an accurate word."

"You are up early, Mrs. Melkiot. Do you have a problem?"

"I was awakened early by the commotion, and once I am awakened I am unable to go back to sleep."

"Well, you shouldn't be up walking around without your security belt and an escort." Stacey grabbed a file at random and checked it. If she was a betting woman Flora would have wagered the administrator didn't see any of the writing inside. "Especially when it's this early and we've just had an upsetting event. It's not safe."

"Just what I told her," Melanie said with dark delight. "I asked Al, but he got called away. I'll take her back to her room."

Flora sniffed. As if she hadn't been walking around perfectly well since she first got here.

"Not just now," she said in a voice firm with resolve. "I think I shall go to the chapel and pray for poor Mrs. Cattermole's soul." Giving a gracious nod, Flora moved serenely but swiftly toward the chapel. She longed to tell them it was her wrist that had been broken, not her legs, and her movement was not in any way impaired.

Once in the chapel she sat, careful to choose a place that could not be seen through the door's small stained glass window, and bowed her head, just in case they had followed her. She hoped it had been an unnecessary precaution. Surely they wouldn't interrupt her in a religious duty? On the other hand, they didn't seem to believe much in either freedom or privacy around here.

Dear Lord, she prayed with ambiguity aforethought, *please see that Penelope Cattermole receives the rewards she so richly deserved.*

It was as close to a prayer for that terrible woman as Flora could come, but at least it kept her from being an out and out liar. A prayer was a prayer, no matter how short or double-edged.

The chapel door had a soft but unmistakable squeak. Flora did not move when she heard it. They had checked, drat them. Didn't they think she could be trusted? Doubtless they would report this sudden religious fervor to Clarissa, but it was a risk that had to be taken. Clarissa had been trying to induce her mother to attend church for years. This little exercise would probably set Flora's position back considerably.

Oh, well, there are some things that just have to be borne.

Flora waited a full three minutes before raising her head. A quick glance around showed she was alone in the chapel, which was what she wanted. She had no doubts that they would gleefully force her to go back to her room if they really wanted to, and she needed to be out here. No, she needed to be by Detective Camacho's side, making sure he didn't miss any clues, but she held no illusions about that ever happening. It would just make solving the case harder, but she could overcome that. Flora knew she could have become a wonderful detective if she'd just put her mind to it. After all, there had been that murder in Dallas; Ashdown would never have solved it without her. And Rebecca too of course, Flora had to add for total if somewhat belated honesty.

Flora had chosen the chapel as a retreat for a reason.

It was on the same corridor as the offices and, if she was careful, she could look out the little glass window in the door towards Miss Enero's office and not be seen from the nurses' station. Of course, she couldn't hear anything that was going on in the crime scene, but it was better than nothing.

For the longest time nothing happened, so much so that Flora wondered if everything had finished up while she had been playing possum. Stacey Enero passed through her field of vision once or twice, her face set and her head down. One of the aides came down the hall; her face was swollen from crying and she was obviously upset.

"Bufanaquishria?" Stacey Enero stopped just outside the door. To Flora's surprise, she could hear rather well. "Are you all right?"

The girl shook her head, setting her curls to jiggling. "It was awful, Miss Enero. I didn't like Mrs. Cattermole, but to see her like that..." A fresh spate of tears drowned her next words. "And that policeman... he acted like I done it!"

"I'm sure he doesn't think that," Stacey soothed. "That's just their way. He's trying to find out who did kill her. Look, why don't you go home? Your shift is almost over anyway. Get some rest."

"All right."

"We'll see you tomorrow."

The girl didn't say anything. In spite of knowing gambling was a definite character flaw, Flora would have laid money the girl would never be back. Some people were just not dependable, and this girl had all the earmarks.

"Miss Enero?"

Flora couldn't see Detective Camacho, but there was no mistaking that deep voice.

"Yes, Detective Camacho? I don't appreciate your upsetting Bufanaquishria," Stacey said firmly without fear or heat. "She's a good girl – a little simple, but a hard worker. You didn't have to be so rough on her."

There was no repentance in his voice. "I wasn't. I just questioned her. Just like I'm going to question everyone else."

"Then it looks like I will be spending most of my time calming down my staff – those whom you don't drive away."

Flora felt a grudging respect for the administrator starting to rise. She fought for her people, and that was good.

"Look, Miss Enero, I had the body taken away as soon as possible just so I wouldn't upset your people."

"Thank you for that. Some of our residents are quite fragile."

"And now I need to talk to you. Can we go in here?"

He had to mean the chapel. Flora was torn. She wanted to hear what they said, but they'd never talk if she were present and if they came in right now she'd never be able to get back to her seat in time. They would know she had been eavesdropping. Of course, she could brazen it out and say she had just been leaving, but then she might be forced back to her room.

"No, one of our residents is in there. I don't want to interrupt her prayers."

"A special friend of the victim's?" Camacho sounded skeptical.

"Mrs. Melkiot? Hardly. Mrs. Cattermole didn't have any friends, special or otherwise."

"I still need to talk to you, Miss Enero, and we still need to set up an interview room."

"You can't use the reception area? No, it's too open. I'd offer you my office, but I've been told it's off limits." Her voice was only slightly sharp. "May I ask for how long? I have a nursing home to run."

"We'll try to have it back to you as soon as possible," the detective said with a professionally vague neutrality.

Policemen are all alike, Flora thought with disgust. *They want everything and won't give anything, even if we're trying to help them.*

"Well, I suppose you can use the bookkeeper's office for a while. It's this way."

Two sets of footsteps walked away, leaving Flora very frustrated. What was she going to do now? She'd love to have a peek at the death scene, but even though she would have no qualms about slipping under the crime scene tape there were still policemen and technicians there who would no doubt take a dim view of such actions. And, to make it worse, the residents – even the ones who had allowed themselves to be shepherded back to bed earlier – were now up and around. She could see them drifting around the cordoned-off hallway entrance, like curious ghosts in their robes or running suits or caftans.

There was movement further down the hall that drew Flora's attention. One of the nurses – Flora had seen her a couple of times, but couldn't be sure if her name was Georgia or not – was pulled in on herself and quite clearly sobbing. Well, that wasn't anything unusual; nurses often became attached to their patients, though it was difficult to imagine anyone becoming so attached to the late and unlamented Penelope Cattermole that her death would bring tears.

What was interesting was that she was being comforted by Al, the handsome young orderly. Flora had never felt quite comfortable around Al since he had given her a bath – a complete bath – her second day here. Naturally modest, Flora found the whole nudity thing embarrassing. Morris had seen her nude, as had Dr. Wallingford, her ob-gyn, and various other medical types, but that was all. Of course he had been totally professional, but to think of a young man handling her body during such an intimate procedure distressed Flora.

He put his arms around the nurse and held her close, which attracted closer attention. This was no kindly coworker reassurance, Flora decided, not from the way he cradled her in his arms. Solidly built and quite matronly, Georgia (Flora had finally decided that it was indeed she) was plain as a mud fence. Could she be his mother or aunt? On the other hand, the way he was holding her and her reaction to it did not seem proper for a maternal relationship, but Flora couldn't see any other reason for such behavior.

Something else she couldn't see was Dewayne. She hadn't seen him since leaving his room earlier this morning when she went to get dressed.

In spite of herself Flora almost giggled. Taken out of context that might have been considered a racy situation, not that Flora Melkiot, cosmopolitan and arbiter of the Dallas social scene, would ever even consider doing something immoral or compromising.

Where was Dewayne? He had said he would see her at breakfast, which was probably still at least an hour away, but had he gone back to sleep? Probably. As usual, the burden of the work fell to her.

Never one to deny when something wasn't working, Flora stepped out of the chapel and tried to look inconspicuous as she moved among the milling patients. It would have distressed her no end that in her terry scuffs and little cotton housedress she fit right in.

Who should she talk to first? Stacey Enero first came to mind, but she was with that policeman. Melanie and Loshonda (or Lorlanda or whatever the girl's name was) were busy, as were a startling number of nurses and aides. They were walking among the wandering crowd of residents, calming and helping and unsuccessfully urging them to return to their rooms.

Flora snorted. This was probably the most exciting thing that had ever happened at Cold Creek Health Care Facility and these silly nurses wanted them to return to their rooms? Death held no terrors for these old people, but a violent death, especially to one who was so universally disliked, was An Event.

"They know!" Tiny fingers clamped with unexpected and painful strength on Flora's arm.

Affronted, Flora yelped then looked down into Eula Badham's watery blue, terror filled eyes. Her face, always soft and somewhat rabbity-looking, had folded in on itself in fear. Around it her candy-floss hair trembled in agitation.

"Who knows what? And you're hurting my arm." With gentle but firm precision Flora began disentangling the old woman's fingers. It was rather like removing a particularly determined kitten's claws – each finger reattached as soon as she moved on to the next one.

"It's started. They killed Mrs. Cattermole first, but they're going to get me next. Maybe even today."

"What has started?" Flora asked purely for politeness' sake, still pulling at the surprisingly strong fingers. "What makes you think you're next?"

"I know," Eula said, tears dripping from her faded blue eyes. "You see, I saw the killer. They'll have to kill me."

Chapter Seven

"And that's all?"

"Isn't that enough?"

Armando Camacho was a good policeman, but even more than that he was a man. Stacey Enero was an eyeful, no doubt – pretty face, great figure – but there was something about her that made him leery. While she might have given him a blow by blow account of what she knew had happened, it was too controlled for his taste. She had a hard edge, a kind of aggressive strength that he found unappealing. He preferred a softer, more feminine type of woman. His Rosalia might have a broader, softer body, but she was sweet and loving and made him feel like a king. He had the feeling that Stacey Enero would give orders like a man.

"It doesn't get us any closer to finding out who killed Mrs. Cattermole. Was her being sent back to the military hospital general knowledge?"

"I hadn't made an announcement of it, but it wasn't a secret. There's no keeping a secret in a place like this," Stacey said, conveniently forgetting how hard and how successfully she had worked to keep her own.

"And nothing was taken?"

"No. Patients aren't allowed to keep anything valuable, and even costume jewelry is frowned on. Anything of real value is kept in our safe. Mrs. Cattermole did keep her wedding band, but it was so tight on her finger it would have to be cut off. We were thinking about having it done, as it was starting to impede her circulation."

"How did she feel about that?"

Stacey shrugged. "She didn't know yet. She probably wouldn't have liked the idea. She didn't like much of anything."

Which, thought Camacho, *was an understatement.* The little he had learned about the victim was that she had been hell on wheels. "What about papers and such?"

"Other than her admission papers and medical history, she didn't have any. Not here, at least. At her home... I don't know."

"What was she doing in your office?" Camacho had waited to ask that question, and he wasn't disappointed in her reaction. The administrator's face didn't change, but something flickered deep in her eyes. It was quick, and she had control again almost immediately, but it was enough. There was something there, and he had to find out what it was.

"I don't know. Do you know what she was doing in there?"

Camacho thought for a moment, then decided to tell her. "She was pulling out employee record files."

Miss Enero's face paled. "Employee files? Do you know which ones?"

"No," Camacho said, even as he thought, *But you have an idea, don't you?* "Can you think of anyone who she might have been interested in?"

She shook her head. "No. She hadn't been here but just a short while, as I said."

"Do you usually keep your office locked?"

"Yes, but it opens with the master key that all nurses carry. Obviously the janitor has one too, and so did the security guard, back when we had one. It isn't much of a lock, though. Sometimes it doesn't catch right and the door opens with just a little shaking. The drug cabinets," she added on seeing the question rise in his face, "are made of steel, differently keyed and very secure. Only the head nurse on each shift, Dr. Jensen and I have keys to them, and the head nurse has to check hers in and out with me."

"And your desk? Do you lock that?"

"Yes, but there's no information that the staff might need in there."

"Did you lock your desk last night?"

"Yes. I do every night. Before you ask, I have no idea how Mrs. Cattermole got it open or if she knew where my spare key was kept. And, since you've undoubtedly looked, you know there's a bottle of whiskey in my bottom desk drawer."

Camacho nodded. It hadn't surprised him. He'd only been here an hour or two, but already he could see how this job could drive someone to drink. "Wild Turkey. Good stuff."

"And it was unopened."

"Yes."

"I'm an alcoholic, Detective Camacho. Six years, three months and seventeen days sober," Stacey said with deliberate precision. "That bottle is my touchstone. It has been unopened for the last six years, and I am working very hard to ensure that I never open it nor any other."

Camacho, who sometimes enjoyed a little too much alcohol, was impressed. No wonder the woman seemed so disciplined. "Good for you."

"I keep it in a locked drawer because there are those here who are not as determined as I. I don't want to be the cause of anyone else's downfall."

And how far down did you fall, Ms. Enero? he wondered.

"Do the owners of this place know about your alcoholism?"

She looked shocked. "Of course. I told them that at the first interview."

"And they still put you in such a position of responsibility?"

Stacey's face twisted sourly. "Of course not. Some of

the owners of this facility are acquaintances of my family. When they found out I was having a hard time getting a job even though I had been sober over a year they decided to give me a chance. I started as a part-time file clerk. I worked here and went to school and worked my way up. It hasn't been easy, but no matter what I've never given this place less than my best."

Even though he was hardened and cynical from years on the job, Camacho was inclined to believe her. This was a big-bucks operation, and from what he could tell it ran like a Swiss watch. That didn't happen with an alky in charge.

He said, "So you don't have any idea of what she was doing in your office, or what she was doing up at that hour, or why she was killed?"

"No. As I said, I had moved her roommate into another room yesterday as I was worried about Mrs. Cattermole's fits of anger. I even took away her cane, but it seems she managed, as well as evading our night staff. Whatever she was looking for in those files must have been very important to her, but whatever 'it' is, I have no idea."

"And you have no idea of what 'it' might have been?"

"None."

"Had you known Mrs. Cattermole before she was sent here?" It was a casual question, one that he asked in some form or another to almost everyone in every murder case, but he was surprised to see her face tense and then almost instantly release with disciplined precision.

Just a little bit too long passed before she answered. Suddenly she was much too interested in inspecting her painfully short, clean fingernails.

"I had met her once or twice. She never paid me any attention, though." Stacey looked up and stared directly into his eyes. "Can I depend on your discretion?"

"Probably not, and definitely not if it touches this case, but you'd better tell me anyway. I'll just find out one way or another."

Her faced worked a moment, then she sighed. "All right. I went into the Air Force right after I graduated from high school. It was the best way I could get an education."

She fell silent, her face drained of color. Camacho waited.

"I liked the service. I got promoted regularly. It was a good life. I got transferred here. My new commanding officer was General Brian Cattermole. He was a hard man, but fair. I wasn't an officer, so there was no social interaction between us, but I did meet Mrs. Cattermole once or twice. She wasn't the type to remember an enlisted woman, so when she came here I didn't remind her of the fact."

Camacho noticed that she was getting paler. What was she hiding?

"Why did you leave the service?"

For one moment Stacey's mouth compressed to a paper cut, then she shook her head as if to fling away bad thoughts. "I was stupid. I fell in love."

"So you got married?"

Another sigh. "No. He died."

There was more there, Camacho thought, but she probably wouldn't tell him now. He'd look into Miss Enero's history. He could bully the story out of her, but he had learned that sometimes a scalpel revealed more of the truth than a sledgehammer.

"Are there any of your patients who have a history of violence?"

Stacey thought a minute. "A few, but nothing of this magnitude. Some food throwing, a slap, even an occasional fistfight, that sort of thing. We keep a special eye on them. This is a care facility, not an asylum, though we do have some elderly residents with mental problems on Corridor F."

Camacho perked up at that. "Mental problems?" *More than the ones wandering around?* he left unsaid.

"Yes, but not the violent kind. Their problems come from age, not mental illness, but they are too disturbed to allow them into the general population. It's for their own safety, not everyone else's. I'll take you in there if you like."

As undesirable as it sounded, Camacho knew it had to be done. He was too good a detective not to investigate, however tenuous the connection seemed.

Stacey went on without stopping. "Her attacks on other people were the main reason we were sending Mrs. Cattermole back to the hospital. We take the safety and comfort of our residents very seriously."

Sounds like part of a sales brochure, Camacho thought. "But still someone killed Mrs. Cattermole."

"Yes." Stacey's voice was bitter.

"When did you stop having a security guard?"

"About a year ago. Having one wasn't fiscally responsible. We put in camera systems instead – one per outside door and one inside focused on the drug cabinet."

"I'll want to see those tapes."

"Our bookkeeper is also our IT guy. He should be in within an hour and I'll have them pulled for you."

"We'll still be here."

Whether he meant it that way or not, to Stacey Enero it sounded like a pronouncement of doom.

* * * * *

Flora Melkiot was both bored and frustrated, which to those who knew her even slightly was a dangerous condition. It was still a while until breakfast and although her digestion was excellent she could not countenance a pre-breakfast snack of chocolates despite the fact her stomach was growling.

Worse yet, she had been unable to find out anything useful even though the entire population of Cold Creek Health Care Facility seemed to be out wandering the halls

– most, she noticed acidly, without any sort of security belt. The nurses moved impotently among them, trying to persuade them to return to their rooms or go to the activities room or the reception lounge and sit down until breakfast was ready, but obviously without success. Everyone was talking about the murder, but no one really knew anything about it.

Flora felt ready to scream, and not only because of the lack of any substantive information. Eula Badham had decided that safety lay only in Flora's orbit and had attached herself like a limpet no matter how politely Flora had tried to shake her off. Of course the poor daft creature didn't know anything about the murder, no matter how Flora's heart had leaped at her startling announcement.

Flora had frozen and looked at Eula Badham sharply. "You saw the killer? When? Who was it?"

The old lady's lower lip had trembled. "It was a ghost... I couldn't see its face, but it was all white and sort of misty. I saw Mrs. Cattermole roll herself into Miss Enero's office and then in a minute the ghost came down from Corridor C and followed her in. They're going to kill me for sure now, I just know it. The nurse who made me go back to bed kept them away last night, but they'll be back tonight and they'll kill me…" Her voice bubbled away to a thread.

Flora had tried to hide her snort of disgust. "If all you saw was a ghost, why would they kill you? You can't identify anyone."

"But the gang doesn't know that. They already know I'm on to them, and now since I saw the murderer they're going to have to kill me." The wrinkled lips, probably a perfect bow in her young years, trembled as a froth of bubbly saliva formed in the corners of her mouth. "They know I can send the banker's son to jail by testifying that he masterminded the bank heist last month."

The lead story on the TV news the night before had been about a banker's son masterminding a robbery. Flora sighed.

"What were you doing out of bed at that hour of the night?" she asked, sounding like a stern schoolmistress.

"I try not to sleep at night, you know, because I have to stay alert – that's when they'll come to kill me. In the night. I have to be awake so I can fight them off."

Fight them off? Flora looked at the small, frail body and wondered if she had the strength to fight off an attacking moth.

"Besides, my foot was hurting and I wanted to see if one of the nurses could make me a hot pack for it. My mother always made me a hot pack when something hurt."

"You didn't use your call button?"

Eula shook her head so violently her thin puffy hair moved as if it had a life of its own. "I didn't dare! It's wired into the gang's headquarters... all of them are. That's how they keep tabs on us. Those who use it too much die – the Death Panels make them kill the ones who ring too often."

Muttering something under her breath that would make Clarissa faint, Flora simply turned and walked away. She wasn't surprised when Eula pattered right behind her.

After fruitless talks with several other residents Flora was convinced that no one truly knew anything. Eula kept announcing to anyone who would listen that she had seen the murderer, but protested loudly that she had no idea of who it was. Finally Flora captured the attention of a nurse, a hard-bitten middle-aged woman whom she had not seen before, explained Eula's problem and suggested most strongly that she be helped to bed. The nurse agreed and as the two walked off toward Eula's room Flora breathed a sigh of relief.

One person she had not seen recently was Dewayne. Had he really had the temerity to go back to bed, leaving her to do the work? Well, that would not do. Besides, after over an hour of trying to get a straight answer from the other residents she desperately needed some sensible conversation.

What she was dreaming of doing to Clarissa and Enrique Rubio for trapping her here was not only illegal but positively messy. At least Clarissa couldn't use the excuse that after the murder at Olympus House she wasn't safe there any longer. This killing was much more close and here she had a great deal less protection than she had at home.

On the other hand, Flora was honest enough to admit, she was becoming excited about the chance to solve another case.

Dewayne's door was closed, but like the seductive wisp of a genie's beckoning finger the scent of coffee curled around it. It smelled like real coffee too, dark roast and strong, and not the pallid colored water served in the dining room.

"Come in," Dewayne called at her knock.

The wisp of coffee became a wave, and Flora's mouth started to water.

"You have coffee?"

"Over there." Dewayne made a quick gesture toward the top of the climate control unit. "Help yourself."

"A one cup coffeemaker," Flora murmured. "How handy." At home she used one of the miniature four cup machines, but the idea of making a cup at a time appealed to her. When they first came out Clarissa had given her one of the single-serving makers that used the little plastic cups. Flora had taken a violent dislike to it and refused to use it, declaring the little plastic cups wasteful, expensive and downright obscene. She was not pleased to see that this one was identical. though in this situation she was inclined to be charitable. Probably the little cups were easier for Dewayne to handle; ground coffee and filters required a certain amount of dexterity.

On the other hand, she did notice with pleasure that a number of the obscene little cups contained French Roast. Perhaps the brand was one with which she wasn't familiar, but it was still French Roast and after days and days of drinking the swill served here she didn't care.

There were no proper cups and saucers, just an insulated mug on the tray, but Flora didn't even stop to think about her dislike of all kinds of mugs. Anything that held real coffee would do. Once the coffee was dripping – oh, the heavenly aroma! – she turned her attention to Dewayne.

He still stared at the screen before him, apparently unaware of her scrutiny. Flora grabbed the carnivorously patterned chair and shoved it up beside him. "What are you looking at?" she finally asked.

"Security tapes."

"From where?"

"Here."

Flora looked at him with skepticism. "You do their security monitoring?"

Dewayne kept his gaze on the screen where snowy pictures kept flashing on and off. "Nope."

"You mean you broke into their system?"

"Yep. Actually, it's so primitive that a child could do it. They should have upgraded a long time ago. But – that's what you get for buying cheapass equipment."

The coffeemaker dinged three times and its light went out, signaling the end of the cycle. Flora took the cup and sipped, feeling the warmth and the unmistakable glow of caffeine seeping through her body. Honestly, good coffee was one of the sacraments of life.

"This is delicious. I've only had one half-way decent cup of coffee since I got here. How did you convince them to let you have your own coffeemaker?"

Dewayne looked up, his one eye sparkling, and gave a lopsided grin. "I'm just special, but it still cost me an arm and two legs."

Flora gulped, then took another slug of coffee. "That's terrible. How can you joke about such a thing?"

He shrugged. "You either have to joke or cry, and I

cried myself out a long time ago. Did you find out anything?"

Flora sat obediently and studied the granulated picture. There were four of them, actually, one in each quadrant of the screen. "That's the entrance, isn't it? I don't recognize the others."

With a start Flora realized she hadn't been outside the building since Clarissa and Bill had brought her here. How astounding! She loved the outside and every morning that was halfway decent had her *petit dejeuner* on the tiny scrap the Olympus House called a balcony. It was such a civilized practice, as was sitting in the shaded walled garden on a lovely afternoon. Oh, how she wanted to be home!

And she would get home soon, she vowed. Clarissa and that fool Enrique Rubio didn't have any power over her. The law couldn't expect her to stay in a place where a murder occurred literally within feet of her. She would call Rebecca for a recommendation for a shark of a lawyer. Flora knew that she could have been a superior lawyer if she had wanted, but the law was so twisty and wily she was secure enough in herself to ask for professional help.

"What are you thinking about? You look like you just remembered something wonderful." Dewayne looked at her closely, the unscarred part of his mouth twisting slightly.

It was wonderful, this realization that she did not have to be subject to Clarissa's rules, but it was not something she could share with Dewayne.

"Just a plan. What are the other three places?"

Dewayne was adroit enough to realize a change of subject, so he merely shrugged. "That's one of the fire exits. That's the kitchen entrance and this one is the ambulance entrance. I can switch it –" which he did "– and it shows four more of the fire exits. Once more, and the last two fire exits."

"One for each wing."

"Right."

"So?"

"I've been studying each tape, trying to see if anyone came or left, or if there's been any tinkering with the tapes."

"And?"

"There's no evidence that the tapes have been edited or doctored or fooled with." His tone was serious.

"You can tell that?"

"Easy. Just run it through a… you don't know anything about computers, do you?"

After a flash of justifiable irritation at being lumped with what he obviously thought was an illiterate section of what he would probably call the 'older generation' Flora felt almost embarrassed, an emotion with which she was not at all familiar. Clarissa had bought her a computer, one of the super-simple ones sold by senior citizen organizations, so they could keep in touch by emails. Flora's refusal to have an answering machine and dislike of telephone conversations in general – *proper communication is done by written correspondence*, she maintained – were legendary in her circle. The computer, still in its original box, sat in the guest room closet of her Olympus House apartment.

"I have a computer," she said with complete truth. "I just don't like it."

"That's okay. A lot of the older generation don't, even though it's not all that complicated," he said, confirming Flora's fears.

Flora bristled. The entire concept of instant communication and heaven only knew what else was distressingly common, something Flora found distasteful especially since she had spent her entire life being not only a proponent but a leading light of gracious behavior. It was unconscionable of him to assume that she could not master the most difficult intricacies of computers if she put her mind to it.

"So tell me what you found out this morning," Dewayne went on, switching directions easily. "I can imagine that the whole place was crawling with people."

"Yes, and not one of them knew anything. Except for that crazy Eula Badham, who is convinced that the 'gang' that runs this place is out to kill her because she saw the killer."

Dewayne sat forward at that, at least as far as his support straps would allow. "What?"

"Don't get excited. She's always saying that they're going to have to kill her because she knows too much. And the murderer is a ghost, if you please… she saw this white amorphous form going down the hall. She had a bad dream and never left her bed, if you want to know what I think."

"And no one else knows anything?"

"No, not anyone I talked to. Of course, the police are still all over the place and the crime scene tape is still up. There are always too many people around for me to slip past it," Flora said bitterly, sipping at her coffee as Dewayne laughed.

"You would too, wouldn't you?"

Flora remembered the whole affair of Laura Fenn Tyler's cordoned apartment and nodded, still pleased at her courage in spite of the way it had ended. "But only when I have a chance of success. I do want to know what was in Miss Enero's office that Penelope Cattermole wanted to see so badly. After all, I heard that Miss Enero had taken her cane away and the woman could barely walk with it, let alone without it. How did she get there?"

"It would have to be by wheelchair, of course."

Flora blinked. Eula Badham had said that the Cattermole had rolled herself down to the office, and she hadn't paid any attention. It was embarrassing to Flora that she should have missed such an obvious conclusion.

"Oh, and you have security tape that proves it?" Flora's eyes widened in horror. "They tape us inside the building? Isn't that illegal?"

Dewayne shook his head. The action pulled on the hardened scar tissue of his face, twisting it grotesquely. "Doctor Bobby says that cameras in the facility would be a violation of the guests' privacy, something for which I think Fred Moretti must be very grateful."

"Fred Moretti? Why?"

The undamaged side of Dewayne's mouth curled up into a merry grin. "It would cut into his nighttime visits."

"Visits? But what – " Flora stopped abruptly, remembering the old man's main topic of conversation. "I thought that was just gossip. He doesn't!"

"He most certainly does, and often. At least, all the gossip makes it seem likely. Thankfully I've never seen him in the act." His half-grin was lascivious, then his expression turned serious. "The only cameras inside this place are fixed on the drug cabinets by the nurses' station. Look." He punched a few keys and the view on the screen changed.

"I don't…" Flora began, then fell silent.

The cameras, two of them, were focused on the enormous metal cabinet that looked more like safes, but there was a small strip of floor that showed. As they watched an image passed, the image of part of a wheelchair wheel and the barest flash of an anonymous hand.

"Is that the Cattermole?" Flora really didn't mean to be flip; she truly believed part of properly genteel behavior was giving someone who had passed on their due respect. On the other hand, somehow in Flora's mind reducing that unpleasant lady to a neutral singular noun seemed more than appropriate.

"Can't tell, but it would seem so. It's the only wheelchair that's gone past since the lights dimmed for the night."

"Is there any sign of anyone else?"

"You mean the murderer? No, but you see that this covers only a couple of inches of the hallway. A marching band could have gone down the other side of the hall and these cameras wouldn't have seen it."

"What time did that shadow go past?"

"Around three. And Princey found her body around three-thirty."

"Thirty minutes…" Flora's brow ruffled in thought. "That's not a very long window of opportunity."

"I wonder if it was an arranged meeting?"

"With whom?" Flora asked dismissively. "I think the question we have to answer is why? The woman's arm was paralyzed and almost completely useless. Think of the effort it must have taken to wheel herself from her room to Enero's office. She must have wanted to be there very badly."

"Unless someone pushed her."

"Is there any sign of someone else on the tape?"

Dewayne shook his head and pushed buttons rerunning the snippet of tape. "Can't tell if there's anyone or not. Can't see more than part of a wheel and a hand."

"So what else have the tapes shown?"

"Nothing."

"At all?"

"Nothing. I've looked at every minute on every camera." Dewayne's voice was serious. Frowning, he stared at the flickering screen as if something new would magically appear. "Nothing shows except that hint of a wheelchair. After the normal shift change no one entered or left by any door until the police showed up this morning."

"That means," Flora said slowly, "the murderer must be here – inside, with us."

Chapter Eight

Naomi edged into the nurses' station almost as if afraid of attack. She had never been where a policeman was at the staff door demanding to see IDs and he wouldn't say anything except that it was orders. She had produced her employee card, happy that she had remembered it. Everyone at Cold Creek knew her and until the facility had been upgraded with a magnetic card swipe system for certain procedures she forgot it more often than not.

Georgia Warneker looked up from a pile of files with weary eyes. Never a pretty woman even in her youth, her normally worn looking face now looked terrible.

"Georgia, girl, what is the matter with you? You look like you've been rode hard and put away wet. What's going on here?" Naomi threw her purse into the cubby beneath the counter and laid a comforting hand on the older woman's arm.

Never one to mince words, Georgia told her.

"Mrs. Cattermole? Murdered?" Naomi blenched. "Lord knows I didn't like the woman, but… murdered?"

"Beaten to death. I've heard her skull was crushed," Georgia answered, her toneless delivery making the words all the more horrible.

"But who would do such a thing?"

The chunky nurse shrugged. "Who wouldn't?"

Her face taut with fatigue, Melanie Jenks strode up and made a notation on a chart.

"Melanie, Georgia just told me what happened. I'm so sorry."

Melanie shrugged her bony shoulders. "Thanks, Naomi."

"It must have been horrible."

"I've seen blood before," Melanie said in a tight voice.

"You look all-in. You took Danita's shift last night, didn't you? Why don't you go home?"

"Naw, can't. All the residents are in a flutter, so it's all hands on deck. Besides, I need the money."

Naomi looked on her with compassion. Between her dickhead soon-to-be-ex trying to take their son and that pathetic new grandbaby (who had been born without a brain, the gossip said) Melanie was certainly between a rock and a hard place. Naomi had things hard, she knew, but nothing like Melanie was facing. The problems Naomi faced could all be solved just with money; Melanie's couldn't.

"Girl, you've worked two shifts in a row, and you're gray as a ghost. You need some rest. Now are you going to go home or do I have to go to Miss Enero and have her order you to go?"

"I told you – I need the money. Harley is…" A suspicious moisture appeared in the corner of Melanie's eyes.

"I know. Harley is trying to take Davy and you need money, but all the money in the world ain't going to do you no good if you kill yourself getting it. Harley will have Davy for sure then. Go home, Melanie. Go home."

For a moment Naomi thought the other woman would fight her and wondered if she really should enlist Miss Enero in this, but then Melanie nodded. "You're right. I'll check out now."

"Good. Go home and get some sleep, and don't think about anything here."

Melanie had already started for the nurses' lounge, but turned and looked back with sad eyes. "You really think I can do that? I'll see you later."

Georgia waited until Melanie was gone before casting a jaundiced eye at the younger woman. "Hope you don't get in trouble because of that."

"I won't, not if nobody knows about it." Her words carried a warning. It was common knowledge that Melanie and Georgia had never gotten along. "This would be her third shift in a row, and if she's that tired it's a risk to the residents. A couple of hours of sleep will make all the difference."

"Idea of staying didn't bother her none."

"Georgia, she's having a really hard time right now." Naomi worked at keeping her tone pacific, especially since she felt like screaming at the sour older woman. "And she needs every dollar she can get."

"And who doesn't? You'd stand up for the devil if you felt sorry for him, wouldn't you?" Georgia frowned and gathered up a handful of files and started on her rounds. "Well, if anything comes of it, it's all on your head. I don't want any part of it."

"It'll be all right," Naomi said to her retreating back.

"Can you save me?"

Naomi whirled around. "Mrs. Badham! Why aren't you at breakfast with everyone else?"

The old woman's faded blue eyes filled with tears. "So they can't poison me. They're going to kill me you, know. I know too much…"

Putting her arm around the bird-like shoulders Naomi sighed. Like everyone else at Cold Creek she knew of Mrs. Badham's mania, but aside from that the woman was sweet. Of course Mrs. Cattermole's murder would upset her.

"Nothing is going to happen to you, Mrs. Badham. You're safe here. Why don't I go with you to breakfast. You'll be all right with me there."

"I'd like that. I want to feel safe…"

"Come on." Without a qualm Naomi left her paperwork. It could wait. The residents were more important. Perhaps it was time for her to talk to Miss Enero about moving Eula Badham to Corridor F. She was certainly becoming more mental by the day.

"Is there a problem?" a harassed Dr. Jensen asked. He was loping down the corridor and, judging from the rare scowl on his face the current situation had upset him. Normally he was so blandly serene nothing touched him.

"No, sir," Naomi answered. "I'm just taking Mrs. Badham in to breakfast. She's just a little upset. We all are."

"Good of you. Glad to see you're still successfully dodging those killers, Mrs. Badham." Tact had never been one of Bobby Jensen's strong points. "Do you know where the police are?"

Mrs. Badham was muttering in barely controlled terror. Naomi held her close and silently called down names on her boss' head. "Shaniqua said that Miss Enero set them up in the bookkeeper's office."

"Good. At least she had the good sense to keep them out of my office." Muttering, he stalked down the hall, looking like nothing so much as an affronted stork.

"Come on, Mrs. Badham. Let's get you some breakfast, and I'll make sure you're not poisoned."

* * * * *

"I wonder who they've got us socialized with today," Dewayne asked. With expert precision he drove his chair through the maze of tables.

"Silly practice." Flora was dismissive. "One should always be free to choose congenial companions, especially for mealtimes. If such a thing is possible here."

"Come now, Miss Flora, that's not very charitable."

"Charitable? That is a strange word choice."

Dewayne looked up, his eye twinkling. "What do you think happens to those who are not congenial?"

"And you do not believe that everyone is congenial to

someone? Why should I have to deprive them of the pleasure of their company?"

Throwing back his head, Dewayne roared with laughter, drawing the attention of the few residents already in the dining room. "You sure are something, lady, you sure are."

"Let's see – who have we been matched with today?" Flora made a great show of looking around. In actuality, it wasn't too difficult to find where Dewayne was assigned. There wouldn't be a chair and there really weren't that many wheelchair-bound patients at Cold Creek. The staff was sadistically set on making everyone walk as long as they could stagger about on cane, crutch or walker.

"Surprise me."

"Here you are," Flora said, sedately pointing to the table closest to the window. "And this morning you get to sit with Eugene Holcomb –"

"A bore, but nice enough," Dewayne said with calculated blandness.

"– and Ora Carroll –"

"Shy, but nice, as long as you don't talk about anything rude or controversial, which covers just about everything except kittens."

"How tiresome. Oh, and here is Marie Williams."

"You know," he said in a different, gentler tone of voice, "I've never heard her say a word. She's a sweet, sad lady."

"I agree," Flora said. When someone didn't bother her, she felt she could be generous. "I wish they had private tables. We need to talk."

"We can go back to my room after breakfast."

"I fully intend to. We can't go to mine because of my roommate." The final word dripped with contempt.

"And how has that unfortunate lady aroused your ire?"

"By existing. That is all she does – exist. And snore. My daughter did not even try to get me a private room."

"She didn't want you to miss all that socialization."

"How, pray tell me, can a lump who snores for twenty-three hours a day and is incapable of speech be sociable?" Flora wandered to the next table, then the next, her expression darkening with each step. "Well, finally! They've put me between that horrible Fred Moretti and Judy Lloyd." She was almost speechless with indignation.

Dewayne, by contrast, was chuckling. "And what's wrong with that?"

"The Moretti man is a lecherous octopus who pinches any portion of female anatomy he can get his fingers on and the Lloyd woman cries at anything, even when someone asks for maple syrup. Well, this just won't do."

After a quick glance around, Flora snatched up her card and switched it with the luckless Marie Williams'.

"There. That's better."

"You have absolutely no shame, Flora Melkiot." By now Dewayne was laughing again. "Do you always arrange the world to suit yourself?"

"Whenever I can," Flora asked with regal aplomb. "I do not see any reason to allow other people to dictate my 'socialization' for me. Now I hope they serve what they call breakfast soon, because I am hungry."

Breakfast had never been Flora's favorite meal, and the breakfasts served at Cold Creek only underscored her dislike. Cold toast, runny eggs always scrambled and without a single thing added to them, some sort of tasteless mystery meat, always fried… Flora sighed and made herself eat. It had taken them even longer than usual to serve it and the extra coffee – what they called coffee, at least – they allowed the residents was an insult to the palate.

Neither could she talk to Dewayne as she wished; normally little more than zombies intent on devouring their food, today the residents were more like a tree full of chattering monkeys. Flora had planned to question their tablemates about the murder, but any hope of sensible conversation was gone.

Really, were all these people mentally handicapped as well as physically? Flora thought in some disgust. Suddenly it was generally accepted by all that modern society was going to the dogs, that it seemed everyone there had individually discovered the body and there were assassins sent by an evil international cartel to kill Mrs. General Brian Cattermole for wildly varying reasons. Opinions as to exactly what reasons only caused two vociferous arguments that had to be broken up by the nurses.

Flora and Dewayne exchanged glances, his amused, hers disdainful. At the table behind them they could hear Eula Badham repeating that 'they' were going to kill her because she 'knew too much' and the protestations of her tablemates that they would protect her, that she had nothing to fear, had no effect. Had Eula's fear been less palpable it could have been a skit from some irreverent British comedy troupe.

Really, Flora thought, *that woman should be in an asylum and under strong medication!*

At their own table Ora Carroll was complaining vociferously that no one had any standards any more as if she had just discovered the fact. Perhaps of all the people there she was the only one concerned that the napkins were made of paper instead of cloth. Flora was unable to decide if she were even allowing herself to hear that there had been a murder in their midst. On the other hand, she decided it was all part and parcel of this entire down-the-rabbit-hole establishment. *At least*, she thought with grim resignation, *it couldn't get any worse.*

Flora was wrong.

"Mama!"

The shriek cut through the excited babble like a sledgehammer through butter. The resultant silence was deafening.

"Oh, Mama, I'm so glad you're all right!"

A vision in tasteful and distressingly modest grey, Clarissa flung herself across the room to envelop a startled Flora in a bear hug.

"Clarissa, what do you think you're doing? And let go of me – you're breaking my neck." Hampered by only being able to use one arm, Flora pushed as well as she could. She really didn't need to gasp for breath, though; it just seemed that way.

As a good daughter should, Clarissa obeyed her mother, but only to an extent. Her arm remained around Flora's shoulders – which thankfully were not necessary to the process of breathing – and her other hand grasped her mother's good arm.

"I'm so glad you're all right. Bill and I were listening to the news as we had breakfast and when they said an elderly woman had been murdered at Cold Creek… I thought my heart would stop, Mama. I thought… I thought…"

It was obvious what Clarissa thought; older and more schooled in guarding her expression, one could only surmise from the dark clouds building up in her eyes that Flora was not pleased to be lumped in the same thought as the words 'elderly woman.'

"For Heaven's sake, Clarissa, behave yourself!" Flora squirmed a little, working to free herself from her daughter's absorptive embrace. It was rather like trying to fight one's way out of a barrel full of cobwebs – clinging and sticky.

"I just had to come over and see for myself that you're all right, Mama."

"I am fine. I assure you no one has tried to murder me."

"Yet," Dewayne muttered under his breath. Clarissa didn't seem to hear, as her gusty sighs of emotional relief was almost capable of bringing in a new weather front, but Flora did and her subsequent glare could have withered flowers.

"Mama, we have to talk…"

"Indeed we do." Using her not inconsiderable strength, Flora disentangled herself and stood up. Clarissa had always been much more Morris' child than hers, even to her lack of height. Flora stood straighter than normal, taking every advantage of the three inches she towered over her daughter. "Let's go see if we can find a quiet corner in the reception area. Things are pretty much at sixes and sevens, as you can well imagine."

"But, Mama, your breakfast…"

"Forget it. It's not worth eating anyway." Flora nodded politely to her gaping tablemates. "Excuse us, please."

The large reception room doubled as a lounge, so there were many chairs and couches, arranged in intimate little clumps. Flora led the way to the furthest, two club chairs done in a surprisingly nice *toile*, close to the front window. While the supposed gardens between the various wings of the building were barely landscaped or maintained, the front of the building was delightful. The sweeping circular drive was edged with low blooming plants – what their name was Flora had no idea, as gardening was extremely uninteresting to her – and under the spreading *porte cochere* meticulously trimmed topiaries in gigantic pots stood guard on either side of the door.

"What brings you here this early, Clarissa?" Flora asked rather uselessly. She knew her daughter's tendency to over-emotionalism and drama – but only in the most genteel and socially acceptable way, of course.

"I told you, Mama. When they said on the radio that an elderly woman had been murdered at Cold Creek I… well, my heart just about stopped, that's all. I was so afraid…" A sob gurgled in her throat. "If anything happened to you, Mama, I don't know what I would do!"

"Oh, for Heaven's sake calm down, Clarissa. There's nothing wrong with me that getting out of here won't cure."

"That's another reason why I came, Mama." Clarissa reached out and grabbed Flora's good arm in a death grip. "Bill and I agreed that there's no way we're going to leave you here in this dangerous place."

In spite of how well she knew her daughter Flora's heart jumped. "You mean you and that rat Ernesto are going to allow me to go home without my having to file charges?"

Clarissa looked shocked. "Home? To Dallas? All by yourself? Oh, Mama, you must be joking. How would you ever look after yourself?"

The tiny flame of the dream of freedom died a swift, guttering death. "There are many ways, most of which I already do myself here."

"No, Mama, we just can't let you put yourself in such danger. Bill and I talked it over and we've decided that you have to come home to us."

Flora could just imagine the discussion they had had. Amiable, workaholic Bill would just have nodded his head to anything Clarissa said while planning his escape to his office. It was doubtful that he had even heard her.

"Home? With you? To your house?"

"Yes, Mama, it's going to be so grand! You know we have that guest suite that overlooks the side garden – "

"You mean that little bedroom and bath over the garage? The one where your maid used to sleep?"

"Only while the maid's room off the kitchen was refurbished after all that termite damage. And we'll repaint it for you. And you can bring down any of your furniture that you want."

Prison doors slammed loudly in Flora's mind. It really wouldn't make any difference if the rooms were repainted or not, because after six months of living with her present-in-body-but-absent-in-mind son-in-law and her punctiliously correct daughter Flora would be ready for the happy farm – the kind with bars on the windows.

"I have a home, Clarissa. In Dallas."

"Oh, Mama, that won't be any problem." Her smile was both beatific and dismissive. "Bill had to go up to Dallas and see one of the suppliers – "

"Who? Which one?" While she had never been a functioning officer of the company Flora liked to keep a finger on what went on. When Morris had passed away she could have taken over the company and done a splendid job of running it, she knew, but by then Bill had been groomed as the new CEO and such a demanding job would have cut dreadfully into her time.

"Oh, I don't know. Does it matter? Anyway, while he was there he spent the night in your condo instead of getting some expensive hotel room – "

Inwardly Flora snorted. She rather liked her son-in-law and had no objection to his staying at her home, but she would have appreciated to have been asked.

" – and he checked your mail and everything, as well as looking the place over to make sure everything was okay. It was all so crazy after your accident, you remember."

Flora remembered little but being kidnapped, loaded into an ambulance even as she protested, and carried off willy-nilly to San Antonio. It would be a long time before she could forgive Clarissa for that. Her jaw tightened.

"I hope you told him to bring down the gold mules I wanted."

"Mama, you know of course I didn't." Clarissa shook her head as if this just confirmed her mother's inability to care for herself. "They aren't safe in your condition."

Just because I broke my wrist why does everyone think I can't walk properly? Flora's jaw tightened another notch, and then several more as Clarissa continued to talk.

The fancy fur-trimmed house shoes were not all Bill had neglected to bring down. Flora liked a certain coachman-cut style of housecoat; she had several, and all in the luxurious fabrics she liked. Clarissa had refused to ask him to bring them, saying they would be too hard to keep clean and would probably be stolen anyway. She had replaced them with a number of little cotton duster housecoats that snapped down the front and plain, easy fastening housedresses for Flora to wear. While she found them hideous, Flora privately admitted they made life with one arm in a cast much easier. She still planned to burn them each and every one as soon as the cast came off and she went home again.

One thing Clarissa had wanted to bring south was Flora's extensive jewelry collection. An avid collector for years as well as the pampered wife of a wealthy jewelry store chain owner, Flora had amassed almost enough jewelry to start her own store… if she could ever decide to part with a single piece. All but a few inexpensive trinkets and what she had been wearing at the time of the accident had been locked up either in Flora's small bedroom safe or in the Olympus House's safety deposit vault, neither of which Clarissa nor Bill had access to, and as far as Flora was concerned they were going to stay there. Flora knew her child well enough to realize that once Clarissa got her hands on those pretties, she'd never get them back.

"But it would be so much more sensible to have you with us. Just think of the fun we could have – lunches at the country club, and the Altar Guild would love to have you as a member, and so would my book club."

Having at one time or another been a guest at each one of these, Flora all but choked. Fortunately, Clarissa – in the fond delusion that she would be pleasing her mother as well as herself – didn't notice.

"Bill checked out the real estate market while he was up there, and there won't be any problem in selling your condo – you'll probably make a marvelous profit – "

"Sell my condominium?" Flora was affronted. "Sell my home? What are you talking about?"

"Well, Mama, it is the most sensible idea. Bill talked to one of the salesmen at Carruthers Realty and he said…"

"By what right did he talk to her?" In her anger Flora forgot the contempt in which she had held Miss Alicia Carruthers during the Tyler murder investigation for being such a wimp in allowing herself to be blackmailed most of her adult life. "I have no intention of selling my home."

"But Mama…"

"Clarissa Anne Melkiot Fullerton, you have badly overreached yourself. I have no intention of moving to San Antonio, now or ever. My home is in Dallas, and I intend to return there just as soon as I can find an attorney to get that idiotic guardianship which allowed you to incarcerate me in here overturned." It was not a lie, even though Flora had only just decided to really call an attorney. *It was,* she decided, *nothing more than a future truth.*

Clarissa looked as if she had been slapped. "But Mama…"

"Don't 'but mama' me. You have acted disgracefully, and as usual it is up to me to set things straight."

"But Mama – an attorney?"

"Of course. You didn't expect me just to sit around and put up with this, did you?"

"But Mama," Clarissa wailed, much as she had when told in the sixth grade that under no circumstances could she get her hair permed like Wanda Eldridge's. She forced herself to take a deep breath and then went on in a much more adult voice, "We can settle that later, Mama. Right now a woman has been killed here and you have to come home with us. What would people think if we left you here in such a place of danger?"

If one's eyes were good enough, they might have been able to see the steam rising from Flora's ears. Yes, Clarissa was her daughter – she had borne her, raised her, taught her manners and the difference between right and wrong. Who was this ungrateful child to be giving her orders? Suddenly if Flora had had any misgivings about taking such decisive action they were whisked away and her mind irrevocably made up. She would not let Clarissa dictate to her either about staying or leaving, even if a knife-wielding maniac were stalking the halls every hour on the hour.

"That is the most specious reasoning I have ever heard, Clarissa, even from you. If such things really matter to you, you would be much better off wondering what people would think about you getting a court order to lock your mother away for nothing more than a broken wrist. Just think of what a juicy piece of gossip that would be for people to chew on. As for leaving this minute, I cannot. I am needed to help solve this case."

Between remembering the brouhaha that followed her mother's last foray into crimesolving and the certainty that her mother would positively enjoy spreading her version of the guardianship arrangement, the relentlessly proper and correct Clarissa Fullerton moaned, momentarily bereft of a cogent argument against either.

As if scripted, a fresh-faced uniformed officer strode up more than a little hesitantly. Facing gun battles and crazy criminals was something that a policeman was expected to handle; to interrupt two arguing women was another thing entirely.

"Mrs. Melkiot? Sorry to interrupt, but Detective Camacho would like to see you now."

Ignoring his outstretched hand, Flora rose unaided and swept from the room.

Chapter Nine

Detective Camacho was ambivalent as he watched Flora Melkiot enter the room. The bookkeeper's office was small and crowded, but it was better than nothing. There was no way he would be hauling these living ghosts of people down to the precinct – too many of them probably wouldn't survive the trip. It wasn't like any of them knew anything anyway.

The Melkiot woman was different. He had known from the first moment he saw her standing outside the crime scene room that she would be trouble. She was tall, so thin she was scrawny and ugly as a mud fence, but even in a tacky cotton dress and bearing a chunk of plaster on her wrist she was still imposing. Of course, she was probably mad as a hatter too. Imagine someone like her helping solve a murder in Dallas. Did all old people get delusional?

"Good morning, Mrs. Melkiot."

She folded fairly gracefully into the chair on the other side of the desk. "Good morning, Detective Camacho. What have you found out?"

"I'm the one who should be asking the questions, Mrs. Melkiot. Any connection with Melkiot's Gems and Jewels?"

Flora nodded with a regal grace. "My late husband began the chain with one store. Now we have more than thirty all over Texas and even more outside. My son-in-law is the current CEO, though I like to keep my eye on the business."

"I got my wife's engagement ring at Melkiot's," Camacho murmured, trying not to remember how much he had paid for it. Luckily the store had had a very generous payment plan.

"I'm glad you had such good taste. I hope they treated you well?"

"Very well. Now about this murder…"

"Indeed. There are some things I wish to know. According to witnesses her head had been savagely bashed in. Do you know yet what the murder weapon was?"

Camacho looked at her closely. Yep, he had been right. Sane or looney, she was going to be trouble.

"I thought I told you I would ask the questions."

"It would be more efficient if we traded information."

"You don't need any information, Mrs. Melkiot," the detective said as his jaw tightened. "You are not a law enforcement officer."

"No, I am actually more efficient than one," Flora said with serene assurance. "We are wasting time, detective. If you had been cooperative we could already be through with this conversation and you would be a great deal closer to solving this case during the golden 48."

Camacho's fists tightened. Yes, trouble indeed. Of course she watched television – what else did they have to do here besides watch television? – so it wasn't surprising that she knew about the so-called 'golden 48 hours' in which they were most likely to solve a crime. Television writers, he decided, had a lot to answer for.

"What did you see, Mrs. Melkiot?"

"A bunch of distressed and disturbed old people standing around an open office door."

"It was very early in the morning. Why were you up?"

"Sleeping is difficult here," she replied with dignity. "It is far too noisy and I am always awakened several times during the night – call button bells going off, someone having a nightmare, nurses checking up on us...

This morning I heard some screaming – panicky screaming – so naturally I got up to investigate."

"Naturally."

She bristled at the sarcasm in his voice, but Camacho didn't find it surprising. She obviously had a very high opinion of herself.

"I did not enter the murder room personally," Flora said. "One of the nurses – the one named Melanie, I believe, though it might have been the one named Georgia – stood in the door and tried to quiet the people. She refused to let anyone in." Obviously the old woman regretted this.

"Very astute of her."

"I had been in Miss Enero's office only once, so from the quick glance I was able to get I could not tell if anything were disturbed or missing." Flora was careful not to mention that her only visit there had been with a furious Clarissa after her abortive attempt to regain her freedom.

"What did you see, Mrs. Melkiot?"

"Penelope Cattermole sprawled across Miss Enero's desk. There was a great deal of blood and from the quick glance I got it would seem that half her head had been caved in. She was sitting in the desk chair; I didn't get a chance to see what happened to her wheelchair."

Camacho didn't move, but his senses snapped to attention. "Wheelchair?"

Mrs. Melkiot looked disgusted. It appeared to be an emotion very familiar to her face. "Wheelchair. A sitting contraption equipped with wheels that enables a person who cannot walk to get around."

"I know what a wheelchair is. Why do you bring it up?"

"What was the murder weapon?"

"Not a wheelchair. What does a wheelchair have to do with it?"

If looks could kill, Camacho knew he would be nothing but a scorched greasy mark on the chair. The silence hung heavy in the air. She was trying to do a trade-off of information, that much he knew. God save him from old hags who watched too much TV and thought they could solve crimes like the professionals. *Writers really did have a lot to answer for*, he repeated to himself.

"It is a crime to withhold information in a murder investigation, Mrs. Melkiot. I ask you again, what does a wheelchair have to do with this?"

Her bony face worked as she thought. She would never have been a beauty, Camacho decided, but even now in her seventies, perhaps even her eighties, she was an arresting woman, even handsome in a way.

She blinked first. "Very well, detective. Penelope Cattermole had had a stroke. She was very much impaired and had great difficulty walking, but that did not stop her from being both unpleasant and combative. For very good reasons Miss Enero had confiscated her cane and her walker. That leaves a wheelchair as a means of locomotion. In other words, she never could have made it from her room to the office without one. Miss Enero's office is quite small and very crowded with furniture. Even with the quick glance I got it was obvious there was no wheelchair inside. Unless the murderer removed it, how did the Cattermole creature get there?"

It was a question Camacho was still pondering after Mrs. Melkiot swept from the office. There had been more conversation, of course, but nothing substantive. Either the woman really didn't know anything else, or she was one hell of an actress. Either way it didn't help him.

Just how had Mrs. Cattermole gotten to the office? The Melkiot woman had been right; according to the victim's medical records she had had a massive stroke, and one arm was useless. Could she have propelled a wheelchair by herself? Could she have stolen someone else's walker or cane? He didn't remember seeing either in the crowded little office, but that didn't mean they weren't there. You expected to see things like that in a nursing home, and so he probably wouldn't have noticed them. He'd check the scene again before he left and talk to the CSIs once he got back downtown.

"Dr. Jensen, detective," said the uniformed officer, peeking around the door, then opening it to admit the doctor.

Dr. Bobby Jensen was not a prepossessing looking man. Average height, a little on the skinny side, balding… Camacho wouldn't have remembered him ten minutes after he saw him. He did, however, remember his family. The Jensens were rich and famous and something of a medical dynasty in San Antonio. They also had a lot of political clout. Camacho would have to tread easily here.

"Please have a seat, Dr. Jensen."

The doctor folded into the chair. His face was blank, as if he were listening to something the detective could not hear.

"Thank you. Dreadful business, this. Death is no stranger in this place, but usually it is a peaceful departing, not a… a…"

"Murder," Camacho supplied.

Dr. Jensen shook slightly, as if a goose had walked over his grave. "Exactly. How can I help you?"

"Do you know anyone who wanted to kill Penelope Cattermole?"

Dr. Jensen gave a fastidious little chuckle. "Perhaps a better question would be who didn't want her dead."

"So she wasn't popular?"

"Hardly. She was difficult, opinionated and contentious. She was being sent back to the hospital, you know. I was against it – I mean, we are supposed to be a place of help and healing, and that woman surely needed help, but Stacey insisted. She said we could not let her endanger our residents and staff."

Camacho had heard a little about Mrs. Cattermole's attitude problems, but everyone heard things a little differently.

"Endanger? I thought the woman had had a stroke."

"And apparently that brought out her worst tendencies. Stacey took away her cane after she kept hitting at people with it."

"Hitting people?"

Dr. Jensen nodded uncomfortably and studied his fingers, wiggling them as if running scales. "Unfortunately, yes. She gave one of our physical therapists a bruise on his shin in the gym and then at lunch yesterday almost hit struck of our most physically fragile guests. And a nurse, too," he added as an afterthought.

"And you don't think her cane should have been taken away?"

"The cane, yes, but not the walker. Mrs. Cattermole would have been incapable of making mischief with a walker, and she could have retained some mobility. Stacey declared her intention of isolating her in her room until it was time for her transfer back to the military hospital. That is in direct contradiction to our stated purpose of intense socialization and reintegration of the patient into as normal a life as possible."

Typical medical pyschobabble, Camacho decided. *Jensen likes the sound of his own voice*. Sure seemed to be a nervous sort, though, the way he kept wiggling his fingers.

"Any reason why Miss Enero would go so far? Did she and Mrs. Cattermole have a history?"

Jensen shrugged. "Not that I know of. Stacey is a dear girl, but she's all spit and polish and rules. Has no appreciation for the ebb and flow of life. I tell her that she can't regulate everything, but she does try." The doctor heaved a sigh. "And I must admit, this place runs so much better since she took over."

Meaning the less for you to do, translated Camacho.

"Are we finished here, detective? There are things I must do." Without waiting for an answer, Bobby Jensen started to rise.

"One more thing, doctor. What was your relationship with Mrs. Cattermole?"

He looked startled. "Mine? Why, none. Other than house physician, that is. I checked her over when she was first transferred over here, like I do all the residents, and I check their charts once a week unless there is some question or immediate health need. And I am on call in case of any problems." He made it sound a dispensation of the highest order. Camacho felt a twinge of sympathy for the patients at Cold Creek Health Care Facility.

"Did Mrs. Cattermole have any problems?"

A singularly impish smile spread over the doctor's bland features. "Other than being physically and mentally impaired by a major stroke, suffering from the various bodily indignities of old age and having the fiend's own temper… no. With good care and a little luck, she could have lasted another decade."

"Thank you, Doctor Jensen."

After the doctor had gone, Detective Camacho sat and thought for a moment. From what he had heard of Mrs. Cattermole it seemed that no one grieved at her passing, but it also seemed that no one had a sufficient motive to kill her. And her death had been a death of anger; there was personal fury in the blows that had crushed her skull.

Who could hate a crippled old woman that much?

* * * * *

"Now that's good… one more time, please."

Flora seethed. Was there no spirit of freedom in this place? No intellectual curiosity? She lifted the weight as instructed, if weight was the proper term. Though it was shaped like a traditional barbell, it was no heavier than a medium-sized can of peaches. Lifting it the required ten times was nothing.

"That's good," Terry cooed, as if Flora had done something worthwhile. "Now I'll get the pedal exerciser."

She bounced off across the crowded therapy room.

The therapy room was more crowded than Flora had ever seen it, as if like sheep the residents were huddling together for safety. Or gossip. *Do sheep gossip,* she wondered. The noise level was incredible and from the few conversations Flora could hear, full of wild theories ranging from presidential assassins and conspiracy theories to space aliens. Flora snorted; she regarded a tendency to blame fantasy instead of finding the real cause as a sure marker of a feeble intelligence. Much to Clarissa's dismay her motto had always been do something, don't talk about it.

"Charlie," Flora said to the young man at the next table. She had waited until Terry was all the way across the room; it was pure luck that she had been captured in conversation by a grossly obese woman in a wheelchair complaining of unwanted attentions from Fred Moretti. It was not an unusual complaint, from what Dewayne had said. That should give Flora a few minutes of freedom.

"Yes, Mrs. Melkiot?" Charlie said, coming to her. Really, he was too pretty for a man, Flora decided. He could be making a fortune modeling.

"Yesterday in here you offered most correctly to help Mrs. Cattermole back to her room and she swung her cane at you. Were you injured?"

Something dark and feral passed over his features and for that moment he wasn't at all pretty. "It hurt like the devil, and it left a whacking great bruise, but injured is a very strong word."

It sounded like a rehearsed speech. So he was ready for that tiresome detective, who would probably take him at face value.

"Did you kill Penelope Cattermole?" Flora believed that a frontal assault was sometimes much more effective than civilized questioning.

Charlie literally blanched. "No! How can you think such a thing? I didn't like her, I don't know anyone who did, but I didn't kill her."

"I didn't think you did, but I had to ask. Now sit down before you faint and make a spectacle of yourself."

He looked suspiciously at her, as he would at a talking snake, but warily sat down. "What are you up to?"

"Just curious. Here –" Flora extended her un-casted hand. "Why don't you give me a massage just so people won't think you're goofing off."

Without taking his eyes from her Charlie began to rub her hand and Flora practically purred with pleasure. Morris used to do this for her, especially when her hand cramped after writing out the hundreds of Christmas cards they had sent every year.

"Was there any reason Mrs. Cattermole attacked you?"

"Nope. I'd never spoken to her before. I knew who she was, of course, everyone did. The staff – " he stopped abruptly.

"The staff was probably warned that an especially difficult patient was coming in and to be careful of her," Flora said sweetly, "just like you all were warned about me."

It had been a shot in the dark, but the guilty flash over Charlie's all too mobile face told the truth. *And who do I have to thank for that*? Flora wondered with poisonous clarity, even as she vowed to find a suitable retribution for her luckless daughter. It was time Clarissa learned once and for all that her mother was not and never had been difficult; determined, yes. Discriminating, yes. Devilish on occasion, yes. Difficult – never.

Flora made herself smile. "Had you known Mrs. Cattermole before?"

"No. Seems like I remember reading something about her husband when he died – he was a big muckety-muck in the Air Force, so there was a lot of press about him – but nothing more."

"But she said quite definitely her husband wouldn't

have you in his unit, so that made me think that you might have served under him at some time."

Charlie's hands tightened around Flora's with such sudden intensity that it was all she could do not to yelp. He released immediately and began to work away the hurt as if it were a visual stain. His voice dropped to a near-whisper.

"It's not common knowledge, Mrs. Melkiot, but I'm gay. It was well known that General Cattermole hated gays."

"You're gay?" Flora repeated stupidly. Thinking about anyone else's sexual life had always been rather repugnant to her, as she regarded such an action as being both voyeuristic and intrusive. Still, the idea of this handsome, personable young man preferring his own sex was distressing. *As if it's any of my business*, she thought. "But you think she knew."

He shrugged. "I don't know how. I haven't told anyone... and neither I nor my partner has anything to do with the military. We live a very quiet life."

So he feels he would have something to lose if it became common knowledge, Flora concluded. "But she knew," she repeated.

He shrugged again. "I don't know how. Sometimes it seems that people like her have a radar for people like me." Charlie raised his eyes and stared her directly in the face. "What do you have, some sort of truth ray or something? I've told you more than people I've known for years."

Inwardly Flora preened. She had always known she had a special gift with people. Modestly she said, "You don't want to be involved in Mrs. Cattermole's murder. Telling the truth is the best way."

"Well, I've told the truth, and I just hope it doesn't come back to bite me. You won't tell anyone, will you?"

Flora looked him directly in the eye. "I thought it was all the fashion today to trumpet your life choices to all and sundry, but obviously I was wrong. I shan't tell anyone unless the solution of this case depends on it."

Charlie nodded with only a slight hint of hesitation.

"Have you hurt yourself, Mrs. Melkiot?" Terry bounced up to the table, the silly-looking pedal thing in her hand. She truly sounded concerned.

"No, I just like holding hands with a handsome young man," Flora replied with an uncharacteristic archness, to which Charlie responded with a practiced leer and a brush of his lips to her fingertips.

"Totally my pleasure, Mrs. Melkiot. Any time."

Terry looked on indulgently as he walked across the room almost quickly enough to be called an escape.

Chapter Ten

"Mrs. Melkiot... Mrs. Melkiot!"

The world was shaking. Had there been an earthquake? Had she been knocked unconscious? How badly was the Olympus House damaged? She had to get her antiques and her jewelry out of danger...

Flora fought her way through the clouds of darkness and at last stared up into the plain dark face of a nurse. She knew this one... Naomi something or other. The one who wanted to be an accountant.

"Wake up, Mrs. Melkiot. It's time for lunch."

"I was not sleeping," Flora replied with aggrieved dignity. "I was merely resting my eyes after therapy." She then ruined her pronouncement with a hearty yawn.

"Of course you are, but it's still time for lunch. Do you need any help?"

Flora Melkiot was capable of and quite practiced in annihilating those who threatened her ideas of her Self and her capabilities, but these were tempered with a self-imposed code of honor. This child was striving to better herself and meant everything she said kindly. Giving her a set-down would be akin to kicking a kitten.

Perhaps, Flora thought grudgingly, *ageing is making me mellow*.

The thought filled her with dismay.

"No, not at all. Run along and help those who need it. I'll be right there."

Naomi looked uncertain at that, but one distinctly un-mellow glance from Flora sent her on her way.

Flora struggled into a sitting position – with, to be sure, no more effort than usual – and shook her head. Normally she detested sleeping in the daytime, but she had been so tired. Of course, anyone would be after such a sleepless night and such an emotionally strenuous morning. As she had gotten older Flora had noted her need for less sleep, which in her mind had been a good thing; sleep was a waste of time that could be better spent doing other things. On the other hand, one did need a certain amount and last night she certainly hadn't gotten it.

As she splashed water on her face to chase away the last cobwebs of sleep she wondered vaguely if Clarissa had gone home or were still lurking about somewhere ready to pounce again with her unreasonable demands and expectations. The looseness of her terrycloth slides were just another irritant attached to her daughter. It would not have killed her and Bill to let her have her pretty mules. She was much more accustomed to them than these tacky abominations.

Flora sighed. She needed to call Rebecca and get the name of a lawyer. The firm she normally used was paid for by the company, which was controlled by her son-in-law, who was controlled by Clarissa. There would be no hope there. Flora sighed again. A woman truly did need to look out for herself.

The dining area was already pretty much full and the decibel level almost to the point of pain.

"Good afternoon, Mrs. Melkiot," said one of the aides. She was serving the table closest to the door. "I think you're over near the tree this time."

Flora forced a rictus of a smile. Of all things to make this day perfect. The tree was a scrawny, sickly ficus, prone to dropping unhealthy looking yellow leaves without warning, usually into something mushy or liquid. Someone should simply toss it on the fire and put it out of its misery.

The trip across the room was excruciating. Of course the murder was still the main topic of conversation, but the theories had gotten much wilder. Apparently whatever Eula Badham suffered from had infected the general population, because the snatches Flora could hear were remarkably similar to the senile old lady's wilder fantasies. Drug lords, money laundering, extra-marital affairs, kidnapping, hidden treasure, and more all featured in someone's theory. Flora felt almost battered by the time she reached her table.

"Well, we thought you weren't going to make it," said a genial older man whose name Flora didn't know.

"The more for us," twittered a wizened little lady. Mrs. Macsomething or other, if Flora remembered correctly. She used the word 'twittered' advisedly, as there was something inescapably birdlike about the woman. Had she started whistling and chirping Flora would not have been surprised.

"I am sorry to have kept you waiting," Flora said regally, sitting and regarding her place card with dislike. It had glitter on it. Glitter was not only vulgar, it was suitable only for kindergarteners.

"Did you hear about the murder?" the bird woman asked, her eyes bright. "I heard…"

The talk flowed on and even though she murmured "Really?" or "You don't say," at appropriate intervals Flora's mind was elsewhere. Once she got out of here she might go to a luxurious hotel where she could actually rest. Then therapists and such could come to her.

Adelita, the little Mexican aide, served, putting plates of some unidentifiable casserole in front of each of them. Dry-looking squares of cornbread – it had to be cornbread, it really couldn't be crumbling masonry – huddled on the edge of the plate.

Someplace, Flora amended, *where they had decent room service*. Compared to this, even a budget chain motel with a diner next door sounded luxurious.

One thing of which she was very conscious was that Dewayne was not in the dining room. Was he fasting, or did he have a special arrangement? Whatever it was, she intended to find out.

* * * * *

"You doing okay?" Naomi asked, gently touching Melanie's arm and making her jump. "I thought you said you were going home."

Melanie shook her head. "I'm fine. And I'll go… just need to finish up a few things first."

Naomi looked askance at her. "Well, you look like pure-dee death warmed over. You really should go home. We can cover for you."

"Thanks, but no. You're overstretched as is, with everyone so buzzed about the murder. Anybody know anything?"

Naomi gave a little laugh. "It isn't like TV, when they solve a crime in less than an hour. The detective still hasn't finished talking to all the residents."

"Like they'll be able to tell him anything sensible."

"Now don't you start being so scornful." Naomi reached around Melanie to grab a pen. "Better note down that Mrs. Barnhill refused to go to lunch – she said she didn't want to eat with a murderer running around loose."

"Ah, whoever did it is long gone." Melanie yawned again.

"Maybe."

"You really don't think that anyone here did it, do you, Naomi? God, who around here is strong enough?"

"Strength can come in many ways, and who knows what anyone can do when they're driven to the brink. Besides, think about it. The doors are all alarmed at night, and no one heard anything. And there are those video cameras on every door."

"Good grief, do those things really work?" Startled, Melanie blinked. "I thought they were phonies."

"I heard Miss Enero talking about them once. They're

real." Finishing her note, Naomi closed the file and almost stifled a giggle. "Besides, it won't be too long before our own home-grown detectives solve the case."

"Our own... girl, what are you talking about?" Melanie brushed back an errant lock of hair and wondered how long before she could sneak away early and still qualify for a full shift.

"You can't tell anybody," Naomi said in a semi-whisper, "but I heard them talking when I went past his room. Dewayne Harbaugh and Flora Melkiot are working on finding out who the murderer is."

"Go on!"

"No, it's true. They were talking about time windows and the video cameras on the outside doors. And guess what? Mrs. Pritchard said that she heard Mrs. Melkiot tell that detective that she helped solve a murder back in Dallas not too long ago."

Melanie made a rude sound. "That Melkiot woman is delusional. Who'd let her near a murder?"

A strident buzzer filled the nurses' station, accompanied by a blinking light on D corridor.

"Oh, law, it's Mr. Moretti again," Naomi moaned. "It's hard to believe he's not an octopus. Did you know he spent the night in Mrs. Abney's room again?" In spite of herself she giggled. Though there was plenty of positive proof that it happened on a regular basis the idea of wild senior sex still astonished her.

"Let me take the call. He won't try any of that shit with me," Melanie said grimly, stalking from the station almost as if pursued, Naomi looking after her with concern.

"Was that Melanie Jenks?" Stacey Enero asked. To Naomi's eyes the administrator hardly looked any better than Melanie. Her face was taut and her color poor.

"Yes."

"This is her third shift in a row, isn't it?"

Miserably, Naomi nodded her head. She hated to turn

Melanie in, but she couldn't lie, and in this state Melanie could easily be a danger to the patients no matter how much she needed the money.

"We can't allow that," Miss Enero said firmly.

"I tried to tell her. She said she would, but – "

"She has no say in the matter – she has to go home and get some rest. Tell her… no. I'll tell her." With a brisk step she started down the hall after Melanie.

That, Naomi thought, *is a scene I sure don't want to see!*

* * * * *

"Come in."

Flora stepped into Dewayne's room, her nose aquiver. A barely touched lunch tray sat on the bed. It did not, she noticed, contain any of the offerings made in the dining hall. A nicely grilled ground meat patty nestled next to a lump of mashed potatoes that actually looked like real mashed potatoes instead of wallpaper paste. Beside them was a healthy serving of bean salad and a partially-nibbled cloverleaf roll. There was an only slightly glutinous slice of apple pie and the scent of real coffee. Flora could feel her mouth salivating.

"You haven't eaten your lunch."

Chuckling, Dewayne glanced up from the computer monitor. "You the food police now?"

"No, but I would be if it got us meals like this. You order out?" Without waiting to be asked she slid into the carnivorous-looking chair and determinedly looked away from the tray. After all, hunger was just an automatic bodily function that a strong will could conquer.

"Nah – Melanie sometimes brings me a tray from the employees' lunch."

"And you tip her generously, no doubt."

He shrugged, and Flora tried to ignore just how grotesque a gesture it was.

"Of course. She's in a hard place – her soon-to-be ex is trying to take her kid."

Some ill-disguised subtle pain in his voice made Flora look at him again. "How terrible. How much money are you giving her?"

"Not much…" He swung around to look directly at her. "How'd you know that?"

Flora smiled. She knew she had a way with people. "Just a guess. You know what it's like to lose a child, don't you?"

Dewayne's normally friendly expression hardened. "I don't talk about that. Ever. To anyone. Now do you want to know what I found or not?"

Her curiosity aquiver, Flora leaned back casually in the seat. Her comment had been just a shot in the dark, but it had certainly hit a tender spot. She backed off; time to find out about that later. "Of course."

"Well, there was nothing on the security tapes in the time frame around the murder, so I expanded the search." His good demeanor almost restored, he grinned. "And guess what I found?"

"Aliens? Drug lords? Political assassins? Those are the most popular theories, according to what I hear in the dining room."

Dewayne chuckled again. "Nothing so exotic, I'm afraid. Two of the aides sneak food out when they leave, but that's not unusual."

"I'm amazed they'd want it," Flora said with some asperity, trying to ignore the tantalizing smell of real meat. "What else?"

"Oh, the usual… people coming and going. The late shift coming in late. Some of the day shift sneaking out early." He smiled, drawing it out.

"None of that can account for the Cheshire Cat look on your face, Dewayne Harbaugh. What have you found?"

"I just find it interesting that our illustrious administrator neither left nor returned from around two o'clock yesterday until now."

Flora gasped. "Not at all? That means she was here last night. Why did she act like she'd been called and came in early?"

"That is the question. She was called true enough, but her main number is her cell."

"So she was here – in the building."

"And Mrs. General Brian Cattermole was murdered in her office."

* * * * *

If she hadn't been so exhausted Melanie Jenks would have been angry at the way that snooty Miss Enero had ordered her to go home then walked her to the door and made sure she left. What did she know? That damned greaser never had to worry or watch as her world was torn apart. Still, Melanie knew that the woman had been right. If anything happened to the patients because she was so exhausted Melanie knew she'd never get over it. She had barely made it home and into her bed. Her mother had made sure that Davy had breakfast and gotten off to school on time. Melanie was glad she could go straight to bed, but was also sad that she didn't get to see him. He was growing so fast, changing almost day to day, and it seemed she never got enough time with him.

It didn't help that from the moment she walked in the front door until she slammed the door to her bedroom her mother was ragging on her, telling her all the problems were her fault, that a man didn't stray unless the wife gave him a reason, that it was a wife's duty to forgive and accept. If Melanie had just been a sweet, gentle, good wife Harley would never have strayed, her mother kept saying. It was all Melanie's fault. She simply wasn't a good enough wife.

Melanie ignored her. They'd said all the words many times anyway. Her mother would never believe that Harley wasn't interested in a sweet and gentle wife, and he sure wasn't interested in good. The woman he had moved in with proved that; she was pure trash in spite of her fancy ways. There was no way Melanie would let that woman have her Davy, no matter what she had to do or endure. That sneaky bastard Harley was too much of a coward to follow through on the threats he had made against her, but they were still worrying.

Teetering on the edge of sleep, Melanie sighed. She was getting too old to work over two shifts straight. Damn Harley Jenks! This was all his fault. He claimed she wasn't a good mother, that she spent too much time away from their son, but he didn't give her enough money to cover the bills and the rent and the groceries so she had to work even more. Now he had that prissy bitch who thought she was so much better than anyone else because she sold real estate and wore pretty clothes, and who wanted not only her husband – whom Melanie would have given her without a thought – but her son Davy as well.

How could she live without her son? Family was everything. She worked like a dog for that boy, and she'd keep it up no matter what it took. Of course Davy was fascinated by that bitch – she took him places and bought him things that Melanie couldn't afford, but she could never love him like his mother could.

Her children deserved the best. She couldn't do anything for Tiffany; she was grown and had chosen her path. She'd chosen to move in with that low-life Earl even though Melanie had told her there was bad blood in his family – a fact proved by that pathetic baby.

Melanie yawned again. She really shouldn't have taken the second shift and certainly not tried for a third, but she needed the money too badly. Her children needed the money too badly. It wouldn't be too long before that loser Earl would dump Tiffany, and of course Melanie would stand by her. And there was Davy, whom she had to protect no matter what. Melanie knew what it was like for a child to be unprotected in a hostile grownup world, and she had vowed a long time ago none of her children would ever know such impotent fear.

* * * * *

Detective Camacho would have run if he could. After a day of hearing about the murder being done by criminals and drug pushers and every other TV crime show staple he was ready to pull out what was left of his thinning hair. *Like most of these poor sad ghosts would know a drug pusher if one stepped on their foot,* he thought in frustration. Yeah, there were some *compos mentis* ones in there, but they were the ones who finally admitted they didn't know anything… all they knew was just what others had said. The real crazies were the ones who were absolutely positive of whatever wild story they told.

How did the nurses here stand it? Seeing the wreckage that age and decay caused? Working with it? Like that pathetic little Mrs. Badham, crying and begging for his help because she knew they had to kill her because she knew too much. And that mad Mrs. Melkiot, announcing that she would help him solve the case like she had supposedly helped solve the one in Dallas. And the shrunken little Mr. Gresham, swearing Camacho to secrecy before finally whispering that he had been a CIA agent during the war, the big one, and knew all kinds of secrets about the government that made him a target.

Even Camacho knew that the CIA didn't exist during WWII.

What he did know was that he hadn't learned a single thing that would help with the case. No one was sad that Mrs. Cattermole was dead. No one had a real reason to make her dead. Very few of them had the physical strength to do half the damage that had been done to the Cattermole woman's head.

Camacho groaned and put his head in his hands. What

had he done to deserve this?

"Detective?"

Looking up, Camacho groaned again, but this time only on the inside. "Yes, Mrs. Badham?"

"I just wanted to ask if you've gotten another place for me to stay. I really can't stay here. They're going to kill me, you know. I know too much."

Camacho had heard what she knew – what she thought she knew, and at length. If she weren't a sweet old white haired lady living in a controlled environment, he would not have been surprised to find out she was high on something. Who knew? In this nuthouse she might actually be.

"No, Mrs. Badham, I haven't, but you can rest easy. I've put special guards around and they'll make sure you're safe."

She looked at him appraisingly. "I haven't seen anyone."

"They're in disguise. No one is supposed to see them. Now why don't you go back to your room."

God, he thought desperately, *I'm starting to sound as crazy as she is. I've got to solve this case quickly.*

Her lower lip trembling, Eula Badham turned around and trotted obediently away.

* * * * *

"I hope you're happy with yourself."

Stacey Enero stared. It looked like Dr. Bobby Jensen, but it surely didn't sound like him. She'd never heard him be so forceful.

"What are you talking about?"

"We're going to lose that military contract and it's your fault. Dammit, woman, we have allowed a general's widow to be murdered here."

"A vicious troublemaker who was a danger to our staff and our residents," she reminded him. "That's why I was sending her back. And what does that have to do with her being murdered?"

The doctor's color rose another notch. "I don't know, but it certainly doesn't look good for Cold Creek."

"Neither would having her injure someone."

"But the military hospital wouldn't have to know about that. We have the bottom line to think of here."

Stacey looked at him with a glare of pure dislike. How on earth had this man become a doctor? There was more to doctoring than just pills and prescriptions, just as there was more to running a nursing home than signing drug requisitions. Unfortunately, she knew there were no required classes in kindness or empathy.

"Our bottom line," she said, enunciating each word with great and poisonous care, "will not be helped by lawsuits, and if she had hurt anyone you can bet there would have been lawsuits. Lots of them."

"Just because you and your staff couldn't control her..."

"I tried to control her by taking her mobility away, and you didn't like that, did you?"

Stacey took a deep breath. In another minute they would be screaming at each other like first graders and however satisfying that might be, such behavior did not mesh with the professional image she was trying so hard to maintain.

"I am afraid we will have to agree to disagree about this, Dr. Jensen. What we need to do now is concentrate on keeping our residents as calm and as safe as possible. This murder has upset all of us."

"A murder," Bobby moaned. His fingers took on a life of their own, skittering up and down his thighs through a series of arpeggios with military precision. Since there was no piano beneath them, however, he looked almost as if he should be at the facility as an inmate in the permanently locked Corridor F. "How will we ever explain this? How can we tell people that their loved ones will be safe here? What is this going to do to our reputation?"

What will Daddy think? Will I be blamed? Stacey translated in her thoughts. She had long ago learned that Bobby Jensen cared more about himself and his father's opinion of him than anything else, including Cold Creek Health Care Facility and its patients.

"We have to do everything we can to help the police," she said sturdily.

"Unless we find something that damages the facility," Bobby said quickly. "We have to protect our image."

Stacey wanted to make a sound of disgust, but didn't. Idiot he might be, but Bobby Jensen could fire her in a heartbeat. "So what do you suggest we do?" she asked carefully.

"I don't know," the good doctor answered in what might be regarded in someone else as a wail. "I just don't know!"

Chapter Eleven

Patience had never been one of Flora's strong points, but she believed anyone could do anything they truly set their mind to do. She had set herself a task, and part of seeing that task successfully completed involved executing the perfect timing, so she had to be patient.

Setting herself in one of the optimum locations of the reception area, she ignored the chatter around her as well as the conversational overtures of the more unwise residents who tried to engage her. She held one of her paperbacks open in her lap, but only made the pretense of reading. She had to stay alert. Besides, the book was boring and nowhere as interesting as the blurbs had led her to believe.

For the longest time there was no opportunity she felt was right and Flora, still tired from the previous night's alarums, was tempted to doze. Keeping awake took an effort of will that, had she not been so sleepy, would have made her proud.

She wished she could have asked Dewayne to sit with her during this, but doubtless he would have put his own spin on things and ruined her plan. Plus, he was better off occupied researching the backgrounds of the suspect pool. As that list included almost everyone in the facility, he would be kept occupied for quite a while.

No, it was up to her, and she had to do it correctly.

It was almost dinnertime before her patience was rewarded. Stacey Enero, at last unaccompanied by staff or some clingy resident, strode through the lounge area. Her face was hard and her mind obviously far away, but that didn't deter Flora, who was suddenly re-energized.

"Miss Enero."

For a moment it looked like she wouldn't stop, but Stacey did, taking a step back to look at Flora. It was obvious that she was working at making her expression friendly.

"Yes, Mrs. Melkiot?"

"I need to have a word with you," Flora said, indicating the chair beside her. "Won't you sit down?"

"Can I talk to you later? I have so terribly much to do right now, and with the police here…"

Flora's smile froze. She was not accustomed to having her invitations rejected. "I think it might be advisable for you to talk to me, Miss Enero, or I shall have to talk to the police myself."

"Haven't you been interviewed yet?"

"Yes, but new evidence has come my way. I wanted to discuss it with you before taking it to Detective Camacho."

"What new evidence?" Stacey asked hesitantly.

"Sit down and we shall discuss it." Flora repeated her indication of the chair. Stacey Enero was not an overly tall woman, but she was standing and Flora hated it when people loomed over her.

It seemed they might just stay like that, two immovable objects in a stasis of conflict, but Stacey blinked first. Pasting an indulgently tolerant smile on her face, one such as she would use toward an obstinate child or mental defective, Flora thought sourly, the administrator sat down as indicated.

"And what is it you think you know?"

More than anything else Flora hated to be patronized, and this made her speak more sharply than she might have otherwise.

"You didn't go home last night," she said in bald truth. "Why?"

Flora had expected sputterings of innocence, accusations, perhaps even a dramatic fainting spell. She was only vaguely disappointed when Stacey Enero's face relaxed to a dull blandness.

"How do you know?" she asked with no more emotion than ordering a Coke.

"I have my sources."

"Probably Dewayne. He always knows everything that goes on around here." Stacey gave a little sigh. "Has he hacked into the video system again?"

"No reputable investigator ever gives up their sources," Flora replied with a haughty serenity.

"Have you told Detective Camacho yet?"

"Not yet, but there's more than just I who know, so getting rid of me won't gain you anything."

Stacey gave a soft little laugh, but it came from genuine amusement. "You have nothing to fear from me, Mrs. Melkiot. I didn't kill Mrs. Cattermole, and I have no intention of harming you. To answer your question, no, I have not told the detective that I was on the property last night, mainly because I didn't want to muddy the waters. As I said, I had nothing to do with Mrs. Cattermole's death."

"She was killed in your office."

"And a big amount of trouble that is going to cause me, but there's nothing I can do about it."

In spite of her natural suspicion, Flora was beginning to believe the administrator was telling the truth. Either that, or she was a most accomplished liar and therefore an incredibly dangerous person.

"Why did you stay here?" Flora asked.

Stacey gave a soft little laugh. "Pure exhaustion. I live about half an hour's drive away. I work hard here and sometimes I'm just too tired to drive home. If there's an empty room, I just crash in it overnight."

"Without anyone knowing?" Flora was skeptical. Even at night there was staff in the facility.

"If possible. I didn't want the night shift to think that I was checking up on them. It's hard to get good people to work the graveyard."

"You sound so sincere."

"Because it's the truth." Stacey looked the older woman straight in her skeptical eyes. "I am lucky to have this job. I am lucky to have any job, and no, I'm not going to tell you the reason why. It has nothing to do with anything that happened here with Mrs. Cattermole."

No one would ever think that Flora Melkiot was a credulous woman, least of all Flora herself, but even though she tended to believe the young woman, she would not let herself lose sight of the fact that proof was needed, and said so rather forcefully.

"It's none of your business, Mrs. Melkiot." Stacey stood gracelessly, almost as stiff as she had been an old, old woman.

"Are you going to explain to Detective Camacho?"

"Not unless I have to. Are you going to make me?"

Flora nodded. "If necessary."

Stacey was saved from the necessity of a reply by Adelita, who tugged at her sleeve and hurried her away to see to some crisis or another.

Flora was not happy. It was not often that someone simply refused to answer her questions. In her heart she felt Stacey didn't kill the Cattermole, but feeling wasn't proof. Besides, she was curious. Being denied was neither pleasant or customary, and she would not tolerate it.

"You look like you're about to do a murder," said Dewayne.

The fact he had been able to wheel right beside her without her noticing was distressing. His electric wheelchair was very quiet, but not totally silent and that she hadn't heard it made Flora furious. Really, this place was deteriorating every faculty she had. She had to get out of here.

"Or is that a bad thing to say?" Dewayne asked, a

pixie-ish grin on the undamaged side of his face.

"Do you have a telephone? Your own line?"

He blinked. "Yes."

Flora stood up abruptly. "Then let's go. There's a call I need to make and I don't want it going through the switchboard."

* * * * *

"Flora?" Rebecca Cloudwebb's voice sounded wary. "I thought you were still in rehab."

"I am," Flora replied crisply, "and I want out of here." With only a little embellishment she recounted all of what had happened, about Clarissa's bossiness and Judge Rubio's treachery and the Cattermole's murder, stopping only when Rebecca gave a snort that sounded very much like a frustrated laugh. "It's all true," she said indignantly. "A woman was brutally murdered and my own daughter has locked me in here."

"I'm sure it's for your own good," Rebecca said, not knowing how far she had plummeted in the older woman's estimation. When they had worked together to solve Laura Tyler's murder several months before Flora had been suitably impressed with the former police detective now turned antique dealer.

Obviously she had been mistaken.

"I'm surprised," Rebecca was saying, "you want to leave instead of solving the murder."

Testy little creature, Flora thought, conveniently forgetting that she definitely intended to do both. *Just because I had to persuade her into helping me solve that Tyler woman's murder she thinks she can smartmouth me.*

"Actually, my safety is more important to me than the rather pedestrian solving of the murder of someone I didn't even like. I need a lawyer."

Even across the miles Rebecca's voice changed, losing its teasing tone and becoming much more serious.

"A lawyer? Surely they don't think you did it, do they?"

For a moment Flora considered the lie, then backed away. Rebecca was a nice woman, but so terribly conventional that she would probably feel obligated to contact Clarissa, and then everything would truly hit the fan.

"No, though I have been questioned, as has every other resident here, since it appears we are all to be considered suspects. No, I need a good attorney to break that accursed guardianship Clarissa has hogtied me with. You know I don't need a guardian."

Across the room Dewayne chuckled. "A keeper, maybe." He had been sniggering behind his hand since the conversation had begun.

"Who's that?"

Flora shot him a sour look. "One of the residents. He has a private telephone which he has been kind enough to let me borrow. Now do you know a good lawyer or must I resort to the Yellow Pages?"

"Obviously he knows you well. Does your daughter know that you're thinking about this?"

"Of course not," Flora temporized and it was the truth. She'd only mentioned that she might get an attorney… hadn't she? Well, it didn't make any difference. Flora was convinced that Justice was on her side, and had to be helped at all costs. "She'd try to stop me. Are you going to give me a name or are you going drive me to imprudent action by tattling to Clarissa?"

"Good Lord, woman, I don't want to run afoul of you. Not again." Rebecca laughed, making the mistake of thinking that the older woman was joking. "If you want a real shark, try A. R. Monroe of Corgill, Watson and Monroe. She's a good lawyer and tenacious as a bulldog."

Having had the foresight to request pen and paper from Dewayne before calling, Flora painfully and, as she was right-handed and hampered by her cast, quite illegibly wrote down the names. She was, however, surprised that

Rebecca would recommend a female attorney. Of course Flora believed that women could be just as effective lawyers as men, but even so she always felt safer dealing with a man.

"Flora – be careful, will you? Murderers don't play around."

"My dear Rebecca, I am always careful," Flora said, then after a few conventional pleasantries hung up.

Dewayne was watching her, imps of amusement dancing in his remaining eye. "That must have been Rebecca Cloudwebb. Your partner in crime."

"Anti-crime would be a more accurate description. I'm sorry the call was so long – I shall of course reimburse you." Flora carefully folded the piece of paper and tucked it into her pocket.

He waved the idea away. "Forget it. My phone plan includes long distance. I enjoyed listening in."

"Didn't your mother ever tell you eavesdropping is a sin?"

"Most fun things are." Dewayne was unrepentant, but his tone was serious. "Did you get a name?"

"I did, but I think it is best I call her from my room."

"Even if it goes through the switchboard?"

"I don't care if that call goes through the switchboard. Clarissa will hear about it soon enough."

He chuckled again. "So you weren't sure if your Rebecca would give you a name, and you didn't want to stir your daughter up for no reason. Very smart, lady, very smart."

"I usually am," Flora said with serene assurance and left.

* * * * *

Rebecca Cloudwebb hung up the phone slowly. How in the world had Flora Melkiot gotten herself involved in another murder? The woman really was a menace, a danger to herself and to others.

When the older woman had frankly blackmailed her into helping solve Laura Tyler's murder at the Olympus House Rebecca had decided she pretty much hated her. Time and circumstance had softened her attitude, though; Flora had not only been instrumental in solving the case, she had shattered the shell of fear and self-pity Rebecca had caged around herself. Yes, her dirty cop ex-lover had killed her partner and tried his best to kill her; yes, her leg was permanently damaged and she would never walk normally again. Those were facts not even Flora Melkiot could change, but without really meaning to Flora had brought her back into the world of the living, and for that Rebecca appreciated her.

Besides that, she was a good customer. She not only patronized C & L Antiques, she promoted it among her friends, with a nice little uptick in business as a result.

And, Rebecca made herself acknowledge, she had come to like the strong-willed old woman – most of the time, at least. Why on earth had her daughter whisked her away almost three hundred miles away to a rehab center in a town where she knew very few people? To a place where there had been another murder? Unfortunately, she had a pretty good guess as to the reason. Clarissa had wanted to take control of her mother – and her mother's money – for a long time.

Rebecca had never really liked Clarissa.

Making her decision, Rebecca reached for the telephone again.

"May I speak to Detective John Ashdown, please?"

* * * * *

Once Flora committed her mind to a course of action, she was ready to do it immediately; any delay was unacceptable. Frustrated and unhappy, she stood at the end of the hallway, looking out at the pathetic clump of rocks and cacti that passed for a garden at Cold Creek.

Normally her roommate was nothing more than a snuffling, wheezing insensate lump that was easy to ignore. Flora had returned to her room fired with the determination to contact this A. R. Monroe woman immediately. She had had no qualms about speaking in front of Mrs. Gutierriez as the woman was incapable of both speech and rational thought; she had not wanted to conduct her intimate personal business in front of Dewayne Harbaugh, who though amusing was distressingly sharp.

That plan, however, was shattered as soon as she stepped into her room. The skimpy curtain that was supposed to make the one room into two was closed, and both the smell and the equally disgusting squishy sounds of bathing indicated that the old woman had had an accident. Again.

Another strike against Clarissa, Flora decided, and retreated to the window to wait, but not patiently. If they didn't hurry up in there business hours would be over and she would have to wait until tomorrow to talk to A. R. Monroe. Flora never waited well.

Looking at the sad little xeriscape Flora thought it was strange that here in San Antonio, where the lush growth seemed almost tropical, they should inflict the grimness of dull brown and grey landscaping on the residents. Of course, this kind of non-garden was easy and cheap to maintain, and it was all for show. Residents were never allowed to go outside to appreciate the Glories of Nature. Flora was a great proponent of nature and paid the Olympus House gardener to keep the potted plants on her condo balcony lush and perfect. Worse of all, there was not even a way to get out there from here in spite of Eula Badham's insistence that there was a hidden door.

Which made it all the more strange that the sandy floor of the 'garden' was scuffed and tracked with footprints. Who could have been out there? Not maintenance – a heavy spraying with weedkiller every month or so would suffice to keep the barrenness pristine – and certainly not anyone trying to get into the facility. Even if the residents were allowed to step outside the building at all only a lunatic would go out there to appreciate the beauty of the place, because there was none.

Flora looked more closely. It seemed that there was more than one set of footprints, meaning that two people had come to right by this window, or one person had done it more than once.

But why? The windows were hermetically sealed and would not open. When Flora had complained about the lack of fresh air, Clarissa had explained that it was for the safety of the residents. Flora had responded that safety was hardly the word, as it was barely four feet from the window ledge to the ground, and far too short a distance to make a serious suicide leap.

Experimentally Flora gave the window a shove upward with her good hand and almost jumped out of her skin when it slid up effortlessly, so easily that if she hadn't grabbed quickly it would have slammed against the top with a crash. Immediately she pulled it down closed again, glancing guiltily around to see if anyone had seen, but apparently no one had. No alarms had gone off, either. Flora smiled in satisfaction. At least now she had a way out of here if became necessary. The memory of being hauled back to her room and Clarissa called when she had tried to leave by more conventional means still rankled.

But why was it here? If some inmate had escaped this way, wouldn't they have found out about it and sealed it? Surely no one who got free of this place would want to break in! Were the residents younger, she might have suspected a Romeo-and-Juliet type meeting place, but try as she would she couldn't picture these senile, superannuated geriatrics indulging in such romantic gestures. Anyway, according to gossip there was enough bed-hopping inside the facility to keep any who wanted such diversions happy.

According to Eula Badham, this window was a door through which she had seen someone entering and exiting.

Flora blinked. Maybe the old lady wasn't as crazy as she had thought. She would have to talk to her and see if she could sift any real information from her clouds of fantasy.

"Well, that's it… you can go back in now," said a bright young nurse who looked as if she should still be in high school instead of holding people's lives in her hands.

At the moment she was holding something else; her hands were full of a tray piled with stained and reeking cloth. Flora admired her courage even as she wished she would get it out of smelling distance.

The smell of aerosol deodorizer was never one of Flora's favorite aromas, even if it weren't a sickly floral scent, but it was much preferable to that which it tried to mask. Keeping her breathing shallow, Flora grabbed for the phone and, after clearing it with the facility operator and being given an outside line, dialed the number Rebecca had given her.

"Corgill, Watson and Monroe," said a chirrupy sounding voice.

"This is Flora Melkiot and I am calling from the Cold Creek Health Care Facility in San Antonio. Rebecca Cloudwebb gave me Miss Monroe's name. I would like to speak with her, please."

"I'm sorry." The voice remained just as professionally cheery. "Miss Monroe is unable to take your call at the moment. May I inquire as to the nature of your problem?"

Honestly, there were times it was just too frustrating to get through to people. Was it all some sort of power game, where whoever finally spoke to the other first lost? Flora's jaw tightened.

"No, you may not. I wish to speak to Miss Monroe, and you may not ask her to call me back as I have great difficulty in getting to use the telephone and have no reason to believe they will give me her call. I am being held against my will and there has already been one murder. I do not wish to become a second victim."

"Please hold just a moment," the voice – not so chirrupy now – said, and some canned and rather unremarkable jazz instrumental flooded through the phone.

"It's time for dinner, Mrs. Melkiot." The gooey-named nurse (Candy? Cookie?) stepped halfway into the room. "Do you need assistance?"

"No, I do not need assistance. I am on the telephone. I will come to the dining hall when I am finished, even though probably there will be nothing worth eating."

"Now, Mrs. Melkiot, you know the rules say that everyone must come to the dining hall at the same time. We can't have you straggling in whenever you feel like it." The woman spoke softly, but there was steel under her tone.

"Mrs. Melkiot, this is A. R. Monroe." Her voice was soft and almost girlish, but there was no mistaking the steel in it.

"Thank Heavens! I need to talk to you."

"Are you in danger?"

"Yes," Flora said remorselessly, if softly. It wasn't a complete untruth; she was in danger of being cut off, for the gooey-named nurse was advancing purposefully on her. "Rebecca Cloudwebb said you were the best, and I need help. I am being held against my will and there has already been one murder – " Her voice dropped almost to a whisper.

"Say goodbye and put down the telephone, Mrs. Melkiot. We're waiting for you." Her name might be gooey, but her fingers were strong as iron as she tried to wrest the receiver away. "You know that telephone calls are not allowed now."

Flora realized she was outmatched; even if she weren't weighed down with several pounds of plaster there was no way she could keep the nurse from taking the phone. Seemingly meekly she released her hold, but as the nurse went to hang up the receiver Flora gave a small scream and cried in a piteous tone, "Don't hurt me!"

"Now, who here would ever hurt you, Mrs. Melkiot?" the nurse asked gently, even as a flicker in the back of her eyes hinted that she might enjoy doing so thoroughly. "It's not nice when you make trouble and worry your friends. Now, let's get you down to dinner."

With practiced efficiency she whipped a security belt from her pocket and put it around Flora's waist, then walked with her to the dining hall, holding as tightly to the belt as she would the leash of an unpredictable dog.

Chapter Twelve

Dinner had been as unappetizing as Flora had expected, but she ate all of hers without hesitation, even going so far as to comment on how good the rice pudding was. Even if the glutinous mass hadn't been. Flora knew that her stunt on the telephone would be remarked upon among the nurses and it did not fit her plans to be carefully watched. Instead she made herself into the model resident, not realizing that such behavior would draw their attention more.

Tonight she was unlucky enough to be seated at one of the large tables, but fortunately her dining companions were fairly congenial. Ora Carroll was on one side, Hortensia Bernal on the other. She recognized Sophia O'Connor, Agnes Rausch, Fred Moretti and Mr. Granowski, but the others were strangers, seen but never spoken to.

When she wished Flora could be both charming and urbane; it was a talent that had propelled her to the heights of Dallas society. When Morris had been alive and they had entertained invitations to any of their parties had been highly prized. During his lingering illness, of course, they had not thrown any parties and after Morris had died Flora found she didn't have the heart for it. She still did her duty with volunteer work and went to other people's parties, of course, but deciding that being a guest was so much easier than being a hostess she had no desire to entertain at home. That didn't mean she had lost her skill.

Before long she knew that Mr. Carrington had been

an accountant and Mrs. Hoffmann ("Just call me Honey.") had been a store clerk before marrying the late Mr. Hoffmann, who had managed a flying school. Flora thought it amusing when the woman admitted she was afraid of flying, but didn't say a word.

Flora had been hoping that Eula Badham or Dewayne might be at her table, but she was seated in a far corner of the room and neither were anywhere close. Well, Flora thought somewhat huffily, she would just have to work with what she had.

Fred Moretti, thankfully seated across the table from Flora, gave her a practiced charming smile, marred only a little by the fact that his large white teeth were most definitely false. "I've seen precious little of you, Flora babe. When are we going to get together and get really acquainted?"

"As we are seated at the same table it is obvious we are already acquainted, and I do so dislike duplicating effort," Flora said in only slightly barbed tones. Honestly, did the man truly think he was a Lothario? Turning to Hortensia Bernal, she smiled. "What new plot has Mrs. Badham discovered?"

So short and round that she resembled a gingerbread cookie, Mrs. Bernal shook her head. "*Pobrecita*! She is still quite sure that drug smugglers are using the home as a headquarters."

"Drug smugglers?" Honey Hoffmann looked up in alarm. "Here?"

"It's so tragic how drugs are ruining our country," Ora Carroll said moistly. Tears were already gathering in the corners of her eyes. Usually it took at least until dessert before she began to weep.

"Mrs. Badham has a very vivid imagination," Flora said with gracious assurance, but she really wasn't so sure. Probably nothing as dramatic as drugs, but there had to be a reason why there were footprints under a window that wasn't supposed to open but did.

"She is always convinced that someone is trying to kill her," Hortensia said, then shook her head. "Poor thing. It must be dreadful to live in such fear, especially when there is nothing to be afraid of."

"Someone killed Mrs. Cattermole." Sophia O'Connor gave a little shudder and looked over her shoulder.

"And who will be next?" a faded looking woman named Arlene Skaggs added in delicious terror. Being in the same building as a murder was probably the most exciting thing that had ever happened to her. "I swear, I've never heard of such a thing."

"I wish someone would carry me home to Devine." Agnes Rausch repeated her dreary litany. "I need to get home. Gotta get my garden planted."

"Is there any more information?" Mr. Granowski asked.

No one said anything until Flora at last spoke. "The police are notorious for not saying a word about an ongoing investigation."

The old man looked sharply at her. "You say that like you have some experience."

Flora preened modestly. "Well, I did help solve a murder in Dallas a few months ago."

The bald announcement had the effect Flora wished. Every face at the table turned to her.

"You never!" cried Honey in awed tones. "You must be awful brave."

"How did you manage that?" Sophia asked, her eyes wide.

"I don't want to talk about murder." Tears were now streaming down Ora Carroll's seamed cheeks. "It's just too horrible."

"If I don't plant my garden soon I won't have any tomatoes," said Agnes Rausch. "Can you carry me home to Devine?"

"A murder? Go on," Mr. Granowski scoffed. "I don't believe it."

The others at the table merely goggled, so in self-defense Flora felt obligated to tell the story of Laura Tyler's murder and her own part – only slightly exaggerated – in bringing the criminal to justice.

"Who'da thunk it?" said Fred Moretti, his eyes glowing with a dangerous admiration. "A real life heroine in our midst."

"Well, you're just like a celebrity!" Honey cooed, her faded, crumpled face alight with unholy delight. "You'll have to help the police solve Mrs. Cattermole's murder."

Even though she intended to do just that, Flora modestly made noises of denial and deliberately changed the subject. Now that this bunch knew of her detective abilities she knew the word would spread, and she would bet that she could count on the residents to give her any information she wanted – and cover if she needed it.

Satisfied to bide her time, Flora set herself out to be charming, even to the extent of agreeing to join a bridge game after dinner, only after swearing the table to a hopefully futile silence about her detecting abilities. Normally Flora loathed bridge, as she did all card games, but she had made herself master it, as every skill was useful in the ever-shifting landscape of social prominence. Besides, playing here beat sitting in her room listening to the snorts and snuffles of her roommate.

She had hoped to get a few words with Dewayne after dinner, but he seemed distracted and was gone from the dining room before she could get over to him. Maybe that meant he was working on a lead? Well, they could talk tomorrow; Flora had plans for tonight.

The bridge game was even more ghastly than she had anticipated, as at first all anyone wanted to talk about was Flora's prowess as a detective, which soon grew to television-superhero-like proportions. Only after Flora insisted prettily that they spare her blushes and change the subject did the conversation grow more general. And, as far as Flora was concerned, more boring. At least Agnes

Rausch had moved on, still tirelessly seeking someone to take her home to Devine and Sophia, pleading fatigue, had gone early to bed. Flora had no idea where the rest went.

Ora Carroll took forever to make a play, more often than once making a mistake that forfeited the hand. Although he was in his 90s, Mr. Granowski was a shrewd and merciless player, the only one there who was close to Flora's skill level. After one hand they tacitly agreed to play against each other, both for the pleasurable challenge of it and because they knew that by partnering they would annihilate the others.

The time passed, in Flora's opinion, simply because it had to eventually, and some of the crowd in the reception lounge began to drift toward bed. Yawning prodigiously, Flora claimed that she was exhausted and made her way towards her room, hoping that such a radical deviation from her normal night-owl attitude would not be remarked upon.

She didn't want to stand out, at least not now. There was much to be done tonight and she didn't need scrutiny when she did it. With agonizing slowness the day wound down; at last the air was full of the sound of water – faces being washed, toilets flushed, medicines swallowed. Some residents were already in bed, snoring or making half-awake cries as they fought sleep. The staff was in full herding mode, rounding up the night owls and escorting them to bed.

Finally the shift changed, always marked with the bed check ritual. It was never completely dark in the Cold Creek building, so all the duty nurse had to do on her corridor was peek in with what she thought was great stealth to see that both occupants of the room were tucked in their beds. Bundled up to her neck with covers that hid her day clothes, Flora made herself lie still with her eyes closed. She would, she decided, lie as if asleep until at least half an hour after she heard the small squeak of the nurse's shoes going back to the central station. By then the skeleton night shift staff would have decided that everyone was settled and congregate in the dining hall as they always did, hopefully leaving the hallways momentarily unguarded.

Flora did not expect to fall asleep.

It was a quarter to four when she woke, startled and angry at her weakness. She had slept right through her best chance of seeing the administrator's office. Flora was by temperament a mild-spoken woman who regarded profanity as a defect of character, but at the moment the words in her mind would have turned the air a brilliant blue.

Of course, she could wait until night, but that would mean another day lost in the investigation, and Flora did not believe in waiting. The day shift wouldn't arrive for at least another hour and it shouldn't take long to look at the small office… Her decision made, Flora slipped from bed and down the hallway, all senses alert. The hallway was dim, the lights down to nighttime level. It was bright enough to see, but not much more, especially considering how garishly it was lit during the day. To her relief there was not a sight of anyone on staff.

Flora clung to the wall, being especially careful of her balance as well as assiduously avoiding anything that might make a noise. It was surprising how much stuff littered the hallway – a walker here, a wheelchair there, a tray table, several pieces of medical equipment she couldn't begin to identify.

Remembering the camera trained on the drug cabinet Flora clung to the opposite wall. From here she could see the windowed doors of the dining room, but at oblique angle. She couldn't see more than a sliver of the interior and unless someone was standing right at the window it was doubtful they could see her. Judging from the laughter coming from inside, it was doubtful anyone on the night shift would even look.

To Flora's disappointment the enormous X of yellow

plastic police tape was still across the door of Miss Enero's office. How long did they intend to keep it up? They had to have finished processing the scene by now. Probably it was there to keep out the morbidly curious – but, she reasoned, such a bar shouldn't apply to an experienced investigator who was just trying to help them.

She grabbed the knob and twisted, disgusted to find it locked. Obviously the police didn't trust anyone. In frustration she gave the door a shake and her heart sang as it popped open. If there were ever any proof needed that she should be working on the case, here it was. Stooping ungracefully, Flora slithered under the fragile plastic tape and, once inside, closed the door behind her.

The lights in the office were out and Flora didn't dare turn any on in case one of the staff should come out unexpectedly, but even though the hall lights were on nighttime dim, there was almost enough light to see. Stacey Enero's office was bounded on three sides by a short wainscoting of sheetrock about three feet tall, but from the top of that to the ceiling was glass. In spite of the glass being lightly frosted a fair amount of light seeped through, and Flora's eyes were becoming adjusted to the dimness. She had always prided herself on her excellent night vision.

The body was gone, of course, but the desk had not been cleaned. A thick darkness that could only be blood spread over the desk top and the enclosed air was thick with the nauseatingly coppery smell. Since it was wood, the desk would probably have to be replaced; Flora didn't see how such a mess could be really cleaned up or the stain removed. There was a fine layer of thin grey fingerprint powder over everything as well; she'd have to be very careful not to touch anything – not that she would ever compromise a crime scene.

A quick look around the small office told her there was no wheelchair or walker, though had there been one the police might have already removed it.

There was the desk, but no desk chair. If that was where the Cattermole had been sitting when she was killed the police had probably taken it. On the other side of the desk was a utilitarian wooden chair without any softening cover or pads. In one of the corners was an ornate iron stand with a somewhat sad looking fern on top of it. The solid wall and two of the wainscot-walls were lined with bookshelves of varying height.

Flora wished she could read the titles; one could always tell so much about a person from the books they read. In this half-light though, the most she could tell was that most of them were thick hardbacks, probably related to the business.

Miss Enero wasn't very neat. The bookshelves were only about half books; the rest were filled with great untidy stacks of paper or, in a very few places, an object. A picture in a carved wood frame of a very handsome young man with a pale silk rose – Flora couldn't tell what color – lying in front of it. Another picture, in a metal frame, of a smiling group of people, from the resemblances presumably a family. Stacey's family? Perhaps. A small vase with an artfully arranged posy of silk flowers.

And one glaringly empty spot.

Flora crept forward to look. The empty space was about eight inches across. The facility was kept much too clean for there to have been a dust outline, but even though she had no idea of what the object which had sat there had been, Flora would have bet it was the murder weapon. The shelf was standard – about ten inches tall and ten inches deep, so the murder weapon – Flora was now convinced that whatever had been there was the murder weapon – had to be smaller than that.

Unfortunately the one time she had been in this office she had been furious and concentrating more on her unjust incarceration here than in taking in the décor, so she had no idea what had sat there, but she should be able to find out somehow. And that idiot Camacho had thought he'd keep her quiet by refusing to share what killed the Cattermole. Flora snorted, as much from disgust as the lingering, unpleasant scents of blood and fingerprint powder.

Creeping carefully to avoid stepping in any of the blood that was still puddled on the floor, Flora moved around to the back of the desk. The bottom drawer, a large one meant for holding file folders, was open, but most of the files were gone. Flora wished for a tiny flashlight so she could inspect what was left, but feared that the police had taken all the interesting papers.

Gently, using a tissue from her pocket, she slid the lap drawer open. Nothing but pens and pencils, a couple of pads of sticky notes, paperclips… just the stuff you'd expect to find in any desk drawer in the country. Neither did the drawer to the side yield anything – a packet of cookies (chocolate chip) and a couple of rolls of LifeSavers (Wintergreen and Butterscotch), an open box of tissues and some loose change. The drawer beneath that had some paper and a couple of cartridges for the printer that was on the bookcase behind. The desk was an old one, with a well and a lift mechanism for a typewriter behind an enormous door to the left, but it was empty. It didn't take a gargantuan leap of logic, Flora decided, to realize that Miss Enero had probably kept a computer in there. A computer which, of course, the police had taken with them.

Disgusted, Flora snorted. How did they expect her to help if they took all the interesting evidence away?

* * * * *

Armando Camacho was at heart a family man. Although he appreciated looking at other women, he loved his plump little wife and enjoyed having his varied offspring around him. He did not enjoy bringing his work home with him. It was department policy that he keep his police telephone near and on at all times, but he preferred to pretend it wasn't there whenever possible.

When it rang showing the 214 Dallas area code he almost ignored it, but he was too good a cop, even though he sat at the dinner table with all his family enjoying one of his Rosalia's incomparable pot roasts.

"Camacho."

"Detective Camacho, this is Detective John Ashdown from the Dallas Police Department."

"Yes. How can I help you?" Camacho asked slowly. Somewhere the name Ashdown rang a faint bell in his memory and he wasn't sure it was in a pleasant association.

"I hear you have a murder in a rehab facility, and that one of your suspects is a Mrs. Flora Melkiot. Is that true?"

Camacho's stomach tightened. Of course. The old buzzard had been the one to mention Ashdown's name. It would be too much to expect that the Melkiot woman would be a felon wanted by the DPD. "Yes."

Ashdown erupted into laughter. "You poor son of a bitch!"

"You know Mrs. Melkiot?"

"Armando, is everything all right?" Rosalia asked, alarmed at her husband's sudden rush of color.

"And how," said Ashdown through his laughter. "I feel so sorry for you."

By now Camacho's stomach was nothing but a tight hard knot. "She said she had helped you solve a murder."

That set off a fresh spate of laughter. When he could speak again, Ashdown said, "She was there when the murder was committed, right enough, and she tried to stay in between me and the case every step of the way. She took down evidence tape, questioned witnesses and suspects alike, poked into everything. Like a damned bloodhound. Or maybe the dark side of Miss Marple."

"And you didn't arrest her for interference?"

Ashdown's shrug was almost audible. "Wouldn't have worked. She knew everyone involved and – " here his tone turned almost apologetic " – she did give us a lot of information about some of the suspects. Plus, her partner in crimesolving was an ex-detective whose brother happens to be a deputy chief."

"Sounds like a rock and a hard place," Camacho sympathized. He'd had to deal with departmental politics before. "Don't guess there's a warrant out for her or anything like that." His voice held a faint hope, but he knew he couldn't be that lucky.

"Nope. You're stuck with her, I'm afraid, unless you can arrest her for something. I'd be careful if I were you, though. She's got lots of money and lots of powerful friends."

Money? Camacho thought of the scrawny, crow-like woman in a cheap duster and a wrist cast, living in a middle-grade rehab/nursing home. "Then what's she doing in Cold Creek instead of some ritzy health farm?"

"From what I hear that's her daughter's doing. Wants her dear mother under her control. Whatever, I'm glad I'm not anywhere near it."

"Lucky stiff," Camacho said with unaccustomed bitterness. To Rosalia's dismay he was still scowling long after Ashdown hung up.

* * * * *

There was no way Flora could learn any more from Stacey Enero's office, at least not in the semi-dark. She'd just have to figure a way to get back in here when there was light… or convince Camacho that it was in his best interests to share information with her.

As if that would happen. What was it that made detectives – especially male ones – so resistant to accepting help?

Maybe if she called Rebecca and had her brother put

a little pressure on him…

No. Even if Rebecca would – and that was a big 'if' – there was no way her brother Deputy Chief Cloudwebb would break with the sacred police line of keeping all their information strictly to themselves.

Using her tissue, Flora slowly opened the door and peeked out. So far, so good. The halls were empty. She stooped under the crime scene tape and quietly pulled the door closed, careful to wipe the doorknob. She had barely touched it, but heaven only knew what they could do these days with just a bit of a fingerprint.

Squeak!

There was the unmistakable shriek of a rubber-soled shoe against the linoleum.

Flora froze. Right now she was in a shadowed area near the central nurse's station, but no matter from which direction they were coming from they would see her. Getting back into Stacey's office would take too long – and who could guarantee that the lock would pop open again? – but there was no way she could get back to her room. She was caught, Heaven only knew what they would do to her. Incarceration in the mental wing, perhaps? The very least they would do was call Clarissa, and right now Flora had too much to think about with the murder to deal with her hysterical daughter.

The chapel! Flora looked toward that sterile little room as if it were the gates to Heaven. It was right here. If she could get in and kneel down in the front pews they wouldn't be able to see her unless they turned on the lights and searched the room.

Holding her breath Flora slipped inside, wincing at how loud the protesting hinge sounded in the near total silence. As soon as she was through she held the door fast, silencing it. Maybe whoever it was would think it was nothing more than their shoes, or maybe an echo. She drew in a silent breath, then almost gagged at the strong smell of urine. Dear God, even here in the chapel?

The shoe squeak in the hall stopped suddenly, as if whoever it was were listening, then started again, this time coming toward the chapel.

Drat!

Inwardly Flora swore. If she was going to get out of this she would have to hide quickly and have a good deal of luck. She turned as fast as she dared in the near-total dark and extended her good hand feeling for the edge of a pew. Her fingers closed around the smooth, rounded wood and she stepped forward, only to fall noisily first against the pew itself and then on top of the large soft disgustingly damp thing that had tripped her. Even her much-vaunted self-control was not enough to keep her from crying out, both from surprise and pain. She had hit the floor with a painful jar.

Outside someone gave a soft shout and there was a thunder of footsteps, incredibly loud in the stillness. The doors of the chapel shrieked open and a blaze of electric light filled the room.

Flora was unaware of how many staff members filled the doorway. She barely heard the screams. Her entire attention was taken by the body over which she was sprawled. It almost seemed that the urine-soaked legs possessed an intelligence of their own and deliberately entangled with hers, while the arms lay across her good one as if in entreaty.

It was all fantasy, of course. Her candy-floss hair spread around her oddly bent head like an obscene halo, Eula Badham stared directly at Flora with sightless eyes. She was quite obviously very dead.

Chapter Thirteen

Detective Camacho looked both angry and disgusted. He disliked being waked before dawn. He disliked even more the number of times Flora Melkiot's name appeared in the dispatcher's narrative. He especially disliked having to run the gauntlet of rapacious reporters herding outside the front entrance. Didn't those nosy vultures ever sleep?

Most of all, though, he disliked the idea of another old lady being murdered.

Arms crossed, he stood belligerently in the home's clinic, looking darkly at Flora Melkiot. She never had looked good to him from the beginning, but now she looked positively pathetic. Even though the blood had been cleaned away, the left side of her face was bruised and swollen around the gash on her forehead from where she had crashed into the pew after tripping over Mrs. Badham's body, while the other side was deadly pale. Just as alarming, the fingers sticking out from her wrist cast were puffy and red; they looked painful, in spite of the doctor's assurance that no harm had been done. None of that, however, mitigated the paper-cut tightness of her mouth and the angry flash in her eyes.

"And?" Camacho repeated.

"And that is all."

"Please stay still, Mrs. Melkiot." Dr. Jensen fussed with needle and thread. "When you frown like that it pulls your skin. I want to stitch this so you won't have a scar. If you relax it shouldn't show, even though it is right on your hairline."

"According to the detective, a scar is the least of my problems." Flora's words were like individual drops of acid as she glared at the policeman.

""You were found with the body," Camacho repeated doggedly. "And you still haven't told me what you were doing in the chapel at that hour of the morning."

"Just because I happen to have some private business which is none of your business you think I am a murderer!"

"The first person to find the body is always suspect," Camacho said, "unless they can prove otherwise."

The door to the clinic slammed open, hitting the wall with a bang like a shot and almost as one everyone jumped.

"Mama!" Clarissa cried and launched herself at Flora. Dr. Jensen barely dodged away in time to avoid being caught in her bear hug.

"Who are you?" Camacho roared.

Flora squeaked in pain, both from the bruises Clarissa was squeezing and from the stab of the needle Dr. Jensen had wisely dropped as it dug into her shoulder.

"Oh, Mama, Mama, are you all right?"

With her good hand Flora managed to push her back a little. "I was until you attacked me. You're hurting me."

Clarissa immediately released her mother, still babbling, but this time apologetically. "Oh, I'm so sorry… Bill was up early – getting ready for a meeting with the silversmith, the one whose name I can never remember – and he heard on the radio about there being another murder here, then when I got here the reporters were just awful and I had to fight my way into the place and the officer in the lobby wouldn't tell me anything but one of the nurses said you were in the clinic…. Mama, what happened?"

"The officer on guard just let you come in?" Camacho asked, fastening on what he could out of her garbled recital.

"He did not!" Clarissa was indignant. "He tried to stop me! I had to kick him to make him let me go."

"And rightly so!" Flora said in smug triumph, her good left hand stroking her daughter's head. There might be hope for Clarissa yet. Just to look at her she could see how distressed her daughter was – instead of her usual polished perfection she wore a disreputable yoga suit and slip-on sneakers. Clarissa had never appeared so sloppy since she was six years old. "How dare you try to keep a daughter from her mother when she's scared to death for her safety?"

Camacho growled deep in his throat.

Free now of fear of attack, Bobby Jensen moved in and pulled the needle from the shoulder of Flora's duster. "I think this is enough," he said, knotting the thread and quickly moving away. "It will hold."

"That is an assault on a police officer," said Detective Camacho.

"My mother was hurt," Clarissa snapped back. "Was I supposed just to stay outside with all those awful media people shouting questions at me? That certainly wouldn't be good for our stores' image."

"May I remind you there has been a murder here? Another one?" Camacho said in deadly soft tones. "Now Mrs. Melkiot, I want you to tell me – "

The door slammed open again.

"Do not say a word, Mrs. Melkiot."

Flora stared. This must be her attorney, as astonishing as it might seem. She was short, probably no more than five feet at the most, had a corona of curly red hair and couldn't be more than in her early thirties. Without effort Flora's mind drifted to the funny papers of her youth and images of Little Orphan Annie, and could be dragged back to the present only with difficulty. What had Rebecca meant, involving her with this… this child?

This child, she noticed on second glance, was wearing a $1,500 dollar suit and some very good jewelry definitely worth a great deal more.

Neither was she alone. Behind her came an older man who, to Flora's mind, looked much more like an attorney should – fiftyish, well preserved and greying at the temples.

"Who are you? What are you doing in here?" Camacho asked, but his stomach was starting to knot again. He didn't know who the bossy redhead was, but he did know the man with her. Abe Rothstein was a crack attorney with a killer courtroom presence, and every law enforcement officer in a hundred mile radius went in well-deserved fear of coming under one of his cross-examinations.

"Detective, I am surprised that you would question someone you regard as a suspect without their attorney present. Mrs. Melkiot, I am A. R. Monroe of Corgill, Watson and Monroe. Your friend Miss Cloudwebb has retained me to be your attorney."

"An attorney? Mama!" cried Clarissa.

"My daughter Clarissa. Ignore her," Flora said dismissively.

"Do you accept me as your legal counsel?"

"Most gratefully," Flora said, extending her good left hand to shake Miss Monroe's rather clumsily.

"But Mama… why do you need an attorney?"

"That's what I want to know, Mrs. Melkiot," rumbled Camacho. "If you're innocent, why do you have an attorney here so early in the morning?"

Ignoring him, Flora turned to the short redhead, whom she noticed was not wearing a wedding ring. "I must admit, Miss Monroe, I did wonder how you got here so fast."

"It's *Ms* Monroe, please. After your telephone call – and a conversation with Miss Cloudwebb – I flew down late last night. Mr. Rothstein was kind enough to pick me up from the hotel this morning and bring me here. This is Mr. Abe Rothstein, our local counsel. We heard the news about the second murder on the car radio."

The older gentleman inclined his head in a courtly manner, but said nothing.

"Mama… what are you doing with her for an attorney? You know Blaisdell and Hamner always take care of our legal matters."

"Yours, and the company's, Clarissa," corrected Flora. "I feel I need my own attorney to see my rights are restored and that da – dratted! – temporary guardianship set aside."

Clarissa turned a most unhealthy color and started to gobble. "Mama! That was for your own good! While you were in surgery for your wrist after the accident…"

"Be quiet, Clarissa. You have had quite enough time to rescind it, and you haven't. You have insisted that I stay here when I most certainly don't want to – I want to go back to my own home in Dallas, and you won't hear of it, in fact you have been talking about selling my condo even though you have no right to do so, so I contacted an attorney."

"But Mama – "

"Which," Camacho all but shouted in a voice that nearly rattled the windows, "is all very interesting, but doesn't matter now because no one is going anywhere until these murders are solved."

"Which could happen much sooner if you'd let me help you…"

Camacho went in for the kill. "So what do you know that I don't?"

"Do not say a word, Mrs. Melkiot. We have to confer before you speak to anyone again." Ms. Monroe had stepped between Flora and the detective, facing him down with supreme confidence in the rule of law, even though it did rather resemble a terrier attempting to stop a train. "Doctor, is there any place I can have a private conversation with my client?"

Bobby Jensen had been edging toward the door,

hoping to be gone before something even more explosively unpleasant happened. He stopped and gulped, then nodded convulsively. "You can use my office… it's across the hall."

"Allow me to help you, Mrs. Melkiot." Mr. Rothstein spoke for the first time as he extended a stabilizing arm towards Flora.

"I'm going with you," Clarissa cried wildly. "I want to know what kind of garbage you're telling my mama…"

"No, Clarissa," Flora replied with admirable calm. She didn't need Mr. Rothstein's support, not really, but as it was so pleasant to have a gentleman offer her his arm she was taking full advantage of it. "You're the other side. What you can do is go home. And please tell that traitor Enrique Rubio I will not forget this." She gave a terrible smile.

While Camacho steamed Clarissa babbled in wordless fury as her mother and the two lawyers swept from the room.

* * * * *

Naomi put her purse into her locker and snapped the padlock shut. Somehow the nights were just too short. She had indulged the kids by taking them out for hamburgers for dinner. Eating out was a treat they seldom had since between school and their needs money was so short, but last night she felt they deserved a treat. Plus she didn't feel like cooking. After they had gone to bed she had stayed up late studying – she had a big test coming up on profit and loss statements, one that she had to pass.

"Mornin'." The single word dripped with sarcasm. Melanie slammed her locker shut and snapped the padlock.

Naomi looked up, startled at the other woman's appearance. If possible, Melanie looked more exhausted and haggard than ever. Her eyes were red-rimmed and her mouth as tight as a miser's purse.

"Good Lord, woman! Didn't you get any rest?"

Melanie yawned and stretched. "A couple of hours. Then Harley and that woman came over."

"You're kidding."

"Yep. Woke me up to talk to me. They tried to convince me that Davy would be better off with them. Again." She ground the words to ragged bits. "How they could afford to send him to a better school. How they could buy him nicer clothes and more toys, even start him a college fund…" She caught her breath with a ragged gasp. "Said that by keeping him I was being selfish and showing that I didn't care about him."

"That's just plain ridiculous," Naomi said. "You've done everything for that boy."

"They don't see it that way. Said that it wasn't good for him to be living in a pigsty."

"I thought your mother…"

"My mom doesn't do anything but sit around and watch her soaps and tell me what a bad wife I was," Melanie said, a profound bitterness in her face. "Keeps telling me she managed to get her husband back and hold onto him until he died." She all but spat the words, then her face changed, tears rising as her hard expression seemed to melt. "They said Davy deserved a better place. They said they'd gotten a lawyer, and he advised that CPS take a look."

"Child Protective Services?" Naomi was horrified. She had heard tales of the outrages this office had done. Harley Jenks was getting vicious.

"Yep. So I stayed up and scrubbed the house from one end to another. They aren't going to have any excuse to get Davy away from me. I won't let them!"

The lounge door opened and Cora Lane, an older nurse who had worked the night shift at Cold Creek for years, walked slowly in. She looked exhausted.

"Mornin', Cora," Naomi said. "Hard night?"

The older woman opened her locker and pulled out

her purse. "You might say that. Someone killed Eula Badham last night. Mrs. Melkiot found the body in the chapel. And I hear she's hired a hot-shot attorney to get her out of here, so her daughter forced her way in. The cop is here too; they're all in Dr. Jensen's office. And the front door is being attacked by the press."

Both Melanie and Naomi were incredulous. "I wondered why there were so many people in the front," Naomi said, realizing that the reporters hadn't yet found that there was a staff door - or they hadn't figured out a way to get past the parking lot fence. Melanie simply swore, muttering about how this might affect her case about Davy.

"Y'all have a nice day," Cora said with dull sarcasm before letting herself out.

* * * * *

Dr. Jensen's office was by far the most luxurious room in the entire facility. Wood paneling, fine furniture, exquisite upholstery and drapes…it was obvious that this room had been done by the hand of a very expensive decorator, it was just as obvious that all the work of the place was done in Stacey Enero's office. There were no glass half-walls here, just a commonplace window overlooking one of the dreary rock gardens; the place might as well have been hermetically sealed away from anything concerning the nursing home. Although Bobby Jensen had been head physician for Cold Creek Health Care Facility for over a decade everything in here looked brand new and practically untouched.

The conversation with Ms. Monroe and Mr. Rothstein proved to be pleasant, as well as productive. Once Flora had convinced them that her rather spectacular injuries had been the result of her falling – she did take full responsibility, as there was no one else to blame save poor Mrs. Badham – and been assured that a member of Mr.

Rothstein's staff was looking into the temporary guardianship she relaxed. She was no lawyer – though she knew she could have been an excellent one had she chosen – but considering that she was both healthy and *compos mentis* the entire guardianship was ridiculous. To her distinct pleasure neither attorney had any doubt that it could be overturned with ease.

"Do you wish to pursue possible charges against this Judge Rubio?" Ms. Monroe asked.

"He is very old to be sitting on the bench still," mused Mr. Rothstein. "Perhaps that could be a hook for us? Proof that it is time for him to retire, especially after making such an unfair ruling?"

Flora listened with some alarm. She had forgotten that one of the problems of swimming with sharks was not to be eaten by them. "Oh, no, that's not necessary. He was a college friend of my husband's. Clarissa just talked him into it."

"Which brings us to your daughter, Mrs. Melkiot." Ms. Monroe was making notes on a legal pad with abrupt little stabs of the pen. "What do you want to do about her?"

"Do about her? What do you mean?"

"Her conduct towards you has hardly been exemplary. Both you and she are quite wealthy, I believe, but she parks you in a middle-class place like this instead of the level of facility in which you might have been expected to be placed. It doesn't sound as if she has your best interests at heart."

"Clarissa has always been a bit of a pinchpenny," Flora admitted, "but she did apologize and said this was the only place she could find on such short notice. And apparently it is the one closest to her home."

The two attorneys looked quickly at each other, disbelief writ plainly on their faces.

"Well," Ms. Monroe said, her tone brisk, "that's as may be, but now we must decide what we are going to do about her. Do you want a permanent protective order sworn out against her?"

"A protective order?" Flora sat forward. "That's a little much, isn't it? She is my daughter."

"It's up to you, of course, but if she did this once, she can do it again."

"She wouldn't dare!"

Ms. Monroe regarded her steadily. "She did this time."

"I for one would like to know why," Mr. Rothstein said with a practiced smoothness. "You certainly seem to be in fine fettle – with the exception of your wrist, and the bump to your head, of course – both physically and mentally."

"And so I am."

"So why did she want to have you in San Antonio so badly that she went to such lengths?"

Flora sniffed. "Because I believe in having freedom to live my life the way I want to. Clarissa is lamentably conventional. She says I embarrass her. She wants me to be the kind of mother she wants me to be – get involved with church, let my hair go white, live with her and bake cookies for the grandchildren." The last thought, coupled with knowledge of Clarissa's robot-like teenagers, made her shudder. Stepford wives? Clarissa would settle for nothing less than a Stepford mother and Stepford children.

"And you want something different," Ms. Monroe said, respect rising in her eyes.

"I prefer to live my life as I see fit. I am well known in Dallas society. I see neither benefit nor enjoyment in ladling out soup to unfortunates or reading to hordes of disadvantaged children who want nothing more than to behave like savages. I would prefer to send rather large checks to deserving organizations and do what I wish with a free conscience."

"But your daughter would rather you did it personally."

"Of course. Then she could brag about what a wonderful mother she has. She finds my social activities rather frivolous and offensively expensive. Clarissa has always been just a little bit tight with money. Don't know where she got it – her father and I certainly weren't."

"Her father – your husband – he is dead?"

For a moment Flora's face softened. She had been truly fond of Morris. "Yes. Several years now. He was a wonderful man. It was cancer that took him. Horrible disease." Then, as if ashamed of showing such a tender, weakening emotion, Flora took a deep breath. "He would have been proud of me, but when I solved the Olympus House murder, I thought Clarissa was going to have a stroke. I have never seen her so embarrassed."

The two attorneys exchanged speaking glances.

"So she wants control over you and your money," Ms. Monroe said bluntly.

"I thought that was what I just said. She would also like to get her hands on my jewelry collection, though I haven't the foggiest notion why. She and Bill never go anywhere interesting. She has even made inquiries about selling my condo, but it's in my name alone, so she can't do anything about that. Can she?"

"Not with me on your side." Ms. Monroe made a slashing note on her pad, then turned to a fresh page. "Now – let's talk about this murder."

"Murders. Actually, there have been two. Which one do you mean?"

The gentleman lawyer's eyes widened. "Are you a suspect in both?"

"I hope not. I didn't do either of them, of course, but this thick-headed policeman seems to suspect me of the last one, at least. And after I offered to help him solve the first one."

For a moment Flora thought Ms. Monroe might be hiding a smile at her indignation, but dismissed the idea as unworthy. They were professionals, both of them. Women had to stick together, especially in the face of male stupidity.

"One of Mr. Rothstein's associates is gathering information on both killings," Ms. Monroe said, all hints of a smile now gone. "Why don't you tell us what you personally know."

Flora had a very organized and logical mind; she couldn't have held the positions of power she had with enormous events like ArtFest and the Crystal Charity Ball if she hadn't. With only a few digressions on points of doubtful interest she outlined all that she knew about the events at Cold Creek Health Care Facility, including Dewayne but omitting her fruitless foray into Miss Enero's office.

Ms. Monroe had been scribbling like mad, her expression one of intense concentration. She looked up as she stretched her fingers. To Flora she still looked like a high school girl wearing her mother's clothes for a play.

"Well, that seems straightforward. I hope you feel up to retelling it to that detective before he chews his way through the wall. Do you wish us to remain with you during his interrogation?"

"Most definitely." Flora knew she could handle the bombastic policeman by herself, but she was humble enough to realize that there were certain esoteric points of law about which she knew nothing and might need an attorney for backup.

Camacho almost looked as if he had been chewing on a wall – not that he had splinters in his lips or anything so dramatic, but they might have been an improvement. His expression was as dark as a thundercloud and his curmudgeonly earlier manner deteriorated to one thin notch above hostility. Accompanied by a weedy looking young man in a badly fitting suit, he stomped into the office and bristled as Ms. Monroe laid out the rules under which Flora would speak. Flora herself was glad to see that Clarissa was not present, presumably having actually obeyed and gone home.

While they talked, Flora divorced herself from the situation and allowed her eyes to roam over the office, deciding that it not only probably had been done by an expensive decorator, it had to have been. This room would have been right at home at any large bank or Fortune 500 corporate office. To Flora's appreciative eye only one thing was slightly jarring. One wall was almost solid with photographs, and dull things they were too, all featuring Dr. Bobby Jensen and all pertaining to Cold Creek Health Care Facility. Here he was doing a ceremonial groundbreaking – presumably for this building – with a gold-painted shovel. Here he had his arm around a matronly-looking woman with grey hair and squinty eyes – the former administrator? Here he was cutting some kind of gigantic ribbon, perhaps for the opening of the facility. Here he was cutting a large and gaudy cake. Here and there he was with powerful looking men, all with tense, humorless smiles that made each resemble a stuffed moose. Here he was shaking hands with a younger Stacey Enero. In every photo his face was wearing the same smug, slightly blank expression and plastic smile. Flora was surprised there were no pictures of him drawing the building plans or connecting the plumbing, since it appeared almost as if he had done everything else himself.

It was too much. Flora had to look away; she could only take so much self-aggrandizement.

"Very well, Mrs. Melkiot," said Camacho in studiedly neutral tones, "why don't you tell me what you've just told your attorneys."

Flora did, trying to use exactly the same words and inflections as before. She had an excellent memory and knew that she could have been a great actress had she chosen, even though was she was saying was the exact truth.

Camacho let her talk, but his glower remained constant. When she finished, he waited a moment, then asked, "And just why were you sneaking around out in the hallways when you should have been in bed? What were you doing that you didn't want anyone to know about?"

Flora remained serene. Any logical person would have seen it coming, and she was prepared. "Older people do not always sleep well, detective, especially in a noisy place like this. I was wakeful, so I thought I might go visit Dewayne if he were up too."

"Dewayne?"

"Mr. Harbaugh. The black man in the wheelchair."

"You and him got a thing going?"

"Detective!" Ms. Monroe's voice was like a shining blade cutting through the air. "That was uncalled for."

"Mr. Harbaugh is severely disabled," Flora replied only slightly testily. "Besides, although some people might have difficulty believing it, decent people do not base every action or thought on sex."

Camacho's eyes glowed with pure dislike. "So this Dewayne will corroborate your story of a meeting?"

"I don't see how he can, as there was no pre-arrangement. I just thought I would see if he was awake. In words of mainly one syllable, it was not planned."

Both lawyers shot Flora a look of caution, but by then she was alight with righteous indignation.

"So you heard someone coming and dashed into the chapel to hide."

"Basically."

"And then you found Mrs. Badham's body."

Flora pointed to her battered face. "I tripped over it, and fell against a pew."

"Did you kill her?"

"Of course not, as I have already told you. She was totally mad and very annoying, but one cannot simply eliminate people who irritate you." Her stare at Camacho was most telling. "No matter how satisfying it might be."

"You are the one who found the body."

"That is not an honor I requested. And if you say

again that the killer is the one who finds the body, I shall scream," Flora said at her most imperious. "Besides, she had been dead for hours when I fell over her."

The detective's eyes flickered, like a predator's when a tasty meal wanders into view. "And just how do you know that?"

"For heaven's sake! Humans are warm-blooded creatures. It takes a while to lose their body heat after death. I have no idea of the statistics, but to go completely cold has to take several hours. When I touched Eula Badham's flesh, she was cold." Flora could not help a small shiver at the memory. "Completely, thoroughly, dead type of cold, ergo she had been dead for many hours and as I was in public view until bedtime and asleep in my bed until just before I found her obviously I could not have killed her."

"So you are a forensic scientist now?"

"Not at all. Merely an intelligent human being."

"Well, thank you, Mrs. Melkiot," Camacho said with patent insincerity as he stood to go, "thank you for your help. I do recommend that you stay in your own bed from now on."

Flora's mouth shut like a bear trap while mutiny blazed in her eyes.

"Didn't you have something else to say to Detective Camacho, Mrs. Melkiot," Ms. Monroe said, sounding to Flora's ears like a grammar school etiquette teacher.

For a moment Flora considered revolting, but the attorney was right. It probably wasn't anything, but in books the people who kept anything to themselves usually ended up murdered.

"It's probably nothing."

Camacho sat back down. "Nothing is nothing. Let me decide, so you just tell me."

So Flora did, repeating the whispered threat she had overheard as best she could recall it.

"You couldn't tell if the speakers were male or

female?"

"No. If you want to be completely accurate I can't say with certitude that they were real people. The televisions here are always on, you see," she said with obvious distaste, "and usually very loud. I suppose it could have been some soap or another, but it sounded real – not like a television show at all."

"And you have no idea of who was speaking?"

"None, at least for the person doing the threatening. As for the other – I must admit my first thought was of Eula Badham. She was afflicted in her mind, you see. She believed that drug money was being laundered through this place and that gangs of thugs lived here in disguise killing people left and right and that she was next because she knew too much."

"Maybe she did," Camacho said slowly, his heavy face puckering with thought.

How ridiculous, Flora thought, but then realized the crazy old lady had died in a violent manner.

She was just about to say so when the screams began.

Chapter Fourteen

Camacho moved with a speed that belied his size. Before Flora could get to her feet he was running down the hall, as was everyone else.

What now? Although she possessed too much common sense to believe in the magical woo-woo new age stuff that seemed to fascinate everyone these days, Flora could not ignore a flicker of discomfort that did not come from her physical body. She knew something awful had happened.

There wasn't much room around the nurses' station, but what there was was packed. Down the hall Flora could see an open door with a young officer standing outside, his face positively green. Flora knew that door. It led to Dewayne's room.

She might be slender, but Flora was strong and, for her age, well-toned. She went through the murmuring crowd of ghost-people like a charging bull, not apologizing for pushing them aside or for the few times she used her cast as a club. She didn't even feel the hurt in her wrist.

That nice young black nurse – Naomi? – and one of the Mexican aides were solicitously leading Melanie down the hall. Her uniform was heavily splattered with blood and her unfortunately horsey face contorted into a mask of agony. It was as if her hands were separate entities, flying randomly at will, perhaps batting at demons only she could see.

"He was just lying there," she kept repeating. "I went

to see if he was going into breakfast this morning and he was just lying there…"

Breakfast? The word seeped into Flora's consciousness as if from an alien tongue. All this, and they hadn't even had breakfast yet?

Clenching her teeth, she plunged forward. The policeman on guard extended his arm in an attempt to keep her out, but she pushed it away without pausing, stopping only when she stood in the doorway.

She had only gotten the barest glimpse of Penelope Cattermole's battered body, and it had been in shadow, but this was definitely worse than Eula Badham or the death of Laura Tyler in the Olympus House exercise salon. This time the ceiling light was on full, illuminating the scene with dreadful clarity. Both those unfortunates had passed with very little blood loss. This was even worse than the fleeting glimpse she had had of Penelope Cattermole lying in a small pool of her own blood.

It looked as if Dewayne Harbaugh had lost all of his.

A nurse Flora didn't know had unfastened Dewayne's support straps and had laid him on the floor. Out of the exoskeleton of his electric wheelchair he looked small and defenseless, sprawled in the middle of a glistening puddle of liquid red as if nothing more than a toy crushed and discarded. Blood covered most of his wheelchair, great drops falling into the puddle with low, sullen splashes. Flora was grateful that his face was turned away and simultaneously thought herself a coward for feeling so.

Detective Camacho squatted just outside the blood pool, trousers carefully pulled up to avoid contact. Surprisingly Dr. Jensen had no such hesitation; he knelt right in the red lake oblivious to the stains creeping into the fabric of his trousers. For the first time in her acquaintance of him Bobby Jensen was acting like a doctor and Flora almost respected him.

The policeman grabbed Flora's arms only to jump backward in surprise as she ungently laid her cast across his wristbone. The karate for seniors class she had taken been helpful after all.

"She can stay, officer," Camacho said, seemingly without looking up. "Well, Mrs. Melkiot?"

"Is he dead?" Flora asked in a voice that didn't sound like her at all.

"No, but I'm not sure how," said Dr. Jensen, still very much in doctor mode. "There's an ambulance on the way. He's tough – he might make it."

Flora sighed and breathed a little prayer. "What happened?"

"I was going to ask you that."

"I've been with you, detective, and this didn't happen that long ago."

"Being a forensic scientist again?"

"The blood is still bright red and liquid."

"She's right." Dr. Jensen nodded, holding out his hand. Somehow the gooey-named nurse had slipped into the room, her hands full of things. She responded to the unspoken demand with a bandage and stood ready, smartly handing each thing as it was needed to the doctor, sometimes before he asked for it, and suddenly she didn't seem so gooey any more.

"There," Bobby Jensen said, his voice full of equal parts of panic and satisfaction. "That should slow down the loss of blood."

"So when did this happen?" Camacho asked.

"Given how heavily he was bleeding, not very long. A few minutes at most, but probably less and definitely not much longer, or he would have bled out completely. Thank you, Candy."

The nurse stood, gathering up the detritus from the supplies. She was neater than Melanie; only the hem of her scrubs pants were touched with blood.

Flora could swear that a look of frustration fluttered over Camacho's rigid face as he looked at her. For the last hour she had been with some authority figure or another, including the detective himself.

So who could have done this to Dewayne? Flora felt more than a little ill. He had a vicious tongue, of course, and a sharp intellect, but physically he was defenseless.

And why? What could anyone gain from attacking Dewayne Harbaugh?

He couldn't have done anything to anyone, unless he knew something. Several new and very ugly thoughts flashed into Flora's mind, but she had no time for them now. There had been the hardly noticed scream of an ambulance and suddenly the room was full of rushing men pushing a gurney and ordering everyone out except Dr. Jensen.

From the hallway Flora watched as they loaded Dewayne's pitiful body onto the gurney. Dr. Jensen followed them out, pausing at Camacho's side only long enough to say, "I'm going with him to the hospital. I'll be back when I can."

The detective nodded. Perhaps there was more to this prissy little man than there appeared. There would have to be, in his opinion.

"Good. Barstow – " he turned to the young officer, who was still rubbing his injured wrist " – go with them. Stay with him and don't let him out of your sight. I want to know if anyone comes near him."

Officer Barstow looked almost relieved and ran after the ambulance crew.

"You do know I can arrest both you and your daughter for assault upon two officers of the law, don't you?" Camacho asked mildly, carefully looking away from Flora's outraged face.

"You wouldn't dare!"

"Neither you nor your daughter have much respect for the police, do you?"

"Both my daughter and I," Flora said loftily, "have the greatest respect for the law."

The distinction was not lost on the detective, who

gave her a look that was half-respectful, half-rueful.

"And you were both under considerable distress at the time," he admitted. "I suppose we should make allowance for that."

Flora smiled and not prettily. "And for the fact that once the media finds out about it your police department would look both heartless for keeping a daughter away when she fears her mother may have been murdered, and spineless when a great strapping young officer claims to be injured by an elderly lady suffering from broken bones."

Camacho nodded, knowing she would make sure everyone knew the story and put the police department in the worst possible light. "You are hardly elderly."

Flora acknowledged the compliment with a regal nod, but did not give. "Not to mention that I have two of the best attorneys in Texas just a few feet away."

"Also true," Camacho nodded, tacitly admitting defeat. "Were you and Mr. Harbaugh good friends?"

"Friends? No. I believe that a true friendship has to grow over a respectable length of time, and I never even saw him before coming here. I did like him, though. He was – is – intelligent, witty and well educated. Those qualities are somewhat rare around here."

The detective nodded. "Do you have any idea of who might have done that to him? Or why?"

The image of Dewayne lying so dreadfully still in that spreading pool of blood flashed in front of Flora's mind's eye and for one moment she feared losing control of herself so much that she just might throw up.

"Mrs. Melkiot?" Ms. Monroe gently touched Flora's arm, pulling her back to reality with a jump. "Are you all right? You're terribly pale. Do you need medical assistance?"

"No, I'm fine," Flora replied briskly. "No, detective, I have no idea of what anyone might have against Dewayne, any more than I do about Eula Badham. How was Dewayne injured? We didn't hear a shot, so I am assuming it was a stab wound?"

Camacho's face tightened. "That's none of your business, Mrs. Melkiot."

Flora's face tightened equally. "And why not? At the rate residents are being attacked I think we should know so that we can be forewarned."

Ms. Monroe coughed. "It is not an unusual request, Detective Camacho. I'm sure you can understand that a number of patients find not knowing much more frightening than the truth. If necessary we can petition the court to instruct the coroner to release the information."

Flora bristled at the intimation that she could be afraid, but was smart enough to keep quiet.

Sighing, Camacho shuffled his feet and looked down. He had stood up to bank robbers and murderers, had been shot at several times, even had a couple of commendations for valor, but there was no way he could win against these two women. It was a wise man who knew when he was outmatched.

"Very well, Ms. Monroe. Dewayne Harbaugh was beaten with a long narrow object. Savagely. We're working on finding out what it was."

Remembering the pool of blood that had surrounded Dewayne, Flora drew in a deep breath and let it out. "Another attack of extreme anger," she murmured, unaware of how vulnerable she looked. It would have annoyed her no end.

"If you don't need Mrs. Melkiot any longer," Ms. Monroe said in a voice that, however soft and well-modulated, was definitely an order, "there are things we must settle."

Taking Flora's arm she started to lead her away, only to be stopped by a red-faced Clarissa. So she hadn't obeyed and gone home after all. Flora saw with some surprise that there were tears in her daughter's eyes, though she couldn't decide if they were from sorrow or anger.

"Take your hands off my mother," Clarissa commanded, answering her mother's unspoken question. "Mama, we need to talk."

"We have talked," Flora replied calmly, "several times, and as I am still incarcerated here against my will, obviously it didn't do any good."

"But it is all for your good!"

Flora snorted.

"You needed care, and I wanted you close so I could look after you."

"Mrs. Fullerton – " Ms. Monroe began, but for perhaps the first time in her professional life was told unequivocally to shut up.

"Clarissa, that is rude. Ms. Monroe is here at my request."

"You don't need a lawyer, Mama. We're family. I just want to take care of you."

"By locking me in a graceless horrible place rife with murders and food that is a crime in itself?"

If she had been younger and less inhibited, Clarissa might have stamped her foot. "I didn't know that, Mama. It seemed a nice place. I was planning that when you finished your therapy you'd come live with Bill and the boys and me."

"God help me!" Flora hadn't intended to say it aloud; the words just popped out of their own accord.

More tears rose in Clarissa's already swollen eyes and began a slow trickle down her cheeks. Perhaps, Flora acknowledged, there really were two emotions at play.

"I'm going to take you home today, Mama. You'll have your own suite upstairs and after your condo sells…"

"My condo? What have you done with my condo? You can't do anything with it. It's in my name only. That is my home, and when I leave here I am going there."

"Mama, all we've done is talk to some realtors. You're too old to be living by yourself, and the condo will sell really fast. It'll make you a lot of money too."

"Which you've already spent, no doubt," Flora said in furiously controlled tones. "Ms. Monroe, I don't care how you do it, but you are to see that nothing happens to my home. I don't want realtors tromping through it. It belongs to me, and me alone. Morris – God rest his soul – put it completely in my name when we bought it."

"We will take care of it, Mrs. Melkiot." Ms. Monroe's voice had a discomforting edge. "You won't have to worry about a thing."

"Forget the condo, Mama, we can settle that later."

"It is settled now, Clarissa."

"Mama, people are being killed here. You have to come home with me so I can keep you safe." By now there was an affecting little catch in Clarissa's voice. It would have impressed Flora more if she didn't know quite well that her daughter could do it at will. "I'm having Miss Enero process your papers right now releasing you into my care."

"Mrs. Fullerton – " Camacho began, but Clarissa turned on him, shaking a furious finger right in his face.

"And don't you dare tell me I can't take my mother to safety! People are being murdered here!"

"I wasn't going to. I think it's a fine idea – we'll just have to know your address and telephone number in case we need to talk to her again."

Flora watched in dismay as her freedom was in danger of being eroded even further.

"I, however, am telling you, Clarissa," she said firmly, determined to put a stop to this right now. "You wanted me here enough to put me here against my will, and so here I will stay until I am able to return home to Dallas. Make it happen, Ms. Monroe."

Already twisted with suppressed amusement, the attorney's lips spread into an unholy smile. "Mr. Rothstein's office is already working on getting a restraining order to block the temporary guardianship and return control of your life to you until we can get a permanent reversion. Then you can do what you want."

"Thank you," Flora said with great satisfaction.

Camacho's face fell almost as far as Clarissa's. "Mrs. Melkiot, I'm not sure that's a good idea..."

Flora had no illusions about what would happen once Clarissa actually got her to that overblown monstrosity in Alamo Heights. Perhaps not the Gothic notion of censored mail and no telephone conversations, but she would doubtless be smothered in cardigan sweaters (which she loathed), cookies and good works, as in Clarissa's vision a proper elderly mother should be. The Altar Guild? Flora shuddered.

Not that she admitted to being elderly, other than when it was useful.

"I am not sure that your opinion enters into it, detective. Good bye, Clarissa. You don't have to call off the realtors in Dallas – Ms. Monroe will do that and insure that they do not interfere again. Say hello to Bill for me." Turning to her attorney without missing a beat she said "You say there are some matters to which we must attend? Perhaps we should return to Dr. Jensen's office. I'm sure he wouldn't mind."

United in frustration, though for different reasons, Clarissa and the detective watched the ill-matched couple disappear down the hall, the elegant Mr. Rothstein tagging along behind.

Driven to extremes, Clarissa did stamp her foot. "Damn, damn, damn!"

Camacho sighed. "Your mother does seem more than capable of taking care of herself," he said in soothing tones. "She'll be able to manage for herself."

"That's exactly what I don't want! Heaven only knows what she'll get into now. She can be a menace to herself and everyone else." Clarissa's hands clenched into angry fists. "She positively likes it when people talk about her!"

"Is it wise to want her in your house, then?" Camacho

asked unwisely. He was rewarded with a blistering stare before Clarissa stomped off toward the exit, muttering words that would have shocked her acquaintances.

* * * * *

"This isn't right," Naomi muttered. With Melanie hysterical and forced to take a tranquilizer, she was now the nurse in charge even though she was only an LVN. Despite the terrible reasons behind it, the temporary promotion made her proud. Miss Enero had told her all she had to do to prepare the pre-breakfast meds was follow the dosage graph on the cabinet wall, put the proper medication in each cup (pre-marked with the room and patient name) and make the notation on the check out sheet. (As if she hadn't been helping with the meds since her second week here!) After that, Naomi knew the aides would give the proper cup to the proper patient and check off on their file what they had taken and if they had refused any. After all, Naomi had done that often enough, and simple though it sounded it wasn't a sure thing. Old people sometimes got funny about medicine, even when it was supposed to do them good.

But something here wasn't adding up. This Percocet bottle held 180 pills. Whenever any new bottle of medication was opened the date was written on the side. This bottle had been opened just two days ago, but there were only 40 pills inside now.

Naomi's brow furrowed. Percocet was heavy duty stuff and very seldom used, usually no more than a dozen doses a month. 140 pills of this would have half the occupants of Cold Creek out of their mind for days. But they were gone. Where? Naomi knew Georgia and Melanie weren't in the habit of checking the bottles when there was no call for that particular medicine, but she wanted to take full advantage of her short time as head nurse. It made her feel important, even if she knew it was just temporary.

Why did this have to happen now?

Naomi held the nearly empty bottle and stared at it as if it could give her answers.

Every time medication was given, it was noted in the patient's file. Every time medication was taken from the drugs cabinets the number of pills removed and what kind they were was noted on the check-out sheet. It was supposed to be a check and balance system that protected everyone.

Quickly Naomi ran down the check-out figures. By this sheet every pill that had been taken out and administered was duly noted – 15 of them. That left 125 pills missing and unaccounted for. But where were they? And who was getting them? These were for severe pain, and she didn't know of that many residents who were in such severe pain. Of course, she didn't know everything about every patient in every corridor, but surely she would have heard something if there were anyone here with such a severe problem.

Naomi frowned again. This just wasn't right. Something just wasn't right. Miss Enero should know…

Sighing, Naomi stifled her original impulse to run to the administrator. All she had was a check-out sheet and a suspicion, and it was too important a matter to make a fuss about on such flimsy evidence. She might even be suspected or even accused of something, and she didn't dare do that.

No, she decided, her job and her future was too important to risk on such a slight suspicion. She'd watch, though, and if something concrete did come along that could in no way bounce back on her, then she'd tell Miss Enero.

Naomi made the proper notations and set about filling the morning med cups.

* * * * *

Breakfast that day was even more of a trial than normal. Speculation was wilder than ever, but in a subdued, fearful way. No one seemed to care about Penelope Cattermole's death – she had been disliked and difficult – but Eula Badham had been if not liked, at least tolerated. Dewayne Harbaugh had pretty much been a favorite.

Stacey Enero couldn't help wondering if it had been someone besides Dewayne would the reaction have been this strained, this haunted. Even though he was still alive he had been attacked, and if he could be attacked, so could any of them. Death was never a stranger to an elderly and infirm population like this, but that was natural death, a slipping away. Not violence and blood and horror.

Stacey prowled the dining room, being careful to speak to everyone at each table, being upbeat in spite of the lead weight in her own stomach. Normally she avoided appearing at mealtimes, but today she thought they might appreciate it. After her second round of the room Adelita practically shoved her into a chair and put a plate in front of her. Stacey literally couldn't remember the last time she ate.

For institutional food, she decided, it wasn't too bad. Bland, but that was recommended for the elderly. At least there was some taste and texture.

"Miss Enero?" His face dark, Detective Camacho loomed over her, seemingly as large and substantial as a building. Or a cliff.

"Detective! I thought you had gone. Will you join us? I can get you a plate…"

Having seen the plates on his way across the room Camacho shook his head with just a little too much vigor. "No, thanks. May I speak with you, please?"

"Of course. Sit down. Perhaps some coffee?"

"I think we had better talk privately."

Something dark in his tone twisted Stacey's gut. Obviously he knew something and just as obviously she probably wasn't going to like it.

"Of course." Dabbing her lips with the napkin, she stood up. It didn't make any difference that her meal was only half-finished; she couldn't have forced down another bite. "Shall we use Dr. Jensen's office?"

How had he found out?

For that matter, exactly what had he found out?

She gulped, fear filling her like dirty water.

Chapter Fifteen

Flora watched as the administrator and the detective left the room. Obviously the detective wanted to talk to her in private. How she would love to be a fly on the wall so she could listen to what was said! How was she supposed to solve the case – cases? – if she was denied all the current information? Detecting was harder work than she had imagined. At the Olympus House it had been fairly easy simply because she knew everyone involved, but also since it had occurred in her own sphere, where everyone knew and respected her – though Rebecca and that tiresome Detective Ashdown would probably have said feared.

It was very frustrating to be treated as nothing more than a nosy old woman, Flora fumed inwardly, especially when she felt she should be treated as a colleague. Who else here had helped solve a murder?

However, she decided, one must work with what one had. Pushing away her almost full plate, she rose to leave.

"Are you all right, Mrs. Melkiot?"

Good grief, can one not move in this place without it being remarked on? Flora wondered in a flash of anger, but her reply was soft. She didn't dare draw more attention on herself than absolutely necessary if she was going to be effective.

"I'm fine, Loshonda. I don't want any more. After all," she said with an arch giggle, "we girls have to watch our figure, don't we? I thought I'd go read for a while."

The aide's look was suspicious, but she didn't say

anything as Flora sailed serenely out of the room.

Flora had learned and learned well the art of subterfuge that was necessary to get anything of value done here at Cold Creek Health Care Facility. She did go straight to her room, prop herself up comfortably in bed and pick up a book, choosing one at random. It turned out to be one of Jana deLeon's humorous mysteries – one of Clarissa's additions, and Clarissa's taste was normally a little too tame for Flora's tastes, but it was still interesting, enough so that a little while later when Naomi stuck her head in the door she was truly engrossed in it.

"You doin' okay, Mrs. Melkiot?"

Flora smiled and showed her the colorful cover. "Fine. Have you ever read Jana deLeon?"

"No, I don't have much time for reading, what with work and school and the kids…"

"No, I don't suppose you do, especially with young children." Flora's voice came out a little more wistfully than she had intended. Those had been good years for her. "It's good to be busy, though. And you do have your children."

"Yes, ma'am, I do, and they's wonderful." Naomi's lips turned upward in a proud little smile. "I'll let you get back to your reading, then."

Flora smiled back. It didn't turn brittle until Naomi was out of sight. The nurse was nice enough, probably the nicest here, but she still had to obey her orders. Was this a care facility or a concentration camp with every move monitored and second guessed? Before leaving Ms. Monroe had assured her the temporary guardianship would be nullified either this afternoon or tomorrow, meaning Flora could pack and leave, probably as early as noon, though on second thought that seemed a little optimistic. She would have to get Clarissa to bring her purse, her charge cards and whatever cash she had carried before she could get an airline ticket or even a cab to the airport, and she knew that would not be pleasant.

Of course, Rebecca would advance her any money she asked for – after all, she had done enough for her and her shop – and Ms. Monroe would probably do the same, but Flora didn't like either alternative. It was humiliating to have to ask anyone for money when thanks to Morris she had more than enough of her own for the rest of her lifetime and then some. She didn't want her daughter's folly to impact the lives of her friends. It had been bad enough admitting that her daughter had completely overridden her!

There was also the problem of her appearance. Flora knew she was not a beauty, but she had always maintained that character, carriage and presentation meant more than a pleasing alignment of features. She had the character and carriage at all times, but the presentation – ! There was no way she was going to travel on a plane and appear at the Olympus House in a dowdy snap-front duster and terry scuffs with her hair striped as badly as a skunk's. Clarissa could not refuse to bring her property to her – Ms. Monroe and company would see to that – but expecting to get her to bring suitable clothes would be nigh impossible. If her daughter were to provide anything, it would probably be the polyester slacks and cardigan sweater Clarissa thought appropriate for an older woman to wear.

Flora frowned. There had to be a solution, and she knew she'd find one once she put her mind to it.

But, a niggling voice in the back of her head kept whispering, did she really want a solution so soon? There had been two murders and a deadly assault – please God Dewayne would pull through. He had already suffered so much. Could she in good conscience just walk away and leave finding the solution to Detective Camacho?

Flora sighed. Of course not. She had always believed having superior abilities also meant having responsibilities.

And, she thought with a savage little smile, solving two murders and an assault would certainly put a spoke in the wheel of those small-minded gossips back in Dallas who called her first case a fluke!

* * * * *

"Well, Miss Enero?" Camacho's tone was demanding, but not aggressive. Not yet.

Stacey could feel the blood draining from her face. She thought she could bury the past if she were just careful enough, but this man had dug up all the old ugliness with insulting ease. How long before he told everyone?

"Yes. I knew Mrs. Cattermole before," she admitted, the words like bile in her mouth. "Are you going to tell the owners?"

"I thought you already had."

"Not everything. Not names."

"Why don't you tell me?" Camacho asked, settling in to a chair. "Everything. With names."

Stacey leaned back in her chair, her eyes roving the luxuriousness of Dr. Jensen's office. She had dreamed of having an office like this instead of her messy little rathole, even as she knew that those who claimed the glory and those who did the work received two different kinds of rewards. Now she'd be lucky to get out with even a part of her reputation intact. No one would hire her after this.

"I told you most of it. I was in the Air Force. I was booted out for alcoholism. My family helped me get a job here – a very low level job. I've worked my butt off making this place the best it can be. You can ask anyone who was here before if it isn't better now. I work hard and keep my nose clean." She looked at him defiantly.

Camacho said nothing. For a moment there was a crackling of power in the air like before a storm. Stacey caved first, looking down at her hands. They were so tightly entangled that her fingers were white as old bone.

"What I didn't tell you was that when I was still in the Air Force I was engaged to a man I worked with. He was a wonderful man. Kind, a good sense of humor, smart… the only flaw he had was that he ragged on me about my drinking. I wasn't a full-blown alcoholic then, but I did drink more than I should. I thought I could show him that I could function perfectly well even with a load of alcohol. One night I took the car keys and drove us home from a party."

"He just let you?"

"No. We fought." Gulping, Stacey covered her face with her hands as if she could hide from the images conjured by her words. "It was a horrible fight. I even hit him when he tried to take the keys away. We were both trained in unarmed combat, remember, and I guess he thought I probably wouldn't pull my punches. I probably wouldn't have, either. I was so determined to prove that I was right I would have gone without him. I wish I had," she said with a little sob.

"Of course," Stacey went on resolutely, her hands falling limply into her lap as she stared straight ahead, "I shouldn't have been behind the wheel. I decided I didn't want to go back to the base just yet, so I took off towards the country. Then something happened – I still don't remember exactly what, but I lost control and we went off the road… rolled over a couple of times down a gully and smashed into some rocks. We were an awful mess… Luckily someone saw us and called for help, but he – he bled to death in my arms before it could get there. I was pretty badly smashed up, but I lived. His last words were to ask me to promise I'd quit drinking. I never had another drink, but it was too late – too late."

Her shoulders heaving with unstifled sobs, Stacey fell forward across her lap as if trying to draw up into a ball.

"And the worst part of it is," she said in a tiny voice that positively pulsed with agony, "is that he forgave me. He was dying in my arms, and it was my fault, and he forgave me. How can anyone live with that?"

Camacho watched impassively, wishing he were

almost anywhere else doing almost anything else. He really didn't like having to do things like this, but he had to know if what he knew was all the truth.

"And?" he asked after a few moments.

Stacey shuddered and gasped, then pulled herself upright. "You still want to hear it all from me? You sadistic bastard," she said softly and without heat. "All right. We were under General Cattermole's command. Everyone knew he was under his wife's thumb, but we didn't know how much. She was on some sort of a morality do-gooder tear, wanting to make everyone act like little plaster saints or something, and she demanded that those of us who were not perfect, those of us who made a mistake or two be made examples of. Which is, if you think about it, kind of funny since her own past was so checkered."

"Checkered? How?"

"Dunno for sure. There was a lot of talk about how she'd been married a couple of times, always in the military and moving up the ranks every time, and how she broke up a couple of families in the process. Hardly the actions of a moral woman, don't you think? But she wanted to be known as a force for good, so we were dragged through the mud. At least Ed – " her voice caressed the name " – was beyond her reach. There wasn't anything they could do to him. I was court martialed and publicly disgraced. I wasn't spared the civilian courts, either, but because of my good service record I was given probation as long as I stayed sober. I have two more years to go on probation. All thanks to Mrs. General Brian Cattermole."

"Were you the only one she made an example of?"

"No."

"Do you think that could be a motive for murder?"

Stacey shrugged. "Sure. I contemplated doing it a couple of times myself, but," she added quickly at the look on the detective's face, "thinking about it is not illegal. I never touched her, nor helped anyone else do so. Did I want her out of here? Of course I did, and I was going to get her out of here, but through official channels and for completely justifiable reasons. She was disruptive and a menace to others."

Camacho sat forward. "So I've heard. Any idea of anyone else who might have wanted her dead?"

"Anyone who ever had any dealings with her, I suppose." Stacey thought a moment, then shook her head. "No, I can't think of anyone here who would go to the lengths of actually killing her."

"What about Eula Badham? Anybody having problems with her?"

"I don't have any idea. She was incredibly annoying, but other than that Eula Badham was as much of a nothing as I've ever seen. I doubted if she knew what day it was, let alone anything that could get her killed."

"Might she have seen something?"

"Around here? Something that could get her killed? Day before yesterday I would have laughed in your face at that question. Nothing ever happens here. Now – " Stacey looked bemused and a little sad. "Now I don't recognize this place. This was a good, quiet facility that ran like a watch. It isn't anymore, and I don't think it will ever get over this. Already we're getting calls from people about removing their family members. If there's a Cold Creek Health Care Facility in six months I'll be very surprised. When you lose the people's trust you lose everything."

Inwardly Camacho nodded. Outwardly he kept his expression stern. "And Dewayne Harbaugh? Did he have any enemies?"

"I don't know. Dewayne is a very special case. He has a vicious tongue when he wants to use it. He can also be funny and very amusing – when he wants to be. He definitely wasn't the easiest guy to be around. And God only knows what he does on those computers of his. He was on them most of the time."

"Is that how he made his living?"

"I don't know."

"Is he rich?"

Stacey shrugged. "I don't know. He came before I was made administrator, but I know he does get special treatment."

"Such as?"

"His is the only private room here. And all those computers and stuff. He even pays a surcharge for extra electricity because of them and has his own private satellite dish. Some special deal with the owners. But there's never been a question about his fees. They're even paid six months at a time."

"Ouch." Part of Camacho's research had shown just how expensive it was to live here as a regular resident. "What happened to – to make him the way he is?" he couldn't help but ask, his question sparked as much by plain curiosity as policing.

"I don't know." Stacey shrugged again, her hands flopping impotently in her lap. "It isn't in his file and he won't talk about it. Presumably the owners know, but all we're told is about his medical stuff. It's not regular policy, but that's the way it is."

"What about visitors? Who came to see the victims?"

"Eula's nephew came every few weeks. Her grandchildren were here when they first brought her in, but they haven't been back that I know of. The only person who came to see Mrs. Cattermole was someone from the military. Definitely a business visit. Dewayne never has visitors."

"Never?"

"Not that I know of." Not looking at the detective, Stacey worried at a fingernail. Her voice changing slightly, she asked, "Do you have any idea of when I can get my files back?"

"When we're done going through them. I think you have all the medical records you need on your computers, right?"

"Yes, for the moment, but there's stuff in those files I need. Not about the patients – about suppliers and things like that. Stuff that has nothing to do with the murders. I do have a facility to run… at least for as long as it lasts."

"We'll hurry." Camacho's tone was easy, but he recognized that there was more to her request than just the day to day running of a nursing home.

Stacey nodded reluctantly, then stood, her hand on the doorknob. "Have you found the murder weapon yet?"

"No, not yet." Camacho watched her with regret. He had begun to respect this girl who had pulled herself back from hell, but that didn't alter the fact that she wasn't being straight with him. "Don't go yet. I want you to tell me why you didn't go home the night Penelope Cattermole was murdered."

Stacey's fingers tightened convulsively on the doorknob, her heart thudding so that she didn't even hear the skittering of footsteps outside.

Chapter Sixteen

Flora put the deLeon book aside with regret – it was a very good story – and pulled notepad and pen from the nightstand drawer. If she really was going to have to solve this by herself, she needed to start going about it professionally and in an organized fashion. All the great detectives had made lists of facts to make piecing the solution together simple; if it worked for them, it should work for Flora Melkiot!

First, Penelope Cattermole. It wasn't difficult to see why she had been murdered; anyone that determinedly unpleasant should probably expect it. Though, Flora thought, it was almost sad that so soon after her death she was already forgotten as a person, having become merely the First Murder.

Second, Eula Badham, who though mad as a hatter had been a gentle soul and was genuinely mourned by most of the residents. Why on earth had anyone killed such a vague and harmless person?

Third, the attack on Dewayne Harbaugh. He was as different from both the Cattermole and Eula Badham as it was for a human being to be. What could someone hold against Penelope Cattermole, Eula Badham and Dewayne Harbaugh?

Flora gnawed the end of her pen, an act that showed just how deep in thought she was. Normally she would neither do nor tolerate anything so common.

There didn't seem to be any reason she could think of, but something else came to mind.

Fourth, the snatch of conversation she had heard outside her room that night, something like 'watch your place, old woman, or I'll kill you.' Flora knew those were not the exact words, but that was the feeling she had gotten from them. If only she had paid more attention – hadn't she learned anything from Laura Tyler's murder? She had actually seen the awful thing and not been able to recall anything but the bubbling horror of the woman's face. How could she be so oblivious?

Because she hadn't been expecting anything, that was why. There was a poster she recalled which had been popular in Clarissa's school days – Life is what happens when you're planning something else, or something like that.

Flora read back over her notes, but without further enlightenment. She then put down where the attacks had taken place, or in Eula Badham's case, the body was found. Flora was not completely convinced that she had been murdered in the chapel, but how else could the killer have gotten her there? Surely even in this place of waiting for Death someone would have noticed someone carrying a dead body down the hallway. If the old woman hadn't been killed in the chapel, where had it been? Again, even after profound thought there was nothing that jumped out at her.

Dewayne had been attacked in his own room, but anyone could have done it. None of the patients' rooms had locks on the doors, a situation Flora found to be an insult to the concept of privacy.

All right, the means of death/injury. The Cattermole had been bludgeoned with a heavy object as yet unknown. Eula Badham died of what appeared to Flora to have been a broken neck; its angle had certainly been enough to sever the spinal cord, which would cause – Flora thought – instantaneous death and the subsequent release of the sphincter muscles. Memory of the frail and broken urine-soaked corpse tugged at Flora's heart. The woman might have been crazy, but she had asked for Flora's help and Flora hadn't believed her. It was a wound Flora would carry forever, and if for no other reason she would do her best to bring the old woman's murderer to justice.

Flora pulled herself back to business. Regrets and guilt would not solve this mess.

Dewayne had been beaten – not shot, not stabbed. Neither had the Cattermole and, presumably, Eula Badham been shot or stabbed. *Murder weapon?* Flora wrote. The Cattermole and Dewayne wouldn't have gone easily – they would have fought back to the best of their ability, slight though it might be. Eula Badham had been so frail that a hard glance could have killed her. All had been up-close and personal, hands-on type murders. Murders filled with rage. That made a definite pattern for this perp. Flora was proud of being able to use the correct term, thanks to the crime shows she watched. Of course, that dratted detective would never tell her if all three had been attacked with the same weapon – or even if they knew what the weapon was.

None of this looked promising. She really didn't have any more here than was flashing around the gossip mill.

All right, place of death. Carefully Flora wrote out the heading to a new column.

The Cattermole had been bludgeoned to death in the administrator's office.

Eula Badham had most likely died in the chapel, but that didn't mean she had first been attacked there. On the other hand, how had the killer gotten her there? Eula Badham had been a small, frail woman, but still carrying or dragging her would have taken a fair amount of strength – to say nothing of having risked attracting attention.

Flora sighed.

Dewayne had been attacked in his private room. He would have died there too had not that nurse – Melanie? – happened to find him.

Flora thought for a moment, her face strained with the

effort of remembering. Melaine had said something about asking him if he was coming in to breakfast. Since she sometimes brought him a meal to his room that made sense. Or she could have gone to see him to ask for more money. Dewayne said he had been helping her financially.

Dr. Jensen said that the attack couldn't have happened many minutes before Dewayne was found because he would have bled out. So who had been seen leaving Dewayne's room a few minutes before Melanie went in?

There was no way Camacho would tell her that either, which meant if she were going to find out she'd have to talk to just about everyone in the place. Flora sighed again. How much more simple things would be if only that dratted detective would cooperate!

Time of death; another column head.

The Cattermole had been killed around three in the morning.

Eula Badham presumably had been killed at night, and not too late for her body to have gone as cold as it was, but the exact time was unknown. At least, if Camacho did know it that was one more thing he wasn't going to share it with Flora.

Glory-grabber, she thought sourly.

And why hadn't Mrs. Bernal said something about her roommate being missing? Of course, Flora knew that Eula Badham sometimes wandered at night. She could have gone out after Hortensia was asleep.

Dewayne… again, time unknown. Melanie had discovered him at breakfast time but it couldn't have been long or he would have bled out.

Flora decided she really did need to know more about medical forensics. When she got back to Dallas perhaps she would ask the medical examiner to give her some lessons. She had a vague memory of his being somehow related to one of her friends in the Dallas Women's Forum.

But that didn't help her now. To solve a mystery, one

had to know why the crime had been committed. She wrote WHY? in the middle of the paper, then in frustration repeated it a time or two.

Again, the main problem came down to the disparity of the victims. What on earth could Cattermole, Badham and Harbaugh have in common that would justify their being murdered?

There was only one common denominator that Flora could see. They all lived in Cold Creek Health Care Facility.

The realization hit Flora like a slap. There were no other points of correlation, at least not obvious ones.

But that wasn't quite right. Eula Badham and Dewayne were permanent residents and the Cattermole had only been here temporarily. In fact, according to gossip, the Cattermole was being sent back to wherever it was she had come from.

So… whatever bound them together had to have happened since the Cattermole's arrival and her death. For a moment Flora was suffused with a flush of triumph, which unfortunately died as soon as it was born.

When had Penelope Cattermole arrived? Drat this place; time here was such a fluid thing that it was hard to pin down actual events into a concrete frame unless they pertained to a specific meal.

Frowning, Flora stared at her page of scribblings, then angrily drew a large X through it. Whatever good this exercise had done for fictional detectives it was a total bust as far as she was concerned. There was nothing there that Flora didn't already know, and putting it down hadn't done any good. No big revelations, no patterns…

Flora sighed and stuck the pad and pen into her nightstand drawer. What a waste. It was ridiculous for her to speculate until she had more facts, but she couldn't help it.

Begin at the beginning, she decided. Penelope Cattermole. For some reason she had snuck into Miss

Enero's office late in the night, at no small cost of time and energy since her cane and walker had been confiscated. Why? What was she looking for? Or, had there been someone with her? The murderer? Or someone else?

Even if he knew, Flora realized Camacho would never tell her. Let him hoard his facts; surely a superior brain should be able to work things out even with the handicap of his uncooperativeness.

So Stacey Enero had something in her office – or the Cattermole thought she had something – that the Cattermole wanted to see or find or whatever so badly that she forced her way down there at night. Had she observed the cameras focused on the drug cabinets or had she just had the dumb luck to avoid them?

Flora sighed. Or did the furtive hand and wheel on the tape even belong to Penelope Cattermole? Had someone else been around? Could someone confined to a wheelchair have the strength to smash a skull like that? Possibly – the Cattermole might be damaged, but she was not wholly defenseless, even without a cane. But without aid or transportation, how had the Cattermole even gotten to the administrator's office? Had another patient or one of the staff helped her?

Was it a crime of premeditation or of opportunity? Had she been lured to the administrator's office or had someone found her there? As there was that missing something from Miss Enero's bookshelf, whatever it was probably had been the murder weapon, which tilted the scales towards a crime of the moment…

Flora sat forward with a jerk. She knew something had gotten past her and derided herself for not remembering it earlier. Of course, a great deal had been going on at the moment, but she still should have been sharper. All the photographs in Dr. Jensen's office! She had only given them the most cursory of glances if that, but now she remembered that some had been taken inside an office, an office that could be the administrator's. If there was a clear shot of the bookcase, she should be able to see what the murder weapon was.

Daytimes at CCHCF were usually a varied time, with many of the patients in physical therapy. Often there were visitors, either sitting with their loved ones in the lounge or watching TV in their rooms. Many of the residents played cards or watched TV in the lounge while they waited for the call to lunch or recuperated from eating it. To Flora it seemed that the building almost pulsed with screaming game and talk shows or the overwrought musical syrup of the soaps. A few residents simply wandered the halls, silent and detached as ghosts. The nurses and aides flitted up and down the halls, their minds fixed on one errand or another.

Trying to modify her confident stride in order not to stand out among these shadow people, Flora headed toward the doctor's office. She and her attorneys had used it this morning, but had only closed the door when they left. Hopefully it was still not locked. The way things were locked up around here, Flora decided, was strongly indicative of a suspicious mindset.

"Mrs. Melkiot?"

Flora stopped with a jerk then forced what she hoped was a friendly smile. Once she had set her mind on a course of action she truly did hate to be interrupted. "Terry. It's unusual to see you in this part of the building."

The therapist shrugged. "With all that's going on our therapy sessions sort of got ignored today, so Miss Enero asked me to help out over here. I've been looking for you."

"Oh? Why?"

"I know you and Mr. Harbaugh are particular friends, and Miss Enero wanted you to know that we heard from the hospital. He's still very badly hurt and on the critical list, but the doctors seem to think he'll make it."

Flora took a deep breath and released it slowly, feeling a depth of gratitude and relief that surprised her.

She would not have said she and Dewayne were friends, but perhaps she might be wrong about that. Doubtless he would say that she was getting soft in her old age, and while Flora might agree with him, for the moment she didn't care.

"Thank God," she said with a rare flush of true belief. "Is he conscious? Has he said anything?"

Terry shook her head. "No, at least I don't think so. They're keeping him in a coma until his brain swelling goes down."

"Poor man – he seems to have had more than his share of trauma. What crippled him?"

Terry continued to shake her head, reminding Flora of nothing so much as a grotesquely oversized bobblehead doll. "I don't know. It should be in his master file, of course, but that's not available to everyone – just Dr. Jensen, I think – unless there is a medical reason."

"But I thought anyone could access anything through the computer."

"Not much of anything is on the computer – not nearly enough if you ask me. Most everything is still done in the old paper files. Dr. Jensen and Miss Enero both are bears about patient privacy even though his patient files are on the computer, most of Miss Enero's are in her desk. The staff's files too. Excuse me, Mrs. Melkiot – there's Enid, and I must talk to her."

"Thank you, Terry. I appreciate your telling me," Flora said to the therapist's back as she ran after one of the nurses. Really, as much as that woman ran she should be a wraith.

Flora was sincere in her thanks; not only did she rejoice that Dewayne was likely to live, but she was most grateful about the information that Terry had given her without even knowing. If there was information about the victims, it would probably be in the files in the administrator's desk. Could those be what the Cattermole had been looking for? But why?

She had said that she recognized several people… Flora couldn't remember exactly who at the moment, but she remembered the woman saying it, spraying everyone close while she did. Of course, that could be a fabrication of an aged mind, but however feeble the Cattermole's body was her mind seemed sharp. What did those files contain and how could she get to see them?

Regretfully, Flora realized that she couldn't. Not only would no one tell her, but the file drawer had been pretty much empty. Camacho had those files, and there was no way he would let her anywhere near them.

"Hey, Flora babe."

Two arms wrapped around Flora and pulled her into a room. She opened her mouth to squawk, only to have a hand clamped over it.

"Hush, Flora babe… it's me, Fred. Fred Moretti."

Flora's thundering heart began to slow. He might be what she would have called in her youth a masher, but Fred Moretti was nothing to fear. She didn't think so, at least.

"That does not instill me with joy," she said acidly when he removed his hand, then wriggled out of his embrace. "What do you think you are doing?"

His eyes sparkled merrily. "Helping you. I hear you're going to try and solve these murders, and I got some information you might want to hear."

"Information? Where would you get information?"

"Outside the door to Dr. Jensen's office, while Miss Enero and that detective were in there."

Flora regarded him speculatively. He was a flirt and a blowhard, but if he had something useful to impart… The only question was, what would he want for it?

"What did you hear?"

His grin was impish, making him look like nothing so much as an Italian leprechaun, if there could be such an impossible creature. "What are you going to give me for it?"

"Nothing." Flora said in a voice that sounded very much like a schoolmistress. "You should think of the greater good, not just your personal gain."

He laughed and spread his hands. "Hey, I was just pulling your chain. Can't blame a guy for trying, can you? Anyway, I got an earful."

"And you just stood there with your ear to the door and listened in the middle of a hallway and no one questioned you?"

"Don't be so skeptical. First of all, the doors in this place are like paper. Second of all, no one notices an old man who has to lean against a wall because he's having trouble with his shoe." He smiled even more broadly. "Besides, I'm a damn fine actor."

Flora nodded with grudging respect. Maybe the man wasn't as much of a fool as he appeared to be, difficult as that might be to believe. "I'm sure you are. What did you hear?"

He told her.

Flora blinked, trying to take it all in. "So Stacey Enero had motive to kill the Cattermole woman."

"Ah, Miss Enero couldn't have done it. She's too nice."

"Nice people commit murders too," Flora said as she remembered the person behind Laura Tyler's death. "Anyone can commit a murder if driven sufficiently far."

"You're a cynic, Flora babe. Well, did I do good? Am I a detective now?" He gave her a burlesque of a leer. "Don't you want to reward me?"

Flora's mind was already leaping ahead. "Your reward is that I don't slap your face for being fresh," she said tartly. "Now go away."

Moretti laughed, apparently loving the chase as much as the capture. He walked toward the door, but turned to shake a gently admonishing finger at her. "You really are something, Flora babe. Don't think I'm going to let you get away."

"One thing – do you know if Detective Camacho and Miss Enero are still in Jensen's office?"

"Nah. They both came out before I got halfway down the hall." With a quickly sketched bow he was gone.

That was a relief; she would have hated to walk in on them without a reason to be in the doctor's office. Of course, she would have thought of something, but it would be nicer not to have to. There could be a problem with Fred Moretti, though; he obviously wanted to be a detective, but she could see his 'help' becoming a drawback. She doubted if he had ever solved a murder, after all.

Flora was almost at the doctor's door when there was a sharp metallic crash and an impressive string of curse words behind her. Turning quickly, as did everyone else in the hallway, she sat that Fred Moretti had run into a metal cart, sending it skittering into the wall. He was bent over and grasping his knee, almost turning the air blue with a decidedly profane vocabulary.

Typical male! So clumsy… Flora stopped. Or clever. He had never been clumsy before, not that she had seen. He was creating a distraction so everyone's attention would be on him while she slipped into the doctor's office. How perspicacious of him to realize that she intended to investigate in there. Perhaps she should take another look at him as a possible helper.

Wanting to draw as little attention as possible, Flora closed to the door to Dr. Jensen's office quietly behind her. The door had been unlocked, for which she was grateful; it was about time she had some good luck.

Another time, perhaps. She was not alone in the office.

There were two people who weren't responding to Fred's diversion. In fact, they weren't responding to anything except each other. In the middle of the room Georgia and Al were locked in an embrace that could by no stretch of the imagination be mistaken for that of mother and son. To Flora it resembled pornography more than anything familial. Even as their lips were glued by a noisy suction their hands were intimately exploring each other. Flora was supremely grateful that they were at least still mostly clothed.

Flora cleared her throat ostentatiously and, as they jumped apart in shock, said mildly, "You should at least have locked the door."

Al was fumbling with his clothes, his face a painfully glowing carmine, but Georgia was made of sterner stuff. Even as she pulled her scrub top down she glared at Flora venomously.

"What are you doing here?"

"I came to meet Dr. Jensen," Flora replied in an unabashed fib. "Obviously he's late."

The two conspirators glanced at each other, their looks speaking volumes that Flora wished she could translate. Then Al ran from the room, dashing around Flora as if she were contaminated.

"I thought Dr. Jensen was still at the hospital with Harbaugh," Georgia said, every word sharp and lethal.

"I didn't ask where he was," Flora replied.

Tension filled the room. For a moment Flora wondered if the stocky nurse would explode into violence. If she screamed for help would someone come to her aid? Would she even have time to scream?

Georgia smoothed her scrubs, then her hair, then said with menacing import, "I would appreciate it if you didn't mention this to anyone."

"What you do is none of my business. I am not a snoop," Flora added with unconscious mendacity.

It wasn't until they both left that Flora exhaled, almost dizzy with relief. She could have been in real danger. Al was nothing but a pretty face – though it appeared Georgia had found him to possess other talents – but the nurse could be a problem. At least now Flora had a pretty good idea of where Al had gotten that new and hideously expensive watch.

Flora was glad she could leave Cold Creek soon. Suddenly staying here just to solve the murders didn't seem so enticing; running afoul of Georgia could be dangerous. She must remember to contact Ms. Monroe to check on the progress of her liberation.

And she had to call Rebecca and tell her to look up some things. Yes, thanks to Fred Moretti she now had a real avenue of investigation.

But now she had to do what she had come in for and get out before Dr. Jensen really did come back – if he ever did spend much time in this office.

Flora stood before the wall of pictures, marveling at the almost egomaniacal self-absorption of Dr. Bobby Jensen. She hadn't been mistaken. He was the center of every photograph.

It was, Flora thought with a snort, *downright unhealthy.*

Unhealthy it might be, but helpful it was. There was a photograph of him, smiling toothily, shaking hands with Stacey Enero. They were standing in what had to be her office, and behind them was the bookcase. Flora smiled. It was a great deal neater than what she had seen herself, but the spot on the shelf above the desk was plainly visible.

As was the murder weapon.

Though small in the picture, the airplane sculpture was perfectly clear. An old style DC3, it was held in perpetual flight by an arch of metal affixed to a thick marble base. Barely fitting on the shelf, the sculpture stood just less than a foot tall and, being of solid metal and stone, was incredibly heavy. Flora was certain of that, because she had the thing's exact twin. Morris – God rest his soul – had been fascinated by airplanes. Cooperating in a rare spirit of amity, Jonathan and Clarissa had given him one identical to this while they were still in high school and Morris had adored it. Flora thought it hideous and totally at odds with her carefully chosen antique décor, but she had put up with it until after Morris' death, when it had been consigned to loving safety in the basement storage room.

Flora almost chortled. She had done it. She had found out what the murder weapon was without any help from that uncooperative clam Camacho. Pure detection had triumphed again. Take that, Detective!

Chapter Seventeen

"You want me to what?"

It was only after a singularly unmemorable lunch spent with equally unmemorable tablemates that Flora had been able to telephone Rebecca. With her door closed as much as allowed and after a single glance at the snoring Mrs. Gutierrez, Flora had outlined her needs to Rebecca, and was slightly affronted at her reaction.

"Calm down," Flora said with more patience than she actually felt. Why on earth did Rebecca have to be so contrary? "It isn't so much, Rebecca."

"Just poke around in someone else's life! I can't believe you're really digging into this. You are not a detective, Flora Melkiot. Three people have been killed there!"

"Two," Flora said with maddening accuracy. "Dewayne Harbaugh is still alive. At least, the last time I heard he was supposed to recover."

"I'm glad, but that doesn't change the fact that people are being killed there. You need to get out and now."

"Rebecca Cloudwebb, I am surprised at you. Yes, I can get out, but what about all the poor people who can't?" Flora's voice took on a messianic fervor as she warmed to her theme. "Those who have no place to go? Those who have no families to look after them? Am I just supposed to go off and leave them in danger?"

"Yes. They aren't your problem. The police are there. It's their job to find the killer."

"They didn't stop Eula Badham from being murdered,

nor Dewayne Harbaugh from being beaten almost to death. Besides, I can't leave here until I hear from Ms. Monroe that it's all legal, and I certainly can't leave here without any clothes or money."

"Hasn't Clarissa brought you your purse?"

"No, though I called and asked for it. She wouldn't pick up, though, so I had to leave a message on the answering machine." Clapping her hand to her mouth, Flora stifled a foul-flavored burp. Luncheon that day had been worse in both food and conversation than usual, which was saying a lot.

"Flora, it could be…"

"All I am asking you to do is find out what you can about Penelope Cattermole, Eula Badham and Dewayne Harbaugh. Please, Rebecca."

Flora seldom said please, at least in that connotation. When uttered as other than a bit of traditional politesse it was a powerful word, she believed – a plea, a beg – and far too much overused and therefore trivialized. When it was used it should be to full emotional effect, and this time it worked.

"All right, I'll see what I can find out. But please – be careful. Don't do any more detecting. Leave that to the professionals. And I want you out of there. As soon as it's legal. I'll send you money if you need it."

Flora made the appropriate noises in spite of being a little offended. She was working on her first assault and her second and third murders, and she wasn't to be considered a professional? Well, maybe an apprentice, if one were to be hard-nosed about it, but hardly an amateur who had never solved anything.

She had been grateful to find that her telephone privileges had not been suspended. She really didn't know if they actually could be, but when Clarissa was in a temper just about anything was possible.

Until Rebecca got back to her there wasn't much she could do. If the police hadn't carried off Dewayne's computers she could have gotten some information off them. It couldn't be that difficult, could it? Just tap a few keys and things appeared on the screen. Dewayne did it without even looking at the keyboard. Surely Flora could have figured it out, but as the computers were now at police headquarters that avenue was closed. Computers didn't seem as difficult as she had thought, Flora decided, so perhaps she should take some lessons once she returned to Dallas. With her grasp of logic learning to use one should be a snap.

A call to Ms. Monroe's office garnered only that she was in court today, and had left word should Mrs. Melkiot call that the court order would be forthcoming soon, probably within a day or two.

Flora sighed. She had hoped to be able to leave tonight – not that she would have, with the murders still unsolved, but she wanted to have the choice. Still, it gave her time to get things ready. She would not walk out of this place looking like this. She had never looked so bad in her life. Not that she cared a thing for public opinion, but if some of those jealous cats in Dallas saw her like this she'd never hear the end of it.

There was a solution to the clothes problem, though, even if she didn't have her money or credit cards. Flora called her favorite salesperson at Neiman Marcus, the woman who had personally assisted her for over twenty years, and explained the mechanics of her problem. Then she gave her an order for two basic outfits, one in black and one in grey, appropriate underthings and a pair of black leather court pumps. Although probably startled by the situation, the saleslady was well trained, agreeing to charge the items to Flora's account and have them delivered no later than tomorrow from their San Antonio store.

There was, Flora thought as she hung up, *a great deal to say for always dealing with a single salesperson.*

Unfortunately, though, she couldn't say the same

thing about her hair. There was no way she was going to go out with her hair chopped off every whichaway and this weird black/white striped bi-color. In spite of the fact he had done her hair for almost twenty years she wouldn't want even Ramon to see her as she looked now. There was a salon here in the facility; she had regarded it with disdain, but at least perhaps they could do something to make her marginally presentable, enough to where she could appear before Ramon without shame. He might be the best hairdresser in Dallas, but he was also the pickiest. To fall afoul of Ramon meant banishment from his Olympus House salon, and there was no way Flora was going to risk that. There was always much too much information to be learned there and Flora did love to keep abreast of what was happening!

The Cold Creek beauty shop was open only during the morning, so to go there now would be useless, and if she couldn't get an appointment by the time she could leave – she almost said 'escape' – she would just go check in at the Menger for a night or two. She and Morris had spent many a happy time at the historic old hotel. Surely the concierge would know of a respectable beauty shop where she could get her hair colored.

Flora approached her last call with a little hesitation. She had no idea that Clarissa would pick up, but just knew – her mother's instinct had always been right on – that she was sitting there listening. Again. When the service beeped, she informed Clarissa that she had ordered suitable clothing and that while there were those who were more than happy to lend her money, she would prefer to handle things on her own, so would Clarissa please bring her purse to the nursing home as quickly as possible. If it were inconvenient for her to bring the purse by, Flora added on impulse, she was sure that Mr. Rothstein would be happy to send someone by from his office to pick it up. Flora made it a point to keep her voice soft and pleasant though she really did feel like shouting. To shout, she believed, showed an excess of emotion and a lack of control, which would give the other person an advantage over you.

Only one more thing to do; while she had stopped believing in the efficacy of lists as a tool of detection, Flora had a tidy mind and, once something was started, she would continue it. Pulling her messy list from the nightstand drawer, she added across the bottom 'Georgia and Al lovers – how long???' It still gave her no solutions, but at least she knew her notes were up to date.

Confident that she had done everything she could for the moment, Flora put the list away, leaned back in bed and reached for the deLeon mystery with a happy little sigh.

* * * * *

"Girl, what are you doing here?" Naomi looked up from counting the post-lunch round of pills, her eyes wide. "You should be resting." Concerned for the other woman's obvious exhaustion and shock, Naomi had sent her to the lounge not half an hour ago.

Melanie shrugged. "Why? I don't have time to rest. If they catch me goofing off they won't pay me for this shift and I need the money."

"You also gotta stay on your feet!" Naomi couldn't help glancing at the young policeman standing just down the hall. He had been there since Dewayne had been discovered and looked like he was going to be there until Judgment Day, which was not altogether a bad thing. He had been most helpful in throwing out a couple of resourceful media-types who had been enterprising enough to find the now-locked employee entrance. That alone had endeared him to the staff.

"I'm doing okay," Melanie said sharply and reached for the tray of waiting medicine cups.

"Are you sure? You had an awful shock, and you're

out on your feet anyway." Naomi snatched the tray back. Miss Enero had made her the nurse in charge, for this shift at least, and she didn't need a zombie doling out the meds to her patients!

"That doesn't matter." Melanie's tired eyes gave pathetic little sparks of anger. "I've been tired before. I need to get money, 'cause if I don't Harley is going to take Davy away from me."

"You don't know that – "

"The hell I don't. He's a sneaky bastard, and so is that whore he's so goggle-eyed about. I won't have that kind of woman close to my son. She'd just as soon knock him around as look at him."

"She's hit Davy?" The idea of someone hitting a child hurt Naomi down to her toes.

"No, I'd have killed her if she had, but you can just bet she will. That kinda scum has a look about them. Oh, she's all gooey-sweet now, just because she wants Harley, and he wants Davy because he knows it will hurt me, but once they get him he won't be safe. I know."

"You know? How?"

"I told you, she has that look. My dad had it too. He was just as nice as punch sometimes, then *wham*! he'd turn around and beat you black and blue without turning a hair." Melanie's face, never pretty at the best of times, went dark and ugly as she gazed into the past.

"And your mother just let him?"

"He'd usually beaten her to a pulp by the time he turned his attention to us. I'm amazed he didn't kill her sometimes. Or us."

"And she just let him?" Naomi could only repeat. Raised in a good Christian home by good Christian people, she had seen a fair amount of arguments – they were human, after all – but had never seen a hand raised against another in anger. Somehow she felt as if the ground had opened up at her feet, leaving a deep and dangerous rift she had never known was there.

"Oh, she left him a couple of times, but she always went back. Each time he'd say it was the last time, and he was getting a new assignment so things would be different there. And she even took him back when he left her." Melanie ground the words so hard Naomi could almost hear her teeth cracking. "She always said that he really loved us, and that if we would just behave and not make him mad he wouldn't get so upset." She gave a harsh bark of laughter. "Upset! Our blood all over the floor and splattering the walls and she called it upset. Sometimes he'd make us clean it up while it was still dripping off us. I tell you, the day he died all us kids danced for joy, but Mama cried, saying he was the only man she could ever love."

"Oh, Melanie, I am so sorry…"

"Don't be. It's over and can't nothing change it. I just gotta do whatever I gotta to keep my Davy out of the hands of those two. I'll kill them both before I let them take Davy away from me. Gimmie that tray."

Shocked to the core, Naomi picked up the tray of waiting medications. Melanie had always been a creature of emotion, given to highs and lows, but Naomi had never heard such venom from her. "Are you sure you're all right?"

"Oh, hell, girl, what do you think?" The dark moment was gone as quickly as it had come, and Melanie gave a flash of her old, impudent grin. "Do you think I'd endanger my patients?"

"No, not deliberately, but you're tired and after seeing Dewayne like that…"

The grin vanished, replaced by a haunted look. "He was a nice guy," she murmured. "I liked him. He was helping me, you know, to keep Davy."

"No, I didn't. And you had to be the one to find him like that – oh, Melanie, that's doubly awful."

Melanie took the tray from Naomi's unresisting fingers. "Yep, but that was this morning. I gotta worry about the now. I gotta worry about Davy."

"Right now you have to worry about keeping the meds straight," Naomi said, very much the nurse in charge. There was no way she was going to let someone under her care be mis-medicated. "Can you do that?"

"Honey…"

"Mrs. Jenks?" Detective Camacho leaned a heavy elbow on the counter. It amazed both women that for such a solid man he could move so soundlessly. "If you're feeling well enough to work, perhaps I could have a few words with you?"

Melanie looked at him with narrowed eyes, then reluctantly handed the tray of medications into Naomi's outstretched hands. "Sure. Why not."

"Shall we step into the doctor's office?" Camacho asked, having taken it for granted that he could use it for a command station.

"Shall we not?" Melanie's reply was uncharacteristically arch. "I've got to help sort meds. Why don't you just ask me here?"

"Very well. I want to talk to you about Dewayne Harbaugh."

* * * * *

Stacey Enero stood in the shadowy darkness of the chapel, looking through the small window at her office, which was still barred with yellow crime scene tape. Small and cluttered though it was, it was still her office. Her place. She had worked hard to achieve it, and harder still to improve the facility. It felt wrong to be banished from it.

Even worse, not to know what they had taken, or how they would react when they read some of her notes in the files. Especially one particular file. Would they believe what they saw, or what she told them?

Or, did they even find what she was afraid they might? Trying as hard as she could, she still could not remember where she had put it. If they hadn't found it, she might have a chance.

If they had…

Stacey gave a little sob. It was like waiting for a sword to fall across your neck.

* * * * *

Flora finished the deLeon mystery with a little sigh of satisfaction. Lighthearted stuff – though murder should most definitely not be lighthearted, at least not in real life – and enjoyable to read. She would have to add deLeon to her list of regular purchases.

"Mrs. Melkiot?"

In spite of herself Flora jumped. She had known from the beginning that there was an intercom system in each room, but hers had never been used before. It was disconcerting to hear one's name coming seemingly from thin air.

"Yes?" Flora was proud that her voice didn't waver in spite of how she had been startled.

"This is the lounge desk – there has been a parcel just delivered for you. Shall we send it back to your room?"

A parcel?

"No, I will come up for it. Just give me a minute." Flora slipped off the too-high bed and groped for the hated terry scuffs. Perhaps she should have ordered some decent bedroom mules while she was at it.

Surely this was the fastest delivery on record. Perhaps the Dallas Neiman-Marcus could take some lessons from the San Antonio one, if they could get an order out this quickly. When she ordered things at home, it usually took twenty-four hours to get something delivered.

Except this was not from Neiman-Marcus, nor from any retail outlet. The box was gaudily colored cardboard, sealed with clear tape, and bore the name of a popular yogurt. Her name was printed on a piece of paper taped to the top, but there was no indication of from where it had come.

Flora regarded the box with interest. Obviously this was nothing she had ordered, and just as obviously was not a gift. No one she knew would send anything in such a tacky way. She had been asking a lot of uncomfortable questions; could it be a bomb? Or an animal head, like in that old movie? Or…

"Would you like me to open it for you?" the receptionist asked kindly.

For a moment Flora was tempted, but if it were a bomb it would be unconscionable to let this nice woman be blown up in her place.

"No, but I would appreciate the loan of a pair of scissors."

Obligingly the receptionist – apparently not knowing how close she had come to being blown up – handed over a pair of scissors. Lifting the box carefully, Flora was not cheered to hear something solid going 'thump' inside. She carried it to the far corner of the room and put it on one of the small tables. *At least*, Flora thought, *if it blows up here casualties and damage can be minimized.* Except to her, of course.

Not knowing how exactly a bomb could be triggered, Flora cut carefully into the tape, lifting each flap of the box with exaggerated care.

It was not a bomb.

Looking at the classic black leather purse Flora experienced a moment of sentimentality. Morris had bought this for her on their last trip to Paris, their last real trip to anywhere, as the cancer had brought him low just a few months after their return home. It was an Hermès bag, and even as he paid for it Morris had protested that it cost as much as a good used car. Morris had been gone for almost a decade, but the bag still looked as if it had just been taken out of the showroom.

The moment of memory vanished, vanquished by a

spurt of annoyance. What had Clarissa meant by putting it in this cardboard box without even so much as a piece of tissue paper to protect it? The edges of the inside flaps were rough and could have scratched the leather.

A quick inspection proved that the precious bag was undamaged, and Flora opened it with no little trepidation – not that she feared Clarissa would send her a bomb, that was foolish – but for what might be missing.

As far as Flora could tell, nothing was gone. The three crisply ironed handkerchiefs without which she never left the house were there, along with all the usual stuff – comb, lipstick, compact, pen, checkbook, even her sunglasses, though they had been broken in the accident. Shame; they had been very good ones. And very expensive.

What was important, though, was her wallet. It was there too, and a quick glance showed everything was inside – driver's license, credit cards, even the Medicare card Flora always carried but never used; she had a deep distrust of the government having anything to do with her healthcare or anything else that should be private. Even the money didn't seem to have been touched; Flora had no idea of the exact amount she had had in her purse, but there was a fair total and it didn't seem logical that anyone would take some of it and leave this much behind.

Now the only question was had Clarissa canceled her credit cards? Was Clarissa even that smart? Of course, canceling the cards would not keep Flora here for more than a day or two, even if she didn't borrow from Rebecca or Ms. Monroe. Mrs. Morris Melkiot could get a credit card from any bank on a minute's notice.

The only thing missing in the box was any sort of apology from Clarissa. There wasn't any kind of note at all. Although Flora knew her child well enough not to expect any kind of apology the lack still caused a twinge of hurt.

Leaving the empty box on the table Flora took her

purse and went back to her room. She'd have to find a safe place to stash her things; one of the things the staff repeated often was that some people weren't as honest as they should be and that was why personal items of value should either be given to family members or locked away in the director's office safe.

It also gives this place even more control over the inmates, Flora thought grimly. *Even if they could get out of here, what would they do for money and identification?* It was frightening. Still, she would have to find a hiding place, because she had no intention of handing her autonomy over to Cold Creek Health Care Facility any more than she had of having it taken by Clarissa.

Unfortunately, her strictly functional room didn't offer any hiding places. Very well, she would just keep it with her. Several of the ladies – the more mental ones – carried handbags, but they seldom contained anything more than a packet of tissues or a couple of mints. One of the nurses had said that the ladies had always carried handbags in their regular life, and carrying one now gave them a sense of normalcy.

Normal? Flora had almost snorted at that. As if anything in this place could ever be considered normal. She regretted the implication of instability that carrying her purse with her might impart, but keeping it in her hands was the safest thing. After a moment's thought, she added the small notepad from her nightstand and a novel by Sandra Parshall. Now she might look addled, but she was prepared. Pity she didn't have any pepper spray – it might come in handy in this place. Clarissa still had her jewelry, but that was all right; fortunately she hadn't been wearing anything spectacular or particularly valuable on the day of the accident except her wedding ring, and she would get that back later. Not even Clarissa would think she could get away with keeping her wedding ring from her, and if Flora couldn't get her daughter to return it, Ms. Monroe could. In the meantime there was no use tempting anyone here with diamonds of that size.

Flora stopped, struck by a sudden realization. Nurses and certainly orderlies didn't make very much, not enough to afford watches like the one Al had been wearing. Seems as if she had heard some gossip about him having a fancy red convertible, too. The nurse Georgia couldn't afford goodies like that, not unless she was independently wealthy, and if she was, why was she working here? Had one or both of them been stealing from the inmates? Or did Al have other generous 'friends'?

The latter was more likely, Flora decided. It was possible that Al and or Georgia had been stealing, but it was hardly probable. The class of patient at Cold Creek wouldn't appear to have the kinds of assets that would be necessary to support such expensive tastes and even if they had they certainly wouldn't have brought them here. A little bit, yes – the occasional chain or crucifix or wedding ring, perhaps even a couple of dollars of spending money, but it wasn't logical there would be more.

Unless Eula Badham was right, Flora thought wryly, *and there was a money laundering operation going on here.*

I have to get out of here, she realized with a start. *If I start thinking someone as crazy as Eula Badham was right, that means I'm going as looney as she was!*

Chapter Eighteen

Chin in his hands, Detective Camacho sat in the doctor's office after he had dismissed Melanie Jenks. Crazy woman who positively hated her husband, and wanted to talk about nothing but how bad he and the whorish woman he shacked up with were and how she would never let them steal her son, but aside from the fact she was groggy with fatigue – which seeing she was on duty was scary– she seemed to be giving him the straight story. That was the trouble. Everyone here was just as you would expect them to be. Okay, he admitted he wouldn't want his life to be dependent on some of the nurses, but this was a long-term care nursing home and rehab center, not a hospital.

All he had really learned was that the killer had to be in the facility; the security tapes proved that. Some of the patients were looney enough to kill, but few of them were strong enough. Any of the staff were strong enough.

Whoever finds the body is usually the killer, Camacho thought, but as much as he would like to he couldn't see Princey Doolittle in that role. The kid was a loser, and definitely a criminal type. His rap sheet was as long as your arm, but it was all petty, juvenile-type stuff. Public intox. Possession. Disorderly. Shoplifting. All of it barely enough to rate a state jail term. Doolittle was strong enough to kill, and probably would if pushed too far or made so afraid he feared for his life. Camacho couldn't see any of the three victims putting the little coward in that position. Besides, Doolittle hadn't been here for the second and third assaults.

Flora Melkiot had found the Badham woman, but although she was a pain in the ass her record was sterling and Camacho doubted she had anything to do with either death.

Melanie Jenks had found Harbaugh, but she was a nurse. It was her job to help people, not beat them to death. Camacho was certain that Harbaugh had been meant to die and that it was just pure luck and the grace of God that he had been found in time.

The question that was driving him crazy was why? What had these three people done to so enrage someone that they would kill? They were all so different. What was the motive? Why these three? Camacho couldn't think of any reason three such different people should have been targeted. As horrific as it was, neither could he ignore the fact that there just might be a homicidal maniac roaming the sterile halls of Cold Creek Health Care Facility. God knew living here could make someone crazy.

Maybe when Harbaugh woke up – if he woke up – he could tell them who had attacked him, but Camacho couldn't wait for that. He had to protect these people from yet another death.

Another thing bothering him was Flora Melkiot. The woman was a danger – snooping around and asking questions and poking into places she had no business being. Ashdown had warned him, but he hadn't realized how true his words had been. The worst thing about her, the thing that was driving him crazy, was that she was in a better position to gather some information than he was. She was one of them, so the patients were much more likely to talk to her than to him. Oh, they had talked to him all right, at great length and with all kinds of crazy theories, but they hadn't told him anything substantial. The Melkiot woman probably knew more about what was going on here than he did.

He really needed to get back to his office, to normalcy, to where he felt comfortable, so he could really look over the new evidence and be able to concentrate on it. To try to make sense of it. He knew there was something here, something he hadn't yet been able to put his finger on, something that could make everything fall into place if he could just find it, but for all his thinking he didn't have the slightest idea of what it was or how to get it.

Camacho sighed and faced the fact that he really didn't want to. It was inevitable. He would have to bring the Melkiot woman into the investigation.

* * * * *

For once in his life music didn't soothe Bobby Jensen. He sat at the baby grand piano that almost filled the tiny room, but his fingers couldn't seem to touch the keys.

Once a humble guest house, and before that a maid's quarters, the little building was now somewhat pretentiously designated as his studio. Here he could come and play at any hour of the day or night without bothering Maxine. She was dismissive of his music, calling it a time waster and a stupid hobby. She never had appreciated his gift, his passion. All she cared about was a spectacular house and fashionable clothes and being one of the leading lights of the country club. A good wife would support her husband's dreams, not laugh at them.

Sometimes he hated her.

Sometimes he hated her almost as much as he hated Cold Creek Health Care Facility. He always felt he could do anything it took to get away from it.

Today had shaken him. It was one thing to evaluate charts and sign drug requisitions and certify that some poor old soul had finally shuffled off this mortal coil, but it was entirely another to have a patient attacked – the third one in as many days – and to have to kneel in still-warm blood, to see the meat beneath the skin, to have a man's life in his hands. It had made him physically ill. The whole loathsome incident reminded him of the messier parts of his med school years and his residency, times he could never remember without shuddering. Body fluids and excretions and pain and mess and inevitable death… to a person of his artistic temperament it was a life in hell.

Things had to change, whatever it took. He was tired of waiting for his family money, money that rightfully should be his now, money that should be supporting his talent instead of suppressing it. He was a musician, a great one if anyone had the intelligence to recognize it. He could earn his living making music. Without the distractions of his job at Cold Creek he could really concentrate and finish something.

Maxine would be angry, but then Maxine was always angry. Another distraction he could live without. He could move his clothes down here, have a bed put in and never be forced into seeing her or going to the house or to the nursing home ever again. Then he could truly accomplish something great.

As if acting under their own volition his fingers crept to the keys, coaxing out the unfailing anodyne of pleasing harmonies and satisfying chords.

* * * * *

After being sure that Detective Camacho had left the facility Stacey Enero sat at the big fancy desk in Bobby Jensen's big fancy office. She had never felt so uncomfortable in her life. Although she had longed for something like this, now she wanted nothing more than to return to her tiny, messy little womb of an office, even though she doubted that she ever could, not really. It could never be the same.

The detective had told her that they would be releasing her office before long, and the first thing she intended to do was buy a new desk. There was no way the owners could object to getting rid of the blood-soaked old wooden one, was there? That was, assuming the place stayed open, and if it did if she still had a job.

A job she'd better start doing; at the moment she was still employed, which meant she should be working. Stacey turned her attention to the box at her feet. Camacho had been as good as his word and returned the files. They were out of order, and positively bristled with uneven pages – so unlike the regimented perfection she preferred – but at the moment that didn't matter. She could straighten them as she worked. Right now it was important to update them from the computer database, so full information was available in both digital and hard copy formats. Records were important in health care; one wrong dose of medicine or one inappropriate treatment could have horrific consequences. Even the mundane records of where and when supplies had been ordered and what a patient had eaten were important. A place had to be tightly run if it was going to be efficient.

Stacey booted up Dr. Jensen's computer, a large fancy model that looked as if it had never been used, and logged on to the medical database for the facility, then picked the first file out of the box. The task shouldn't take too long; there had been no major incidents or changes since they had been removed.

Such dedication was admirable, but impossible to sustain. She had barely finished updating her second file before Stacey gave up and sat on the floor by the box. Telling herself that it would be much more efficient to have the files in the proper order, Stacey riffled through them, her throat catching as if she were being strangled when she realized that the one file she really wanted wasn't there.

* * * * *

An afternoon's worth of thinking had done Flora little

good, leaving her more than a bit cranky even though she would never have admitted it. She always regarded her own temperament as consistently and elegantly level. Not even the consumption of a large number of chocolates had helped – an unusual indulgence, as Flora really did like to preserve her figure. The trouble was that she had no definite information on which she could ponder. Nothing was solid – nothing that she knew of anyway, and the police certainly weren't being of any help.

No, what she needed to know she would have to find out herself. Like who had been seen going into Dewayne's room before Melanie; if she knew that she was almost certain she would know who the murderer was. Unfortunately, that could mean talking to everyone in the place, and who knew if they'd tell the actual facts or come up with all kinds of weird tales about space aliens and drug lords.

She was so deep in thought that when the telephone rang she actually jumped.

Just another example of how deleterious being here is, she thought crossly, snapping a curt 'yes' into the receiver.

"Wow! What's got you so ticked off?" asked Rebecca Cloudwebb.

Flora shook her head, knowing that Rebecca couldn't see it. She was indeed slipping, allowing her emotions to show like that.

"Frustration," she answered in civil tones. "If you aren't crazy when you come in here, you most certainly will be before long."

"How's that revocation of the guardianship coming along?"

"It should be finalized by tomorrow at the latest. At least, I hope so."

"So how are you getting home?"

"I haven't decided yet. I am having some clothes delivered, so I can look decent traveling, and Clarissa did return my purse, so I shall not have to depend on others for financial aid."

There was a moment of dead air, then Rebecca's words spilled out in a torrent as if escaping. "Would you like me to come down there and get you?"

Flora was touched. She and Rebecca had been friendly, but never really friends, never what Flora had always regarded as friends, but this was a generous offer.

"Thank you, but I shan't put you to such effort," Flora said in as warm a tone as she could muster. "I do appreciate the offer, though."

"You aren't staying there just to try and solve the murders, are you?"

Flora's warm and fuzzy feelings evaporated. How could this – this stranger! – know her so well? Or be so rude as to make it sound like an accusation?

"I do feel that I should give them the benefit of my expertise."

"Oh, Flora – " Rebecca began, then gave a sigh so deep that even through the telephone receiver Flora could almost feel the breeze riffling her hair. "Well, if you're determined, and I know you are, you'd better listen to what I found out about those people."

"You have answers already?" Flora asked, impressed in spite of herself. "That was quick."

"There's probably more – this is just a down and dirty first look. Who do you want first?"

"Dewayne Harbaugh. He's still living, and if someone is out to get him we need to be able to stop them."

Rebecca sighed again, but wisely said nothing more. "Okay… Dewayne Harbaugh was a big-shot computer programmer. Worked for one of the big governmental contractors. Turns out there was some hanky-panky going on – don't know exactly what yet – but he turned whistleblower. Testified in front of a congressional committee and everything. Then all of a sudden his car blew up. No one ever caught for it. It was a miracle he survived. He got a really big settlement and the story kind of got hushed up; apparently it would have embarrassed too many people if everything was made public. Now he freelances in computer stuff."

"So that's where his money comes from," Flora murmured. "I hope he negotiated a very good deal."

"What?"

"Nothing. Anything more?"

"Not on him. And there's nearly nothing on this Eula Badham. Born into a decent farming family eighty three years ago, married her high school sweetheart, lived in the same small town all her life, had two children – both dead now – and lived an absolutely blameless life. Only other thing that I could find out about her was that she liked to arrange flowers. Won a couple of prizes, in fact."

"A Federal whistleblower and a small town flower arranger. Doesn't make sense," Flora said. "They had nothing in common. What about the Cattermole?"

Rebecca sighed. "Penelope Cattermole was a real piece of work. There's a lot of information about her, including some she'd probably rather no one knew. Raised by a single mother who supported them by working as a barmaid-slash-prostitute, she ran away from home when she was sixteen. Probably some abuse going on there, I think, but no record of it. She married a soldier, and found her milieu. As far as I could determine she had six husbands before marrying the General, except he was only a Colonel then. Got to be a General only after marrying her."

"Probably was afraid not to," Flora said.

"She was a player, that's for sure. Broke up a few homes in her marital career. Always married a serviceman and always married up in rank. Even changed forces – went from Army to Navy and then back to the Army and finally ended up with the Air Force. After she married Cattermole she became all holier than thou and highly moralistic. No one dared set a foot wrong around her. Made a lot of enemies, too. Nothing worse than a reformed rake."

"Do you know what company Dewayne worked for and when?"

Accustomed to Flora's mental twists and turns, Rebecca dug in her notes before naming one of the government's largest contractors and a date only a few years before.

Flora thought furiously for a moment, then said, "General Cattermole was still active duty then, wasn't he?"

"And Dewayne's company did business with the Air Force." Rebecca was indeed quick. "Do you think there was something between them?"

"I don't know," Flora said slowly. "I wouldn't put it past the Cattermole to be using her husband's rank to sell influence, but you didn't see her. She couldn't speak without spitting – " here Flora gave a reminiscent shudder " – and could hardly get around unaided. Besides, why would either of them wait so long if there were bad blood or anything between them? No, I think there's a third player in this. Remember, nothing happened until the Cattermole came here. And she was killed before Dewayne was attacked."

"So you think there was someone who was afraid if they got together and compared notes something damaging could come out?"

"It makes sense." Which was a ridiculous affirmation, Flora knew, as all her ideas made sense.

"What about Eula Badham? There's no evidence that she had anything to do with any of this."

Flora shrugged. That point had been bothering her, too. "She was always saying that she knew too much. Obviously she was as mad as a hatter, but this third person might not have known that. He or she might have regarded her babblings as a threat. Or perhaps she just got in the way. She was just a crazy little old lady, and someone who has already killed might not even think twice about another murder."

"God, how cold." Rebecca's voice held a shudder of horror that her years as a police detective had never been able to wash away. "I'm going to do some more digging on this. And remember, I'll come get you whenever you say. I'd be a lot happier if you were out of there."

It wasn't until after they had hung up that Flora admitted to herself, "So would I."

"Mrs. Melkiot?" The tinny voice came out of the intercom just as Flora put her hand on the door to leave. This time she didn't jump, but for one millisecond thoughts of being constantly watched ran over her like stinging ants.

"Yes?"

"This is the front desk, Mrs. Melkiot. You have a visitor."

Perhaps Clarissa come to apologize? It startled Flora how that idea pleased her. It was not right for a child to be so defiant of a parent, and Clarissa should be mature enough to admit it. She would never stand for any of her boys to act like she had.

Smiling, Flora put her bag over her arm and walked down to the lounge.

It wasn't Clarissa. It wasn't anyone she had ever seen before. A nice looking man just on the cusp of middle age and wearing a very good suit, he stepped forward as soon as Flora entered.

"Mrs. Melkiot? I'm Jonathan Buckman, of Rothstein and Partners. Mr. Rothstein asked me to give you his sincerest apologies for not coming himself, but he is in court today."

Flora extended her hand and shook his, murmuring something polite.

"Here are the papers rescinding the guardianship your daughter instituted. We have already given copies to the management here, both on site and the corporate offices, but Mr. Rothstein wanted you to have yours personally."

Probably so they can bill me for another hour, Flora thought ungraciously, but her polite smile didn't slip. "That is most kind of all of you. Now these papers mean that I can go when and where I please?"

"Indeed. You are now your own boss. We want to thank you for letting us help you and assure you that if you ever need legal assistance or advice again, Rothstein and Partners will be happy to assist." He even gave a little bow.

Flora assured him that were she ever in need in San Antonio again she would be certain to call. After a few social platitudes he left with all the dignity of an anointed king. As she was sticking the unopened envelope into her purse Flora wondered if there were some special master class for expensive lawyers where they learned to walk like that.

Now she had her own life back in her own hands. Finally! Flora almost did a little jig of happiness. Her purse was once again in her possession and she had a sheaf of papers legally assuring her that she could do what she wanted. Once her new clothes were delivered she would be ready and able to leave when she wished. It was turning out to be a very good day, Flora decided, walking back to her room.

Now she just had to find out who had been seen going into Dewayne's room that morning.

Chapter Nineteen

Naomi was determined. Melanie might be working, but she was so exhausted she was almost staggering. It didn't matter how badly she needed the money, she didn't need to be working this shift, especially not with all the stress she'd been under recently. While she might be fine for straightening covers and helping patients to the bathroom and other minor tasks, Naomi was positive there was no way she was capable enough to take care of dispensing the evening meds. And there was no way she was going to let her.

Miss Enero was in the doctor's office, and a policeman had brought back a big box of files, probably the ones they had taken from her desk. That meant the administrator would be busy for quite some time. She hadn't told Naomi to continue being Head Nurse, but on the other hand she hadn't told her not to. Georgia, the regular Head Nurse on the day shift, didn't seem to be around anywhere, and with Melanie so unreliable at the moment Naomi simply decided to continue with her duties. After all, she still had the drug cabinets key.

Except it wasn't needed. Although the door was closed, it wasn't locked and one glance inside showed why. Every shelf was a mess, and the tray with the Level Four meds was totally empty.

Naomi's first impulse was to run screaming in panic, but then she was stopped by the thought that she was Head Nurse. Head Nurses didn't run screaming, they handled things in a controlled and businesslike manner. She was in charge; she should act like it.

Taking a deep breath, Naomi closed the doors and locked them, then made herself walk calmly down to Dr. Jensen's office. She knocked, but did not wait for an answer, instead stepping right in.

"Miss Enero, we have a problem."

* * * * *

Her plan of action solidified in her mind, Flora wandered down the hall with seeming disinterest. The patients seemed more active than usual; perhaps everything was not all bleak. The murders and the assault on Dewayne seemed in some perverse way to have stimulated all of them.

Perhaps, she thought, *what they need is not so much gentle care as it is mental activity.* She made a note to investigate such an idea. The concept intrigued her so much that she almost fell over Sophia O'Connor's motorized wheelchair.

Frail though she might be, Sophia's mind was untouched; so, apparently, was her taste, as her eyes widened at the sight of Flora's handbag.

"Going upscale, aren't you? That's a lovely purse."

Flora caressed the smooth leather with her fingertips. "Thank you. It was one of the last gifts my late husband gave me."

Raising an almost transparent hand, Sophia touched the leather almost reverently with a shaking finger. "He had good taste, obviously. You can always tell quality, can't you?"

Flora agreed; such a belief was one of the cornerstones of her life. She had always detested anything that was cheap and shoddy. The image of her exquisite condo back in Dallas flashed before her with a pang of overwhelming desire. Even though she had wanted to leave as soon as possible, now that she had the revocation of Clarissa's guardianship she knew in her heart she couldn't, not until this mess was cleaned up. If she did, she'd be haunted by Eula Badham's plea for help, the plea she had ignored. It wasn't often that Flora felt ashamed.

"One certainly can. Sophia, I need your help. Did you happen to see anyone around Dewayne Harbaugh's room before Melanie Jenks found him?"

Sophia's eyes sparkled before her expression clouded. "So you are investigating the murders and poor Dewayne? I had heard gossip about that, but wasn't sure. To answer your question, I was in my room when I heard Melanie screaming. I hadn't been out of it until I came out to see what was going on. Poor Dewayne… I've heard he's holding his own."

How much Dewayne would hate hearing himself called 'Poor Dewayne,' Flora thought.

"We can only hope that he survives," Flora said with a deep sincerity. "He's obviously been through so much."

"Aren't you afraid the killer will target you for nosing around?"

Flora shrugged. The idea had occurred to her, but in her assurance that she could handle anything it didn't bother her much. After all, after Laura Tyler's murder she had felt uncharacteristically vulnerable and had taken a self-defense class for seniors offered by the new owners of the exercise salon at the Olympus House. The instructor had complimented her several times on her progress during classes.

"He – or she – won't be able to do anything once he's caught."

"Can I help? Do you want me to ask around about anyone entering Dewayne's room?"

Smiling, Flora felt entirely justified. Everyone wanted this killer caught, and the more eyes the better. *The killer*, she thought in almost certainly probable error, *couldn't murder everyone!*

"Hey, two of the prettiest babes in the place!"

Strutting like a banty cock, Fred Moretti strolled up, a gleam in his eye.

"And one of the blindest men," Flora retorted without heat. As much as she liked compliments, she was unfailingly honest.

"I got some information you might like," he said with a grin towards Flora.

"Really? What?"

His grin widened. "What'll I get for it?"

Flora's eyes hardened. "You will get a deep and sincere thank you, plus the knowledge that you did the right thing."

"Hey, ain't no fun in that."

"Oh for Heaven's sake, Fred, this is no time for your jokes," Sophia said with annoyance. "People are dying."

"People die here almost every day," he said without spirit. "But hey, you're right. We all gotta pull together, right?"

"So what do you know?"

"It's like this, Miss Flora, there's some serious shit going down here. Someone's been stealing drugs."

My God, Flora thought as the pit of her stomach plummeted, *drugs. Eula Badham was right, and no one believed her!*

Aloud she asked, "How do you know this?"

A little of his cocksureness came back. "I was standing in the hallway a little while ago, just to see what I could see, you understand, and that cute little darkie nurse opened the meds cabinet to dole out our evening happy pills. Well, she took one look inside and went dead white – as white as she could, you understand…"

"Get on with it, Mr. Moretti," Flora ordered crisply, her distaste for his crudity vying with her desire to hear what he had to say.

"Well, I could see the inside of that cabinet. I've seen it before, you know – it's open to anyone to see when they're dealing out the pills and you happen to be close by."

"Fred!" Sophia snapped.

"There's a reason, there's a reason… normally it's as neat as a pin. Every bottle in place, and the thing dang near full. This time it was about half empty and it looked like it had been picked up and shaken. I mean, bottles everywhere, on their side, everything."

"And you're sure some were missing?"

"Of course. I said it was half empty, didn't I? That means lots of 'em are missing. Well, this little girl didn't scream or anything. She just closed the doors, locked them and went straight to Miss Enero."

"As she should have. What did they say?"

He shrugged. "I dunno. She closed the door and there was too many people around for me to get a good listen."

"Mrs. Melkiot?" Looking a little nervous and standing just a bit further away than necessary was a young policeman. Flora couldn't be sure, but he might have been the one she had hit with her cast when he got in her way.

"Yes?"

"Detective Camacho would like to see you in Dr. Jensen's office. Now, if you please. I was sent to bring you." He looked as unhappy about it as Flora felt.

Well, it didn't make any difference what the police knew about her activities now. She looked at Sophia and Fred and said, "You have to help me. Talk to everyone you can and see if you can find anyone who saw someone entering or leaving Dewayne's room before Melanie found him."

They both nodded and split in different directions. The young policeman was wise enough not to offer her his arm, and in fact stayed more than an arm's length away from her.

"You shouldn't have done that," he said mildly. "You might have put them in danger."

"Young man, we are all in danger. It is the police

department's job to keep us safe, and as far as I'm concerned, you have been doing a wretched job of it." Flora said tartly. "If you all had done your job properly, Eula Badham would still be alive and Dewayne Harbaugh would not be in the hospital fighting for his life."

The officer looked suitably chastened, but said nothing. He merely opened the door to Dr. Jensen's office and said, "Mrs. Melkiot, Detective Camacho."

* * * * *

Detective Camacho had not really been surprised by the call summoning him back to Cold Creek. The surprising thing was that it had been from Stacey Enero.

"So you're missing drugs."

"Yes. Lots of them."

"Don't you have controls on that?"

"Yes, of course we do!" Stacey snapped. "That's why I've suspected theft for a while, but couldn't prove anything. There's never been anything on this scale, however. Nothing this blatant."

Camacho's face was unreadable. "And you're just now finding this out?"

"You've obviously read the file I've been keeping, so that's a silly question. I've known there have been drugs missing for quite a while now, but it's seemed like just a few pills here and there – not that that's acceptable, but I had no way of tracking down who was doing it."

"But now you do?"

"I have an idea. When I logged on to Dr. Jensen's computer today and started checking the drugs he had ordered against what was registered in to the system I realized something was very wrong."

"You're the administrator," Camacho said in cold tones. "Didn't you know what was going on?"

"I told you I suspected. I couldn't prove anything other than a couple of pills were missing from every order.

I did tell Dr. Jensen about it and I emailed the owners about the situation, but it ended there. Bobby Jensen is notorious for not seeing what he doesn't want to see. I don't know about the owners, but that's what I was supposed to do and that's what I did. That's why I started keeping the file you found, so when I had enough evidence I could go to the owners personally."

Camacho kept his mouth shut and his face neutral. It wasn't easy; as far as he was concerned Stacy Enero was at the very least stealing drugs from the nursing home. The file she had been keeping of shipments and drugs missing was an indictment – though he did think it was clever of her to come up with the cover story of keeping an eye on the shortages. He couldn't really figure out why she had killed the two women and tried to kill the black man, but he was sure the reasons would come out as his investigation went on. He tried a different tack.

"The medicine supply cabinet is kept locked, isn't it?"

"Of course. All the time except when the medicine is being dispensed or – rarely – it's opened when there's an emergency. It's one of our most stringent rules."

"Mrs. Case said the cabinet was unlocked. Not broken into, but unlocked."

"Yes." Her mouth, normally classically sculpted, tightened into a hard knot. "And that's not supposed to happen."

"Who has the keys?"

"There are just three keys. One is kept in the main office downtown, where the owners keep keys to all their holdings in a safe. One is mine, and one is kept in the safe in my office and given to the Head Nurse at the beginning of every shift." Guiltily Stacey realized that she had given the key to Naomi and never gotten it back. She trusted Naomi, but… it was a breach of protocol, and her fault. Damn!

"Was it unlocked earlier?"

"Not that I know of." Stacey gave a little sigh. That was such a wimpy, cop-out answer. She was supposed to be in charge, to know everything, and yet all kinds of horrible things were happening. The world she had worked so hard to create was becoming a nightmare, crumbling about her as she watched, and it seemed that she could do nothing.

"Do you think Mrs. Case is part of it?"

"No. I'd stake my life on Naomi Case being a straight arrow. She's a widow with several children and she's going to school too."

"So she could probably use some easy money," Camacho said, amazed that the Enero woman could give him such an open shot. Of course, if she were trying to protect herself she could have deliberately thrown the black nurse under the bus.

"Who couldn't? Nurses are notoriously underpaid, especially in a facility like this. So," she added with an unexpected wry humor, "are administrators."

"Could the key have been copied?"

"Do you mean is it one of those fancy ones that can't be duplicated? No, it's not one of those, just a normal key. I suppose it could have been copied, but I don't have any idea of where or when. It wouldn't be easy, not with our schedules. You'd have to leave the facility with the key… I'd have said it was impossible, but obviously it's not. Of course, there's the key in the corporate office. I assume there are people there who can open the safe."

"Who are the owners?"

Stacey held out a piece of paper covered in her scrawly handwriting. "A consortium of doctors. Here's the company name, and I've added as many of the individual doctors as I could find. There may be more; this is a tax thing for them, so they aren't really forthcoming about any of it."

"Do you think they might have something to do with the missing drugs?"

"I don't know. Yesterday I would have said no – I mean, these guys are top level doctors from all over the country. As a group they probably gross as much per year as some states do. Why would they risk it all for what would be small potatoes for them? It doesn't make sense."

Camacho took the paper, but said nothing. Sometimes when people got a chance to make easy money they'd do it no matter what, and rich people were the worst about it.

"So who do you think is behind this? Dr. Jensen?"

Stacey looked troubled. "It looks like it, doesn't it? But I don't believe it. Bobby Jensen is not a crook. He's too stupid to be one. Anyone with any smarts would have avoided leaving a paper trail like this to himself. For one thing, there aren't any copies of official requisitions – requisitions I might add, that have to be countersigned by me. They're multi-part forms; I keep one, Dr. Jenson keeps one, one goes to the main office and one goes to the supplier. There's a monthly report that goes to the state. And, since I've been here a copy has been scanned into a computer file."

"Paper copies?"

"These are Level Four drugs – heavy duty stuff. There has to be a paper trail."

"State law?"

Stacey smiled. "Better than that – owners' law."

"So there's no record of all these pills that have gone missing? How do you know, then?"

"By the bills. However they were ordered, they had to be paid for. When the first bill came in I thought it was just a mix-up. I hadn't been in charge for long, and the place was a terrible mess. The previous administrator… well, she didn't do much."

"But Dr. Jensen signed the orders."

"Yes. After I had been here for a while and gotten things pretty much under control, there had been two orders like this. I paid the bills, of course, but I also wrote our supplier and asked for copies of our orders. They sent them, and they just had Dr. Jensen's signature."

"What did he say about it?"

"He just shook his head and said there must have been a mix-up. I reminded him that drug orders had to have both our signatures on them."

"What did he say?"

"He just nodded and said 'of course.' I don't believe he was even listening. He was working on his music… in his head. I can always tell. His fingers… it's like he's playing the piano."

"I've seen him."

"Anyway, I put a bug in our supplier's ear that no order was to be filled unless it had both our signatures on it, and that they were to send me a copy of every order we got from them… without telling anyone."

"And they did?"

Stacey flashed a quick smile. "We buy a lot from them… Besides, they wouldn't like to get a bad rep from us. Cold Creek is a small outfit, but the owners are heavy players with lots of facilities that buy from them. And to answer your question, yes. I've gotten a paper copy of every order they've received. And each one has had two signatures – one of Dr. Jensen's, and one theoretically of mine."

"A forgery?" Camacho asked, a new vista of possibilities opening up in front of him in spite of his perpetual cynicism.

"Dr. Jensen's looks real enough. I'm not an expert, but I've seen enough of his signatures to believe that it is. I do know that mine was a forgery, because I didn't write it. It doesn't even look like mine."

A good way to pass off a real signature as a forgery, the detective thought, *is to make it so obvious that no one will believe you wrote it.* Aloud he said, "So it is Dr. Jensen."

Stacey shook her head. "I don't think so. Oh, I'll bet that he signed each of those orders, but like I told you,

Bobby Jensen is stupid. He'll sign anything stuck in front of him, especially if he's in a hurry to leave. It's a joke around here."

"That doesn't seem very safe."

"It isn't. One time on a dare one of the nurses had him sign a letter authorizing her to take six months paid vacation. Luckily she didn't hold him to it."

"If he's that bad, how has he held on to his position here?"

"He comes from a family with money, detective," Stacy said in a voice heavy with bitterness. "He doesn't have to worry about holding on to his position. His father is one of the major owners."

"Oh." *That*, Camacho thought bleakly, *put a completely different spin on the problem.* "What do you think this drug theft has to do with the murders?"

Stacey's face clouded. "I have no idea. All three victims were residents. I can't see how they are connected, but they must be. Maybe one of them saw something, but all three? I don't know. I just don't know."

Camacho didn't either.

There was a preemptory knock just as the door opened.

"Mrs. Melkiot, Detective Camacho."

Chapter Twenty

The silence in the room thickened as Flora and the detective stared at each other. They sat in the two visitors' chairs, the space between them no more than a yard or two of carpet, though it might as well have been a bottomless chasm. Sensing a battle of titans to come, Stacey Enero had quit the field, saying she had some things to attend to on the floor.

"Well, detective," said Flora at last, using her most autocratic voice, "you wanted to see me?"

"Yes, Mrs. Melkiot," Camacho replied. It was amazing how his throat had tightened, how he was having to force the words out.

"About the murders, the attempted murder or the drugs?" Flora said briskly and was gratified at the flash of astonishment that went over the policeman's face.

"Are you telling me you know about the drugs?"

"Are you telling me you didn't?" Flora saw no reason to tell him she had only known about them for a few minutes. Though she would have, she thought mournfully, if she had only believed Eula Badham earlier.

"How did you know?"

"How did Eula Badham die?"

"Strangulation and a broken neck. Your turn, Mrs. Melkiot."

Inwardly Flora smiled. Now that he was obviously out of his depth Detective Camacho had decided to turn to her. Finally.

"Only a short while." He didn't have to know just

how short.

"How did you find out?"

"Detection and interviewing, Detective. What you would probably call plain old gossip. And observation. Many of the inmates here are just old – not blind nor stupid."

"And they talk to you."

"Because I listen to them. I don't interrogate them, pity them or dismiss them because they are old. And they know I will believe them."

Most of them. Eula Badham…

"And doubtless you've solved the case." Camacho didn't like being forced into a defensive posture, and so became sarcastic.

"I think I might have," Flora said, enjoying the look of shock in his eyes. "You might look into an orderly named Al. I apologize, but I don't know his last name."

"An orderly… What makes you think it might be him?"

"First of all, his watch. No orderly can afford a watch that expensive on the salaries they pay here. Even Melkiot's sells only a few per year in our most affluently located stores." Flora made a mental note to talk with her son in law Bill about further upgrading some of the higher end merchandise in their better stores. "And when I mentioned how lovely it was, he told me it was a family heirloom his grandfather left him."

"Maybe it was."

Flora's expression became even more haughty. "That particular watch has been made for only three years. I hardly think that's adequate time to be considered an heirloom."

Camacho nodded. It merited investigation, at least. "So how do you think this Al got into the medicine cabinet?"

"With a key, of course, as the lock wasn't broken." *Honestly*, Flora thought with some asperity, *does he expect me to do all his work for him?* but she kept her voice civil and sophisticated.

"And how did he get this key?"

Flora sighed. "I can think of several different ways that it could be done fairly easily, but the most obvious is that he had an accomplice – someone who had legitimate access to it."

Stacey Enero, Camacho thought in a wave of vindication. "Do you have a guess as to who this accomplice is?"

"I don't have to guess," Flora said in tones of unmistakable authority. "But let's be fair in our little information trade-off. Have you found the airplane model that killed Penelope Cattermole yet?"

Badly shaken, the detective jumped. "How the hell did you know about that?"

"Detection again, detective." Flora really was trying hard not to sound smug, but it was difficult. "Detection and observation, pure and simple. Have you found it?"

"Yes," he admitted after a pause that was just a little too long. "Buried in the bottom of one of the bins of dirty sheets. And before you ask, it was clean. Looked like it had been washed with bleach."

"Pity. I'll bet the finish was ruined, and those things were outrageously expensive in spite of being fearsomely ugly. My husband had one, you know."

Surprised that her late husband had not done her in with it years ago, Camacho struggled with keeping his face straight. "Miss Enero's father was in the Air Force. That had belonged to him. He crewed on one of those planes."

Flora thought that the matching statue, now hidden deep in her storage room and unwanted by either of her children, might have a new home. After a decent length of time she would see about sending it to Miss Enero.

"Mrs. Melkiot, how did you know?"

With her good hand Flora made a graceful gesture toward the wall of pictures that was – mercifully – behind her. "A good detective can't overlook any source of information," she said sweetly. "And what weapon was used on poor Dewayne?"

The detective sighed. "A steel tray like the ones used to bring his meals when he ate in his room. It's one that fits on those smaller rolling carts."

"Fingerprints?"

Camacho shook his head. "Lots. We're trying to match them now, but most were just smudges."

"Of course," Flora said as much to herself as the detective, "there would be lots of fingerprints. Everyone here has most likely handled those trays and I fear that this place's attitude toward sanitation is not altogether ideal."

An idea was beginning to form in Flora's mind, only to be extinguished by an anguished scream from the hallway. She was quick to her feet, but exhibiting a speed unexpected in a man so stocky, the detective was out the door before she was all the way up. There was, however, as she had been telling people, nothing wrong with her legs and she caught up with him before he could slam it in her face.

Drawn to the sound of drama as moths are to light, the residents were flowing into the hallway. Camacho went through them like an icebreaker, Flora following in his wake. As if it were a stage, the area around the nurses' station was empty, except for what seemed to be a goodly number of the staff. Forced into leaning against the desk, Stacey Enero held the solid, sobbing body of Georgia Warnecker.

"Don't cry so, Georgia," the administrator said with little effect.

Cry? Flora thought with a fastidious distaste. *More like wail. Howl. Screech.*

"He's got to be here," Georgia wailed. Never very attractive to begin with, her doughy face was contorted into a horror mask from a nightmare. "I called him this morning and he said he'd see me at work, but when I called here they said he hadn't come in. I drove by his apartment, but his car wasn't in the parking lot, and he's not at my house, so he has to be here! He said he was working an extra shift so we – So we – He has to be here!" That little exercise in illogic served only to send her off in a new paroxysm of wails.

"Stop that caterwauling at once!" Flora ordered, stepping forward until their faces were almost touching. "It is only delaying us finding him."

Camacho moved as if to push Flora to the side, but stopped still when Georgia obeyed, her cries fading to soft little hiccoughing sobs. Stacey gave Flora a grateful look, but did not turn loose of the chunky nurse.

"But where is he?" she asked in a pitiful voice.

"He came in early this morning, Georgia, and picked up his check. Said he had to leave because of a family emergency – his grandfather." There was a moment's pause, then Stacey added, "He said he wouldn't be back until his grandfather was better."

"You just gave him his check and let him leave?" Camacho was incredulous. "Miss Enero, there is a murder investigation going on."

"I am not going to keep a man from going to the side of his dying grandfather," she replied with steely spirit. "The man's name and address are in our records."

"The same grandfather who left him the watch?" Flora asked in acid tones.

"He doesn't have a grandfather," Georgia screamed, clinging to Stacey as if to a life raft. "He was an orphan. He doesn't have anyone but me."

"And you were lovers," Flora said. It was not a question.

The mask turned from one of grief to one of hate. "You should know that, you snooping, interfering old witch! You couldn't stand it, could you? You couldn't stand it that someone handsome like him could love someone like me. He told me how you kept looking at him, how you kept following him around, hinting that you had a lot of money, that he should leave me for you."

"Then he was a liar as well as a thief," Flora said crisply. "And you are a fool. Who thought of stealing the drugs? You or him?"

"I… I…" Georgia seemed to crumple in on herself, squashing Stacey even more against the desk. "There just wasn't enough money. Even though I worked extra shifts there just wasn't enough money. I wanted him to have nice things – he'd never had anything, you see, growing up in an orphanage and all…"

Flora stifled an urge to snort in disbelief. Even if the young man had been raised in an orphanage – which she doubted – it was extremely likely he had picked up a lot of 'family' of the female persuasion.

"Georgia," Stacey said in gentle tones, "he listed several family members on his application form."

"He told me he did – he said he did that because people didn't like to hire orphans. He said they thought they were unreliable." Her voice, calmer now, threaded away into reluctant belief. "I even gave him a car, so he wouldn't have to ride for such a long time on the bus. He'd never had a car."

"Girl, you gave him that big fancy red convertible?" Naomi asked in scathing tones. "How could you afford it?"

"I couldn't, not after a while… but he loved it so. I just couldn't ask him to give it up. But he – he knew what trouble I was in, and said that he knew someone – a guy he met in the orphanage – "

This time Flora couldn't restrain a snort.

" – who was kind of a rough-and-tumble guy and that he could sell some pills on the street and get us some money. It was just a few…some of those pills sat in the cabinet for months, some got so old they had to be thrown out… I didn't think anyone would miss them. I'd take just a few and then hand them to Al…" her voice almost broke on his name, "… and he would hand them out to his friend late at night."

"Through the window at the end of my corridor," Flora said. It too was not a question.

"What about the key?" Stacey Enero asked. Her tone was soft, but there was steel beneath it.

"Al took mine while we were doing the meds one morning and had it copied. Then he had a friend fix some sort of electronic gizmo that fit on the security tape machine. I don't know how it worked but it only showed the cabinets – not who was there. Al was so smart… he just never had a chance," she added pathetically.

"He was a dope dealer," Flora said with brutal truth, "and you are his accomplice. Eula Badham saw him passing out the drugs one night and mistook the window for a door, but no one would believe her. He threatened her, didn't he?"

Georgia nodded jerkily.

So it wasn't a TV show, Flora thought, her belief in her powers of observation vindicated. Camacho was snarling into his phone, giving orders for everyone to be on the lookout for a red convertible even as he grilled Georgia.

"What make was the car? Do you know the license number? Do you think he'd take off for the border?"

Georgia only stared at him, as uncomprehending as if he were speaking a foreign language.

Once again Flora had to take things into her own hands. "Eula Badham was a harmless old lady. Why did Al murder her?"

Georgia howled again, and Camacho grabbed Flora's arm. "That's enough, Mrs. Melkiot!"

"If you don't want my help…" Flora shrugged and stepped back. She'd done the heavy lifting. Even the police should be able to wrap this drug thing up now. She should put her powers of deduction onto the other murders. *One murder and an attempted murder,* she thought punctiliously. Please God Dewayne Harbaugh was still alive.

Words spewed out of the nurse's mouth. "He didn't murder her. She wouldn't shut up. She kept telling everyone about it, but since she was crazy no one took her seriously. She even started following him. He didn't mean to kill her, I swear. He was so upset – all he did was give her a little push and she fell and broke her neck against the chapel pew."

Flora couldn't help it. Just how stupid could this woman be? "Before or after she strangled herself?"

"Mrs. Melkiot, I'm warning you – "

Georgia's doughy face went papery white. "Strangled?"

Camacho stepped in closer. "Why did the two of you kill Mrs. Cattermole and attack Mr. Harbaugh?"

Papery white turned into transparent. "We didn't. He didn't. We didn't touch them. Why? They didn't bother us."

To Flora's ears her denial had the ring of truth.

"When did you start writing orders to buy pills?" Stacey asked, clasping the nurse closer. Georgia seemed to be melting, bonelessly slipping down through her arms.

The stocky nurse gasped and almost stiffened, but apparently a denial was not only useless, it would take just too much energy. Her body seemingly boneless, she relaxed and slid down another inch or two. "Just before you came. Mrs. Hammond didn't notice, and Dr. Jensen would sign anything. It was the money again… we earned so little and it went so fast. Al said we needed to get away and make a fresh start together, just the two of us, but we'd need a nest egg to tide us over…"

The detective motioned to a uniformed policeman, who stepped up and clasped handcuffs around Georgia's wrists, in front out of respect for her weight. Flora almost protested that such restraint would be unnecessary – the nurse was beaten, totally incapable of resistance. Georgia looked at everyone as if she had never seen any of them before in her life.

"Georgia Warnaker, I am arresting you for narcotics violations and being an accessory to murder. Lethbridge, read her her rights and take her downtown."

"You have the right to remain silent..." the young man began, but that was the one thing Georgia didn't do. Finally realizing the reality of her situation she began to howl again, so loudly that it was clearly audible until the front door shut behind them.

"Well, that solves that," Camacho said, heaving a sigh of relief.

"What about Dewayne and the Cattermole?" Flora asked astringently. "Surely you don't think those two had anything to do with those?"

"Of course they did. She would be sure to deny it, but it all has to be linked. We'll find out."

Flora's face radiated disbelief. "Linked? How?"

"I said we'd find out, Mrs. Melkiot. Now I thank you for the information you brought, but it's time for you to step back and let the professionals take over."

This time Flora's snort was gargantuan. "Georgia is a fool, and you are an idiot!" She wheeled angrily, right into Fred Moretti's waiting embrace.

"Flora, girl, you did it," he said, giving her big wet kisses. He had aimed for her mouth, but with her usual quick reflexes Flora turned her head adroitly, forcing his lips to land on her cheek before she banged her cast against his funny bone. He quickly let go, and although it hardened the smile didn't leave his face. "Boy, you're sure feisty, and I like that. You solved the case!"

Flora's expression was more fury than feisty. "My room. Now," she said, tromping off down the hallway, the crowd of residents parting before her like the Red Sea.

* * * * *

If Fred Moretti were anticipating a romantic dalliance, he was doomed to disappointment. Before reaching her room Flora had picked up Sophia O'Connor, Mr. Granetti and Honey Hoffman, all of whom trailed behind her in a mixture of pride at having been chosen and apprehension for the same reason.

Flora jumped up to sit on the edge of her bed. The room was small and the extra people – and especially the two wheelchairs – crowded it. Mrs. Gutierrez gave a heroic snore and turned over. Intent on her thoughts Flora didn't even bother to glare at her.

"All right, did any of you find out anything about who went into Dewayne's room this morning?"

"No one I talked to saw anyone. Most of them were still in their rooms, asleep," Fred said. His words were followed by a chorus of agreements, all somewhat shamefacedly given, as if in confessing a lack of information they had somehow failed.

Flora sat staring, her eyes focused on the wall across the room. Just before Georgia had started screaming she had thought of something, something important to the case, but whatever it was had vanished, dancing away from the edges of her mind. Such intransigence on the power of her brain to recall what she directed when she wanted it angered her.

Well, that was no excuse not to work. The thought would return. It had better, because somehow she knew it was important. Flora expected her own mind to obey her even if that stupid policeman wouldn't.

"When Dewayne was attacked he was dressed and working on his computer," she said, trying to fix a solid picture in her mind. "That means he had been working all night."

"How do you know that?" Fred asked, a smirk on his face.

Flora glared at him. "Because of his injuries he was incapable of dressing himself or strapping himself into his wheelchair. That means he had to call someone to help dress him very early in the morning, and none of the staff said they had attended him during the night, ergo he had never gone to bed. Dewayne was a special case, as you know, and not subject to the rules that dominate the rest of us."

There was a soft murmur of assent. Mrs. Gutierrez merely shifted and began to snore, but for once it didn't penetrate Flora's concentration.

"So, do any of you know what he was working on?"

There was a moment of silence; if one could hear heads shake, there would have been a cacophony of sound. Finally Fred said, "Dewayne could be a nice guy, and was most of the time, but he was secretive. I don't think he ever told anyone what he was doing."

"He was certainly adroit with those computers," Sophia said. "He helped me straighten out my bank account once."

"And he helped me order some stuff online and have it sent directly to my granddaughter," added Honey Hoffman.

"He found my grandson's email address for me after I lost it. He even helped me send some emails. He was marvelous with those machines," Mr. Granetti said, his rheumy eyes jealous. "Wish we'd had them when I was young."

"But that's all simple stuff. He wouldn't need all that fancy equipment just for things like that," Flora murmured, thinking madly. He might have been a programmer before his accident, but what was he doing now? Just what had Dewayne Harbaugh been up to?

Candy knocked as she opened the door. "It's time for dinner. Y'all come on."

Obediently everyone trooped out, including a thoughtful and unaccustomedly acquiescent Flora.

Chapter Twenty One

There was always such a good feeling when he wrapped up a case. Armando Camacho felt quite smug as he drove back to the station. Of course, now what he always regarded as the real work of the case had to be done – the paperwork necessary to take the case to the DA.

Sometimes he didn't like the way cases turned out. That Al was a slimebag, taking the money and killing those old people. While it wasn't technically a crime, it was criminal how he had bamboozled that old nurse, Camacho thought, conveniently ignoring the fact that Georgia Warnecker was probably the same age as he. The detective would have bet that she wasn't the first woman Al had wooed and used, either. Slimebag, indeed.

"Detective, we've finally cracked the security code for Harbaugh's computer," said an impossibly young officer. He was holding a sheaf of papers. "Most of it, at least. Dude was working on some heavy stuff."

Camacho looked up. "Like what?"

"As near as we can tell, he was a hacker for hire. A white hat, though," the young officer said. There was a tinge of admiration in his voice. "High-end stuff."

"Criminal? He was breaking the law?"

"We don't think so – at least, not from what we could find. He had a great setup, though. Must have done a lot of the programming himself."

Beyond email and basic programs like word processing and simple tax preparation, computers were a mystery to Camacho. His children could make the things practically sit up and dance, like all kids could today, but he was happy with what he knew.

"Any idea of what he was working on?"

"Industrial espionage. He was looking for a mole who had been selling off information from – " and the young officer named an international company who had more assets than most of the world's countries. "It was legit – he was on their payroll as an independent contractor."

"He was doing that from a nursing home?" Camacho was equal parts impressed and skeptical.

"Why not? The internet goes everywhere." The young man shrugged. "Anyway, we thought you should see this. It's about the nursing home."

Camacho took the sheaf of papers, but shook his head. "I'll put this in the file, but we've wrapped up the case."

The young officer looked startled. "You have? Do you have the perp in custody?"

"No, he skipped before his partner rolled over on him." While fairly standard, that particular phrase brought an unpleasant visual of the Warneker woman and the young stud in bed to Camacho's mind and he shuddered. "We've got a BOLO out on him. Should have him in custody before long."

"I still think you should read that, sir." There was an undercurrent of pleading in the young man's voice. He couldn't order a superior to do anything, no matter how much he wanted to.

"I will," Camacho lied. The case was closed, so this could go to the DA with the rest of the paperwork. There were other cases demanding his attention and he shouldn't be wasting time on a case that was wrapped up as far as he was concerned. There had been a stabbing at one of the universities and a shooting on Broadway and half a dozen other things that needed solving. The killings at Cold Creek Health Care Facility were closed.

Feeling virtuous and just a little triumphant as he

always did when a murderer was exposed, Camacho worked diligently on the necessary paperwork to send to the District Attorney.

The only thing was, those papers sat there mocking him, almost glowing with a demand for attention. Detective Armando Camacho was a good policeman with a reputation for meticulous detail; honest and thorough and with a closure rate that proved both. He finally gave in to his training and grabbed the papers. There were only a few, and the type was decent sized, so it didn't take him long to read the entire bunch.

He went slower the second time he read it, and even slower the third, as if he was checking to make sure he was truly seeing what he was seeing. At the end of the third reading he gave a great sigh, half out of chagrin that he had come so close to missing the true closure of the case and half out of frustration that Flora Melkiot had been at least partly right. It was not a slam-dunk, but it gave an entirely new slant on the murder of Penelope Cattermole and the attempted murder of Dewayne Harbaugh.

Damn!

Calling to a uniformed officer to come with him, Camacho strode through the station toward his car.

* * * * *

Dinner was somber. It was also as close to inedible as any meal Flora had been served since her arrival – macaroni boiled to the consistency of runny oatmeal and drenched with thin soupy cheese, then studded with slivers of cheap hot dogs that were more filler than meat. Flora forced down a bite or two – noting with fastidious displeasure that the liquid cheese slipped through the tines of her fork and dripped down on the front of her duster.

"They should be calling this soup instead of macaroni and cheese," she muttered and put down her fork. Once again she would dine on Rebecca's candy in her room.

Honestly, this place was enough to put her off chocolate for the rest of her life.

Honoria Rogers scooped up a spoonful of the mess and manfully swallowed a mouthful. “It’s not really so bad…” she said with not quite enough determination to wipe out a tone of disbelief. “Hunger is the best appetizer, you know.”

“So you’ve said.” Many, many times, Flora could have added, but it wasn’t Mrs. Rogers’ fault the food was so bad. Flora wasn’t quite sure exactly whose fault it was, but whoever it was could be sure that once she was away from here she would find out who the principals of the company that owned this place were and they would hear from her. She might be an older woman, but Melkiot was a name that demanded respect in the financial world and she intended to use it to the fullest extent. “However, I am not yet that hungry and hope I never shall be.”

“Excuse me!” Raised to a volume and an authority unheard since her military days, Stacey Enero’s voice cut through the low babble of the dining hall. “May I have your attention, please?”

Every head turned toward the kitchen doors, where the residents were treated to the unprecedented sight of their administrator not only with her suit jacket off and her blouse sleeves rolled up, but wearing an apron. A very dirty and ill-used apron.

“I want to apologize for the quality of this meal,” she said in a voice that rang with equal parts of sincerity and embarrassment. “This afternoon all but one of the kitchen staff just up and left. I guess after the events of the last few days it shouldn’t be very much of a surprise. Two of the nurses and I worked on this dinner, and I guess you’ve figured out that none of us are very good cooks.”

A weak wave of obligatory laughter skimmed over the room.

“But I have spoken to the owners – ” here the tone of her voice hardened, leaving very little doubt as to exactly what she had said, in spirit if not in actual words " – and they have assured me that we will have a full kitchen staff again, starting with breakfast in the morning."

Applause, stronger and more sincere than the uncomfortable laughter, flared briefly.

Stacey raised her hands, betraying a large stain on one sleeve. "I know things have been difficult and scary the last few days, and I'm sorry for that. It's going to be different, though. I give you my personal word. Now – I know dinner has been pretty unpalatable, but I've ordered some cakes from the H.E.B. and they've just come, so I can guarantee dessert will be good."

This time the applause lasted longer. Everyone loved cake.

And good cake it was, too. Of course, Flora thought, it was nothing compared to the hand-made creations they served at the Olympus House restaurant, but for a grocery store cake it was excellent. Of course, H.E.B. had always had a good reputation. Clarissa wouldn't have shopped there if it hadn't. When Miss Enero said that anyone who wished could have seconds, no one left the dining hall – except Flora. She would have enjoyed a second piece, but restrained herself. She had never ingested so much sugar in her life as she had here. Just because of her current unfortunate circumstances she should not let herself put on weight.

The hallway was totally empty. Giving in to temptation, Flora scurried down to Dewayne's room. The crime scene tape was gone – doubtless thanks to that idiot detective – and since none of the patient rooms had locks, which heretofore Flora had noisily deplored – she slipped in without any trouble.

The floor had been sketchily cleaned, a fact for which Flora was profoundly grateful. Of course Dewayne's computers were gone, leaving the desk looking empty. It wasn't, of course. There were the things one found on all desks – note pads, a pencil holder, his coffee mug which probably held the remains of his last cup…

Flora felt her throat tightening. Dewayne Harbaugh didn't deserve what had happened to him. What kind of monster could do that to a man so badly crippled? There was anger in that attack, personal anger, just as there had been in the Cattermole's death. What could two so disparate people know or have done to rate such treatment?

It kept coming back to the fact that the only point of convergence in their lives was that they were at Cold Creek Health Care Facility.

So far as anyone knew.

Had they touched lives before? Probably that stupid policeman hadn't investigated such a possibility. He was interested only in easy fixes. Georgia and Al were guilty as sin – and of sin – but only in Eula Badham's death, the drug scheme and their personal lives. Flora simply could not believe they had anything to do with either the Cattermole or Dewayne.

She pulled up one of the visitor's chairs to the desk. She simply could not make herself sit in his wheelchair, which she pushed out of the way. One by one she opened the drawers, finding nothing that shouldn't be in a desk drawer – snacks, papers neatly filed into hanging folders, pads of sticky notes, paper clips, a ruler – all the normal stuff that lay in probably 99% of all the desks in the country.

Except for one thing – an elegantly framed photo of a bright-eyed and handsome boy, probably no more than ten or twelve. His curly hair was cut short, his skin the color of expensive chocolate. His black eyes snapped with intelligence and his full lips curved into a small, friendly smile. The picture ended at his shoulders, but still Flora could tell he was wearing a nice-looking plaid shirt that appeared to have been carefully ironed.

Flora looked at the photo carefully. There was no name, no place of origin, no photographer's stamp. Just the image of a boy on the verge of laughter.

Was this Dewayne's son? She couldn't see any similarity of feature to Dewayne, but considering the extent of his injuries that was not surprising. Flora carefully replaced the picture where it had been. She didn't want him to know that she had been prying into his private life. The last report on Dewayne was that he would definitely survive and had been taken off the critical list, both of which seemed to be small miracles.

There were still the shadows of dark smudges on the floor where Dewayne had lain. Flora was very carefully not looking at them. When he returned she wanted everything to be just the way it had been, and if the staff didn't do a better job of cleaning this room she would personally hire a cleaning service to do it.

On a shelf above the empty hole where the computer had been were violently colored plastic notebooks – the old fashioned three ringed kind like children carried to school. The one on the end stuck out a little from its fellows.

Was that the one Dewayne had handled last? Or had the police looked through it and replaced it carelessly? Flora wondered.

It didn't make any difference. Clumsy because of her cast, she pulled it down and laid it on the table.

It was a diary of sorts, written on three-hole lined notebook paper. Not a personal one – who would need one in the sterile sameness of life at Cold Creek? – but it held what looked like business notes. There were dates, each on a separate page – or pages – and all from this week, and lots of notations in a combination of abbreviations and initials and what could only be computerese, none of which Flora could understand. There were also some frightfully large numbers which could be money, or telephone numbers, or some arcane code, or just about anything else.

Decidedly frustrated, Flora knew at least some of the

answers to her questions had to be buried in this gibberish, but she had no idea of how to get them out. Had Camacho even looked at this? Or made any effort to figure out what it meant?

Why should he? she thought with a wave of bitterness. *He had Georgia and Al, and thought they were all he needed to mark the case closed.*

She turned to the last page, about a third of the way through the notebook. This was dated the day before Dewayne was attacked, and all the rest of the pages were blank. The sheet only had one line of lettering, but it was heavily underscored. Worst of all, there were brown spatters on the paper, which Flora very much feared might be dried blood.

MJ/PC 1990(?). AFR/SAPD. Nix.

Flora read the line several times, but it made no sense. The only things that the scribblings matched in her brain were PC - which even she knew stood for Personal Computer - and Nix, which was a slang word for 'no' many years before, and she didn't think either of those definitions were accurate. MJ meant nothing, as did AFR or SAPD. Margaret Jean, like her long-dead cousin? Air Force Raid? Special Action Protective Division?

Shaking her head, Flora stared at the scribbles with mounting frustration. Those cryptic notes could mean just about anything. She could think for days and not even know if she hit the right combination.

"What are you doing in here, Mrs. Melkiot?"

Startled, Flora jumped. Really, was it a rule here that the nurses creep around on tiptoe? She had been so deep in concentration she hadn't even heard the door open.

"Snooping, aren't you?" Melanie said, not giving Flora a chance to reply. "That's not allowed, you know. You probably think you're hot stuff because you helped solve a murder back in Dallas – or so you say – but apparently you didn't hear the detective say that this case is closed."

"Do you think Georgia and Al did it? Killed Mrs. Cattermole and beat Dewayne within an inch of his life?"

The haggard-looking nurse shrugged. "Know what? I don't care. I've got too much to worry about to care about things that don't affect me. Now come on. You're going back to your room, and you're going to stay there." She whipped a security belt out of her pocket and motioned impatiently for Flora to stand.

Knowing herself to be outmatched physically, Flora arose with a dignity that seemed as if it were her own idea and picked up her purse.

"I shall be leaving here in the morning," Flora said with a condescending dignity. "The guardianship my daughter forced on me has been rescinded, so I can leave when I want."

Melanie yanked the heavy webbing tighter than it needed to be and steered Flora toward the door. "Well, whoop-de-do. One less problem for me to worry with."

"You've had a lot to cope with, haven't you?" Flora said gently. There had been gossip about the trials Melanie had been facing with her looming divorce and the possible loss of her son. Even Dewayne had said he had been helping her…

Flora's mind began to fire again.

Dewayne had been helping her, too, Flora realized. She had asked him to look into the background of the victims and those who worked at Cold Creek. Had he found something? Had that something gotten him attacked?

Inwardly Flora shivered. Had Dewayne been nearly killed because of something she had asked him to do? It was a horrible thought.

I need to talk this over with someone, Flora thought, suddenly assailed with an unfamiliar rush of guilt. *I'll call Rebecca as soon as I get back to my room. She's a former police detective, so surely she's been in this situation before. She'll know what to do.*

There must have been thirds offered on the cake, because the hallways were empty and there was the noise of happy talk coming from behind the closed doors of the dining hall.

Melanie obviously believed that nothing was wrong with Flora's legs, for she hurried down the hall, dragging Flora with her at an uncomfortably near run.

"Come on," she all but snarled. "Don't drag your feet."

"I'm coming as quickly as I can," Flora replied regally even as she dragged her feet as much as she dared. Something felt very wrong, and though she didn't quite know what, she was very uncomfortable. "I would like to go back to the dining hall."

Melanie glared at her, her reddened eyes harsh. "Sorry – you were caught snooping, so you have to go to your room. Now!" She gave a savage jerk to the security belt, almost pulling Flora off her feet.

Oh, for Heaven's sake! Flora thought in annoyance, her eyes flicking up and down the deserted halls. *Usually you can't go ten feet without running into someone. Where is everybody?*

And why was Melanie so intent on taking her to her room? Something was just not adding up. Melanie had never been one of Flora's favorite members of the staff – if pressed, she didn't have any – but there had always been something edgy and unpleasant about the horse-faced nurse.

Flora considered her options. She could simply stop and dig in her heels, but Melanie was both younger and stronger and could drag her by force if necessary. If she screamed, could she be heard over the noise in the dining hall? She could strike out with her purse (too light to do much damage) or her cast (which Melanie could probably deflect) but that would not guarantee her releasing her hold on the security belt.

They were almost at her door. Flora knew she had to

do something and quickly, as her unease was reaching panic proportions, and panic was something totally unfamiliar to Flora Melkiot.

Chapter Twenty Two

Never let it be said that a confident, capable woman like Flora would give in easily. Deciding a two-pronged attack would be best. she took a deep breath and readied her casted arm for a roundhouse punch, but Melanie, accustomed to dealing with recalcitrant patients, had anticipated her. She yanked the security belt with a sudden movement, jerking Flora into a state of perilous imbalance and forcing all the air from her lungs.

"Don't you even think of screaming, or trying to fight me. I've worked with crazies like you for years and I know all your tricks, you old witch." Melanie said in a low, threatening tone. She dragged a gasping Flora into her room and shut the door behind them, then wheeled Flora around to face her.

It was, Flora thought vaguely, the first time she had ever seen that door completely shut.

"You know," Flora wheezed, "that I will report you to the highest management for this treatment."

"Yeah, like hell you will."

Melanie said something else, but Flora didn't hear her. With the idea of making a scathing report she had focused on Melanie's name tag, then belatedly her mind began to make connections.

Melanie Jenks.

MJ.

That meant PC wasn't Personal Computer, but was most likely Penelope Cattermole.

Flora couldn't remember any of the rest of

Dewayne's note, but somehow it must all tie in. Inwardly Flora gulped.

Melanie was shaking her shoulders viciously. "I asked you, what do you know?"

There was no hope in prevaricating. Melanie was unbalanced enough to assault her no matter what she said. "That you killed the Cattermole and attacked Dewayne."

"So he did tell you."

"No, you just did with the way you're acting. Why did you attack him? He was helping you."

"Because he was digging into things, finding out things that didn't concern him. Or you. Or anyone." Melanie was devolving as Flora watched. Her reddened eyes resembled those of a rabid animal and her face tightened, becoming something that was less than human. "He snooped into the Air Force records, and the San Antonio Police Department records, digging into things no one has a right to know. He even went into my family's medical records at Nix."

Too late Flora remembered Dewayne's note. Nix. Nix Hospital, downtown. She should have known that – Clarissa had been there for her appendectomy years ago.

Medical records? Did Melanie have a mental problem? And, if she lost her job here, Flora reasoned, *what would happen to her son? Would she see that risk as worth killing for?*

"Was that a reason to kill him?"

"He could have told someone. He could have kept me from keeping Davy. I had to kill him." In contrast to her contorted face, her voice held the ring of sweet reason.

It's nearly always the one who finds the body, Flora thought with almost frivolous irrelevance. *That detective will be pleased.* Then, her mind working at a super speed, she realized that was why Melanie's clothes had been so covered with blood after finding Dewayne when Candy, who had worked so hard to save Dewayne's life, had hardly any blood on her at all.

"But you didn't. They're saying he'll get well."

Melanie's face hardened even more. "He can't do that. I have to protect myself. It's my right. I have to stay here and look after my son and keep him away from his worthless daddy and that whore."

Which was worse for a child to have as a mother, Flora wondered, *a whore or a murderess?*

Ungently Melanie shoved Flora back against a bed. She had turned loose of the security belt, but held Flora in an unbalanced position where only the snoring lump that was Mrs. Gutierrez kept Flora from falling. Wildly she glanced around the room, obviously looking for some kind of weapon. Flora was grateful for the sterile, clutterless area and tried to think how she could break the nurse's restraint. It wasn't a formal hold, just one hand clamped around Flora's throat while her forearm pushed painfully down on Flora's chest, pinning her against the bed – and the flaccid stolidity of Mrs. Gutierrez – and keeping her off balance.

Perhaps falling might help, Flora thought, wildly seeking ways to get the nurse's hand from her throat. If she could get her off balance too…

On the other hand, the fall might even tighten her grip on Flora, making things even worse than they were now.

And, Flora realized, even as exhausted and strung-out as the nurse was, she was both younger and more limber, and would probably just go down with her without turning loose. Still, she couldn't just lie here and give up!

Trying to pull free of Melanie's grip, Flora struggled and flailed and even kicked. Melanie didn't even seem to notice. Raising her casted wrist she slammed it against the nurse's head, but either the angle was wrong or Flora was too weak.

"Stop it, you old bitch!" Melanie's hands, strong and wiry as stranglevines, locked around Flora's throat. "You'll tell. I've got to keep Davy, and you'll tell and they'll take him away from me. Stop it!"

Another belated realization, irritating in its lateness. Melanie's scrubs were a pale off-white – something that could easily appear as a ghost to a half-blind, addled old lady.

Why, Flora wondered, *was it always so easy to see things once it was too late?*

"Did you kill Eula Badham?" Flora croaked, trying to force air through her constricted throat.

Melanie laughed, an incongruously happy sound. "No, why would I? Al did that. Crazy old woman, as if anything she said mattered. He did right to kill her, whether he meant to or not. She's better off dead."

And what will she say about me? Flora wondered. She was still flailing, but somehow her arms weren't obeying her very well. Melanie didn't appear to be aware of the blows.

"Why did you kill Penelope Cattermole?"

"Does it really matter?"

"I want to know," Flora gasped. In the crime shows she watched the villain was always more than happy enough to talk about their crimes, giving the hero – and Flora had no doubt she was the hero – an opportunity to save himself.

"Snoopy to the end, aren't you?" Melanie gave a laugh that was nothing more than a crazed cackle, but the ploy worked. Her hands loosened almost imperceptibly, yet it was enough for Flora to grab a lungful of much-needed air. "She recognized me. She said she knew me, and was looking at my file. She'd have told everyone about me, and I'd have lost Davy."

"What could she have said that would cause you to lose your son?" Flora asked in wonder.

"It's none of your business." The respite was over. Melanie's hands tightened again. "You're going to die, old woman. You've snooped too much. We'll all be better off without you..."

There were flecks of black at the edges of Flora's

vision and she wasn't getting any air. Melanie's hands were like iron around her throat.

This is it, Flora realized with a spurt of anger. *If I don't do something I'm going to die, and how pathetic to die like this, in a second-rate nursing home while wearing a disgusting cotton housedress!*

Once again she flailed out wildly with her cast as the darkness crept ever closer.

* * * * *

My God, Detective Camacho thought as he hurried through the empty nursing home, *what's happened? Where is everyone?*

The drive over had given him time to realize how important it was that he be at Cold Creek, that there were questions he had to ask – questions that he feared he already knew the answer to.

A burst of laughter from the dining hall answered that question. Followed by Robertson, the uniformed officer he had dragooned into coming with him, he dashed into the room. The place was happier than he had ever seen it before, the residents talking animatedly – most of them, at least – and the tables littered with cake-smeared plates. Dirty and disheveled and in an apron, Stacey Enero stood in the corner, a satisfied smile on her face, even though she looked exhausted she also looked ten years younger.

He didn't see the face he was looking for, though.

Stacey's face fell as she saw the policemen, and started toward them, but Camacho was too impatient to wait even those few seconds and shouted.

"Where's…?"

The rest of his question was drowned in a blast of sound that at first he thought was a siren heralding the arrival of his backup before realizing that it came from a human throat.

Turning on his heel, Camacho sprinted back through

the swinging doors and, trailed by a number of the staff and, more slowly, by a cloud of the residents, followed the sound down the hallway. Acting on instinct as well as hearing, he shoved through the only door that was closed where he was confronted with a scene that would stay with him for years.

A large Hispanic lady sitting bolt upright in her bed, the sheet pulled up to her chin as if she were an affronted young maiden, her eyes bulging, her mouth open as she screamed loudly enough to wake the dead. A healthy stream of blood slid from her nose downwards to drip off her chin onto the sheet.

Flora Melkiot, her eyes closed and her mouth open in a greyish face, but with her arms still flailing wildly, bent backwards over the large Hispanic lady's legs.

Melanie Jenks with her hands wrapped tightly around Mrs. Melkiot's throat, looking up with wild eyes and a grimace that made her look like a ravening beast.

Camacho and Robertson plunged forward, grappling with the nurse, who maniacally kept screaming "No, I have to do it. She'll tell! I have to keep my son!" and refused to let loose of the rag doll that was Flora Melkiot.

Not thinking of possible lawsuits or charges of police brutality or any of the other ridiculous unfairnesses that were making policemen afraid to do their job, Camacho made a fist and slammed it into Melanie's jaw. It wasn't hard enough a blow to knock her completely out, but it stunned her enough to loosen her hold on Flora's neck and send her staggering back into Robertson's arms. It was the work of seconds to get her handcuffed and as full consciousness returned she began to struggle madly.

Deprived of the support of Melanie's hands, Flora began to slip downward bonelessly. Leaping forward, Stacey caught her and, unable to lift or hold her, eased her down into a sprawl on the floor. Close behind, a short butterball of a night shift nurse called in for emergency service rushed forward to comfort the wild-eyed Mrs.

Gutierrez, stanching the blood with the already stained sheet and hushing her inarticulate cries.

"Breathe, Mrs. Melkiot! Breathe!" Stacey ordered. "Someone call 911. We need an ambulance here now!"

An ambulance? For whom? Flora wondered vaguely, merely glad that the horrid pressure on her throat had ceased, and wishing that her head wasn't so swimmy. There was something important she had to do, something she had to say…

"Breathe!" Stacey ordered again, as Naomi bent over Flora.

"She has a pulse," Naomi said, then slapped Flora across the face. "Breathe, Mrs. Melkiot!"

"Get some oxygen in here," Stacey shouted and from somewhere in the hall there was the sound of running feet.

Flora drew in a large breath, oddly startled that it felt as if she were breathing liquid fire as the air penetrated her starved lungs. The next breath was equally painful, but the swimmy feeling in her head was fading fast.

"Did you enjoy that?" Flora croaked in a voice that sounded totally unlike her own. Simultaneously Naomi and Stacey gave breathless, relieved giggles.

Camacho's worried stare was almost tactile and his own breathing suspended, but once Flora spoke he turned to Melanie, now immobilized in Robertson's no-nonsense grip.

"Melanie Jenks, I am arresting you for the murder of Penelope Cattermole and the attempted murder of Dewayne Harbaugh. Robertson, take her outside and read her her rights."

Robertson ungently shoved the now quiescent Melanie toward the door. Although she was still, it was a dangerous stillness, like a crouching beast just before it attacked.

"Wait," Flora said in a small, rough voice. "You attacked Dewayne because he found out something you wanted hidden, something about you and Penelope

Cattermole. Why did you kill the Cattermole?"

Now more than ever Melanie resembled a rabid animal. Her face worked and tightened into an ugly grimace. She was silent so long Flora feared she would never answer, but when the words started they came out in a flood, like the foulness from a lanced boil.

"Because the bitch deserved it! Someone should have killed her a long time ago. She recognized me, and dug in the files to prove it. She said she would stop me from keeping my son. An unacceptable family history, she said, and then she laughed. She just sat there and laughed."

"And you thought people would believe her?" Flora asked, then swallowed heavily. It felt as if great chunks of granite were being forced down her throat.

"Why wouldn't they? She always got everything she wanted. Did you know she stole my father? He was married and had three children, and he left us all to go with her. My ma cried and cried, but I was happy he was gone – that bastard beat us all whenever he felt like it, beat us until we bled. But after they were married an officer started paying her attention, and suddenly she decided that my father was too rough for her, too uncouth, that he wasn't the man she had thought. Of course, he was just a sergeant, an enlisted man instead of an officer so all of a sudden she had an attack of conscience – " her voice ground the word to a bitter powder " – and said that he should go back to his wife and children, that she couldn't live with him anymore. And my mother took him back!"

Surely that was a good thing, Flora thought. *The man was a jerk, but at least he returned to his family.* She reserved her opinion of the mother.

"She took him back, just when I thought we were finally rid of him!" Melanie's voice became a wail, like that of an affronted child. "She took him back, and didn't say a word when he started beating all of us again, worse than before. She didn't even say a word when he beat her. She never had. She took him back!" She gave an inhuman cry of grief, crumpling into a sobbing heap and would have fallen had not she been securely held. "Why couldn't the Cattermole bitch keep him? Why did she send him back? That damned woman should have kept him!"

"Get her out of here," Camacho said, his voice rusty with disgust. Then he turned to Flora and spoke reluctantly. "You were right, Mrs. Melkiot."

Flora thought about telling him he was most gentlemanly to admit it, but as just the thought of speaking made her throat hurt she contented herself with nodding graciously.

"Let me help you up," Camacho said, reaching down. "Can you stand?"

Flora reached up with her left hand, only to fall back with a shriek as he touched her.

"Mrs. Melkiot…!" cried Stacey.

"What's wrong?" Camacho asked.

"Damnation!" Flora cried in an unaccustomed fit of profanity. "I've broken my other wrist!"

About the Author

Janis Patterson is a seventh-generation Texan and a third-generation wordsmith who writes mysteries as Janis Patterson, romances and other things as Janis Susan May, children's books as Janis Susan Patterson and scholarly works as J.S.M. Patterson.

Formerly an actress and singer, a talent agent and Supervisor of Accessioning for a bio-genetic DNA testing lab, Janis has also been editor-in-chief of two multi-magazine publishing groups. She founded and was the original editor of The Newsletter of the North Texas Chapter of the American Research Center in Egypt, which for the nine years of her reign was the international organization's only monthly publication. Long interested in Egyptology, she was one of the founders of the North Texas chapter and was the closing speaker for the ARCE International Conference in Boston in 2005.

Janis married for the first time when most of her contemporaries were becoming grandmothers. Her husband, a handsome Navy Captain several years younger than she, even proposed in a moonlit garden in Egypt. Janis and her husband live in Texas with an assortment of rescued furbabies.

www.JanisPattersonMysteries.com

www.ingramcontent.com/pod-product-compliance
Lightning Source LLC
Chambersburg PA
CBHW071130260626
47162CB00003B/736
* 9 7 8 1 9 4 1 5 2 0 1 6 1 *